COLD LIGHT

THE AFTER SERIES
BOOK 2

TRACI L. SLATTON

parvati
press

This book is a work of fiction. Names, characters, places and incidents are either the product of the author's imagination or are used fictitiously. Any resemblance to actual persons, living or dead, or to actual events or locales is entirely coincidental.

Cold Light

The publisher does not have any control over and does not assume any responsibility for author or third-party websites or their content.

Cover designed by Gwyn Kennedy Snider
http://www.gkscreative.com

Cover art: Copyright © Shutterstock 146305565, Vintage winter landscape in the forest; Shutterstock 122085325, Collection of silhouettes, iStock 158620, squiggle4b; iStock 19409679, tropical butterflies

Published by Parvati Press
http://www.parvatipress.com

Visit the author website:
http://www.tracilslatton.com

ISBN:
978-0-9860611-0-3 (Paperback)
978-0-9846726-9-1 (eBook)

Library of Congress Control Number: 012910210

Version 2013.010.10

BOOKS BY TRACI L. SLATTON

IMMORTAL

THE BOTTICELLI AFFAIR

FALLEN

COLD LIGHT

FAR SHORE

DANCING IN THE TABERNACLE
(poetry)

PIERCING TIME & SPACE

THE ART OF LIFE
con Sabin Howard

THE LOVE OF MY (OTHER) LIFE

PRAISE FOR *FALLEN* AND *COLD LIGHT*
BOOKS 1 AND 2 OF THE AFTER SERIES

 This series continues to haunt me. I fell in love with the characters in the first installment, **Fallen**. Within this story [**Cold Light**], the characters have changed for the better. The tension was high throughout the story. As the reader joins in the adventure, they continue to wonder if Emma will be in time to save her daughter, if she will give into the overwhelming love and desire between her and Arthur and if the mist will catch them. The surprises were thrilling and sprinkled within the story adding fun to an already compelling plot. The ending is left open allowing for the possibility of third installment. For which this reader, hopes is more than a possibility. I have loved both books in this series.

HC Harju, *Night Owl Reviews*

 Slatton displays exceptional storytelling abilities in **Cold Light** by weaving fragments together at the end in a way that was delightfully unforeseen. And her poetic prose spirit the reader away into complete submersion. She also leaves a few mysteries behind to make you ache for the third book.

Rebecca Skane, *Seacoast Online*

 It [**Fallen**] is well-written, and I love the sci-fi aspects of it, the paranormal activities. It makes for a great read. . . . This book is incredible. It puts life into perspective for me. . . . It's not for the faint of heart. It is for women who want to hear their voice

and are as comfortable chopping wood, as wearing make-up. As the world changes, I like to read about women who make their own decisions, have opinions, and possess inner courage and strength. We older women worked long and hard to fight against antifeminist media and men. We want all of us to have choices; our sons and daughters, grandsons and granddaughters.

I love the main character, Emma Strong; knows her own mind, down-to-earth, smart, talented, powerful, not unlike the author! I highly recommend it!

Jennifer Jilks, *Country Cottage Reflections*

 **Cold Light** picks up over a year after **Fallen** left off. Emma has made it back to the Safe Zone in Edmonton, Alberta with Haywood and the girls, and quickly brings the reader up to date on how it happened. Even though my heart broke at the end of **Fallen** when she left Arthur, I understood her reasons . . . an excellent story that I wouldn't hesitate to re-read in the future. New characters are introduced early, and many of them are easy to like and amazingly relatable considering the circumstances of. My favorite early on was Gaff but edged over to Kangee by the end. Emma is still the survivor, Arthur is still the leader, Gaff is the resourceful kid, Kangee is the enigmatic mystery; the rest have their own unique attributes as well. Ms. Slatton did an excellent job creating believable characters and situations based in a hard to imagine postapocalyptic world.

Daysieanne, *My Book Addiction Reviews*

 I read **Fallen**, loved it. I read **Cold Light**, loved it. Now I must wait for what will seem like an eternity for the last of this amazing trilogy? . . . **Cold Light** leaves us with another heart-wrenching, cliffhanger ending. I cannot WAIT for the last book. I must know what happens. I NEED to know. Grrrr.

If you haven't started reading **Fallen** yet, do it *NOW*. Then read **Cold Light**. I believe you will be as spellbound as I am by these marvelous reads.

Julie, *Books Complete Me*

 I have long awaited this second book, **Cold Light**, after the way **Fallen** ended. I was NOT disappointed! Emma's daughter has been kidnapped by a rogue group and she goes on a suicide mission to get her back. I was very excited to be reunited with a few of the cast from **Fallen** and am still in anxious need of book three now to see how this all wraps up.

Emma is one strong and determined woman but Arthur is just as determined. I am torn on which way I want Emma to go because with the one man her husband she has the strong history and children but she shares something with Arthur that I don't think she and her husband ever really had or ever will.

I can't say much more without a spoiler comment but I will say I didn't really like the way **Cold Light** ended. I would not want to be in Emma's shoes and have to make the choices she is being forced to but it's time . . . there can be only one victor in this war.

Jennifer, *Gimme The Scoop Reviews*

 There are a lot of twists and turns . . . . **Cold Light** is a book of survival, fighting all the odds and trying to rebuild what has been lost. It is a love story between Emma and Arthur, only will Emma make the right choice? Does she live with a man she doesn't love for her children's sake while living in misery without the man she loves? This is a situation that many people have faced throughout history.

The book is a cliffhanger, as was book one, and I am one of those people who hate that and almost always give a poor rating because of it. The reason I didn't in this case is because the story is just too absorbing, the characters are amazing and the author's description of post-apocalyptic Earth is fascinating. I read at least a book a day. Often times when an author leaves you hanging at the end, by the time the next book comes out, you don't remember all the details of the book you just read. That is not the case with Ms. Slatton she brings the reader up to date on what happened prior so I know I will not be floundering about wondering what happened before. I can't wait for the next book in the series.

Linda Tonis, *The Paranormal Romance Guild*

 This book [**Cold Light**] in one sentence: A haunting, heart-wrenching, action-packed emotional roller coaster of a read that will leave an impression on you long after your finish the book.

To say that I love this book or this series would be an understatement. Traci Slatton has done an impeccable job with what I thought would be an impossible hurdle for her two main characters to overcome after the ending of **Fallen**. Not only did she do the impossible, but she made me love the characters and the new additions to the book even more.

Evelyn Amaro, *Paromantasy Blog*

 The After trilogy is a post-apocalyptic romance story that is as heart-breaking as it is realistic. Earlier this year, I dove into Slatton's **Fallen,** quickly immersing myself in a world that sucks you in and characters that keep you enthralled in their very existence. As I began reading **Cold Light**, I immediately felt like I was home again. The way of life for the survivors of the mists really keeps you cheering the characters on. I couldn't imagine living in the After world. It's disturbing on so many levels. I have to admit that some of the survivors really do make the best of their situation, revealing a spark of hope amongst the darkness. . . .

Slatton once again has created a brilliant post-apocalyptic world that will have you on the edge of your seat. I couldn't read it fast enough. The *After* trilogy is, by far, one of the most exciting reads I've read all month. I'm dying to find out how Slatton will end the trilogy. The worst thing about **Cold Light** is that it ended leaving me wanting more of the After.

Jennifer, *Fictitious Musings*

 Slatton's ability to weave a tale that is filled with adventure, loss and love is unmatched. Her writing makes it so easy for you to fall in love with the characters so much so that you find yourself riding a roller-coaster of emotions. One minute you are mad, then your lips curl into a smile, and sometimes you cannot help but reach for a tissue.

The Mists are changing, and our favorite Russian cut-throat is back in **Cold Light**. But don't get me started on the ending. I only hope that the final installment comes out quickly, and things work out the way I want them to. (I am totally on team Arthur!!)

An exceptional series that will keep you reading and ignoring your family. So grab **Fallen** and **Cold Light**, grab a bottle of wine, head to your favorite reading spot and be ready to spend the next four to eight or so hours falling in love with this series.

A MUST have series!

Annette Marie Guerriero Nishimoto,
Gothic Mom's Book Reviews

Emma's courage is only matched by her determination to find her daughter. But her heart is torn between the man whom she married and the man to whom she has fallen in love.

. . . Arthur's relentless pursuit of Emma is both heartbreaking and remarkable given the circumstances of the day. Finding a woman like Emma is a once in a lifetime occurrence, but his love has forced many of his friends into life-threatening situations. But like family, they argue and fight, and in the end, the survival of one means the survival of them all.

Cold Light is an amazing look at one person's passion to find someone they love- Arthur's pursuit of Emma and Emma's hunt for Beth. The storyline is slow to evolve as Traci takes the reader on a cold, dark and deadly trek across the snow covered fields of Alberta, but once Emma reaches a survival Outpost, the interaction of the characters quickly uncovers a series of plot twists and anxiety ridden re-introductions to the colorful characters from the series first book. Arthur's reunion with Emma is heart-wrenching and painful knowing he has travelled thousands of mile and 18 months to find the only woman he will ever love.

The character development continues as each of Arthur's family members seeks to find a place to where they belong. And survival 101 after an apocalyptic nightmare can also mean finding someone to love for all of the right and wrong reasons.

Sandy, *The Reading Café*

Traci Slatton nails it with her follow up to **Fallen**. In **Cold Light** Emma is faced with hard decision after hard decision—and we're not talking about decisions on simply where to live or who to be with. We're talking life and death decisions in a place that is just simply not pretty.

The end of **Fallen** leaves of with the reuniting of Emma with her family. She leaves behind someone she's grown attached to and does what is right and honorable. But now her life in Europe has followed her to Canada—in more ways than one.

What I appreciate about the After trilogy is how the world can be so bleak, but yet there is so much hope in the story. There's love, and thoughtfulness, and honor in a place where those just don't seem like they'd exist anymore. And what I love even more is how honest Traci's writing is. She doesn't hesitate to do what needs to be done to move the story forward. When writing a story like **Cold Light** (or it's previous book), there are hard things which need to be done to give the story credibility. You cannot write about bad people and have them not do bad things. This is not a young adult dystopian or post-apocalyptic story—this is hardcore, knuckle-whitening stuff and it kept me riveted from page one.

Lydia, *The Lost Entwife*

**Fallen** is another captivating story about the end of civilization as we know it. . . . Knee-gripping suspense and a host of great characters bring the post-apocalyptic world to horrifying life in **Fallen**. . . . I eagerly anticipate the next installment.

Margaret Marr, **Nights and Weekends Reviews**

Slatton is a fantastic storyteller. . . . **Fallen** awakens emotion and captivates with the turn of each page. . . . From every angle, **Fallen** is a captivating adventure with just enough romance to keep you enthralled and begging for more."

Jennifer, *Fictitious Musings*

Fallen is an exhilarating post apocalyptic thriller that contains superb twists and spins, which keep the reader wondering what next. The fast-paced story line grips the reader early on with the vivid description of a world gone mad and never slows down. . . . An exciting end of the world thriller.

Amazon Hall of Fame Reviewer Harriet Klausner
for *Alternative Worlds Reviews*

Excellent book [**Fallen**], I mean Unbelievable! So I tracked down the author because I was dying to know when the next one came out. . . .

Taking Time for Mommy Blogspot

The reader is forced to consider previously stable definitions of time, obedience, psychic powers, science, and most importantly, love. Powers exist, perhaps, that enhance long-ignored mental skills but is the power of memory too strong to allow for new ways of relating and the freedom to explore same without guilt and ignoring the instinctive inclinations of the heart?

Many, many questions arise as one reads this story [**Fallen**] that defies what can be falsely read as a simplistic story/plot. Traci L. Slatton is a writer to watch closely, including in whatever sequels follow this unique, well-written sci-fi novel!

Viviane, **Crystal Book Reviews**

 This is so not a world I want to live in—a mysterious mist that kills, rogue bands of survivors who round up women and children for far more nefarious purposes than you could imagine, dwindling food supplies . . .

I like Emma. She's strong, she's resolute, and she's fearless in standing up for those who can't help themselves—almost to the point of getting herself killed . . .

The plot is simple (survive), the story is moving. I enjoyed reading **Fallen**, and the realization at the end makes me antsy to find out what happens in the sequel to this first-in-a-trilogy.

Drey, **Drey's Library**

By the end of the book [**Fallen**], I wanted to know more about everyone. What will they do? How long can they survive? Will they find happiness? The book ends with a very emotional cliffhanger. This is the first of a trilogy, and I can't wait to find out what happens."

As I Turn the Pages Blogspot

Slatton's natural storytelling ability takes over and the reader finds themselves engrossed in another well envisioned story world. . . . Slatton has once again allowed her ability with words to develop a post apocalyptic world that draws the reader in, and allows them to work towards the struggle of survival right along side the characters. The characters are compelling and real. . . . They have weaknesses, and compulsions that are both horrifying and ennobling. Slatton has developed characters that have the courage to face a failing world, while at the same time demonstrating not only everything that is right about mankind, but everything that is wrong, as well. . . . I look forward to the future installments of this trilogy.

Lisa, **The Book Worm's Library**

In the post apocalyptic world of **Fallen**, survivors are tormented by a mysterious mist that can disintegrates animate and inanimate objects alike. Many have also developed psychic powers, like Emma's ability to heal. Emma was in Europe with her young daughter when the mists descended and the apocalypse began. As they travel to find a safe haven, more children joined their group and Emma protects them from both the mists and the roving bands of marauders. When they come across Arthur and his men searching for provisions in a dead town, Emma strikes up a deal. . . . Slowly, they fall in love, but Emma is torn between her new feelings and the husband she left behind overseas. When Arthur's devastating secret is revealed to her, she doubts the strength of her feelings for him.

Fallen has a very vivid world populated with interesting characters.

Laura Lehman, **Bella Online, The Voice of Women**

 What would you do if your daughter was stolen by Raiders? This is a story [**Cold Light**] that will stir every parental emotion in you and then take you for a ride. Emma's daughter was taken by raiders and there is nothing she will not do to get her back. The books plot and pace was stunning with its action packed story line and the dangers lurking around every corner. But she is not alone, she has loyal companions along the way. The world building is set in a post apocalyptic world. The characters were creatively built and I love how much they were relatable. Over all a great addition to the 1st book in this series.

Melissa, *Were Vamps Romance*

The second exciting "After" post-apocalyptic thriller moves forward on two fronts: Emma's relationships and the anticipated suicidal Armageddon Mists war as Traci L. Slatton deftly blends both subplots into a superb dystopian tale through her quality cast. The triangle participants fear the repercussions on the young at a time when nightmares are prevalent yet none of them can leave. Readers will wonder who will quote Dickens' A Tale of Two Cities: "It is a far, far better thing that I do, than I have ever done; it is a far, far better rest that I go to, than I have ever known."

Amazon Hall of Fame Reviewer Harriet Klausner
for *Alternative Worlds Reviews*

I haven't read the first book in the *After* Trilogy, but after reading **Cold Light** I have already ordered it on my kindle and will be reading it within the next few days. The way Traci L. Slatton has created the After world is amazingly real to a reader. I can picture it easily in my mind without even trying too hard. The characters in the book are very easy to relate to as well. The way people have to live now really hits home and makes me wonder if I would even be able to do that. Life without phones and computers and even tvs… kinda scary. As I previously stated I haven't read the first book but the way the author fills us in at different places in the book tells some of what I missed in the book. I didn't feel lost at all.

Jen's Corner Spot

 **Cold Light** is absolutely thrilling, even better than **Fallen**, but a bit shorter. I burned through the book in a couple of days and it left me longing for the conclusion to the story.

Once again, I love the characters in Slatton's story, as well as the intense and horrifying storyline. This is post-apocalyptic storytelling at its best. I'm a sucker for disaster movies and stories of post apocalyptic survival and I can visualize Slatton's stories as if they are a movie in my head. That's what great storytelling is all about. Highly recommended.

Game Vortex

 I've fallen for Fallen . . . Let me just throw this out there: I love dystopian books. . . .

A few other things you might want to know about me is 1) I love science fiction, 2) I love the conflict of man against nature gone wrong, and 3) I love a hearty romance thrown in there for good measure. Fallen had all of these ingredients, and more.

Full of action, adventure and a very intelligent read, I absolutely loved this story. . . . **Fallen** ends in a place where you know there will be a sequel, and this was fine by me, because I wasn't ready to let go of this world Traci L. Slatton had created so beautifully.

L. V. Lewis

 If you'd read **Fallen**, there is no way you can forgo **Cold Light**. I read this immediately after reading **Fallen**, but am just now getting to review. However, don't let that lead you to believe that this book isn't as stellar as the first. In fact, this book is more action-packed and the stakes have gone even higher than Emma and her family just avoiding the mists that can consume them. This is a do-or-die, life-and-death story that leaves you guessing at every turn—How is Emma going to get out of these newest pickles? Read **Cold Light** and find out.

This is a dystopian romance for the mature set, (Hunger Games and/or Divergent on steroids). Don't ignore this wonderful series.

I give **Cold Light** Five out of Five Stars!

L. V. Lewis

 From page one I was riveted to this bleak world where hope and honor can still exist. Yes, there was evil, greed, fear, bad people taking advantage of others, but love, strength and the will to live still existed, too. The author told an amazing story, brutally well. **Cold Light** is Book 2 in the *After* Series, following the book **Fallen**.

Tome Tender

Fallen is well written with twists that keep you reading. Traci L. Slatton does a good job describing the scenes, you feel like you're there with them. The characters were well-rounded, having good and bad sides, which helped make them feel real.

This is a solid, enjoyable story for fans of the post-apocalyptic and/or dystopian genres."

To Read Perchance to Dream Reviews

 **Fallen** definitely had my attention from page one. It is an intense post-apocalyptic action/romance that's so well written you feel like the mists exist; (and you will probably avoid fog after reading). Being a fan of the survival-horror genre, I didn't know how a "survival-romance" would mesh, but Traci Slatton made it work. Her writing style is really descriptive and has a great flow to it; one minute your heart is racing, and the next minute you can't help but smile. The characters, Emma especially, had an authentic quality to them. They weren't just cookie-cutter characters, but 3-dimensional, and the dialogue fit them perfectly. As for the plot, it was very well developed, fast-paced, twisty, unique, and you won't see the ending coming. I personally can't wait for the next book in the trilogy!

Allizabeth Collins, *The Paperback Pursuer Blogspot*

 I was pulled into **Fallen** from the first few pages. Traci L. Slatton's apocalyptic world seems eerily possible. . . . **Fallen** is billed as the first of a trilogy. . . . This is not a girly romance. Slatton has written an apocalyptic novel with a romance built in— like most good stories should have. **Fallen** is excellent. I'll have to watch for the sequel.

Jandy's Reading Room

To

Julia Howard

and Madeleine Howard

and to

Carole and Stefano Acunto

COLD
LIGHT

1 MY DAUGHTER BETH WAS DISAPPEARING WEST-
ward into the snowy horizon, caught up by a raider on
horseback, and my husband threw his body over me, to
keep me from going after her.

"No, Emma!" Haywood yelled. He covered me with his
body, circled my struggling torso with his arms. "You can't
save her. We can't lose you, too. Everything else is gone.
Please, Emma! Not you too. Calm down." He pressed his
cool, pale cheek close to mine, willing me to calm. His
breath, tart with morning coffee, came in short bursts.

Gun fire and war cries, screams of terror and hooves and
explosive charges, rattled and boomed and whistled through
the frigid air. I hadn't heard the sounds of battle in a year
and a half, but I knew them like they were branded onto the
skin of my consciousness. I would never forget. The end of
the world had brought chaos and madness. Inevitably, battle
ensued. Even here in the Safe Zone of Edmonton, Alberta.

"Let me up," I gasped. "We have to go after her!" I writhed
against crunchy snow. My red ski hat pulled off my head and
bitter sharp ice pebbles lodged in my scalp. I had to get to
Beth. *She's only nine. What will the raiders do to her?*

I knew too well what they would do. I redoubled my
efforts to escape from Haywood.

"Not right now," Haywood said. He clutched me fiercely.
"I can see, Emma," he whispered. "I can see the paths. If you

go now, you'll die. So will she. In every path. It's horrible."
He lifted his head and his dark eyes burned into mine. His
pupils were engorged; he was under the spell of prophecy. It
had come upon him after the apocalypse, this skewed ability to read possibilities in the near future. They fanned out
in front of him like multiple parachutes opening, several at
once, and then they closed. Which, if any, would come to
fruition? What choices would alter them? How could he pre-
vent further catastrophe? It tormented him.

I lay still and breathed through my open mouth. The air
was so cold that it seared my throat. The pain, as it always
did, brought me back to myself. Haywood was right. There
was no retrieving Beth in this moment: a bloody melee of
shouting people, whooping men on horseback snatching up
women and children as their horses raced past, and unarmed
men throwing rocks and getting shot down where they stood.

Haywood sensed my surrender and rolled off me.

I stood and looked into the west, after the disappearing
cavalcade of riders. I could just make out the gleam of Beth's
blonde hair as it wafted out like a flag from where she was
perched on the withers of a stocky black draft horse. A raider
in a ragged gray parka rode with her captured in his arms. She
was too far for me to hear her screaming, though my heart
knew she was pleading for help.

A few feet away her pink fleece hat rolled toward me and
then lay still on the ground near some shell casings. I walked
over to pick it up, not taking my eyes from her as the bouncing dot of her blonde head grew smaller and smaller in the
distance. My sweet oldest daughter was standing right next
to me when the raiders thundered up around us. I turned
to look—how had her hand slipped from mine? Suddenly
she was shrieking, and our walk in the park had turned into
a nightmare. I could still see the terrified look on her face.
Why hadn't I been taken in her place?

I'll get you back, Beth, I promise that, on my life.

"They rode right up through the river valley, through the park system," Brendan said. He trudged over to us, clutched my arm, and peered up into my face. His black eyes, from near my waist, searched my expression. His woolly black beard had caught white flakes. "'The latter end of joy is woe,'" he muttered. I knew it to be a quote but couldn't place it. Shakespeare, maybe. Or Chaucer or Milton. Brendan was an African American dwarf who'd once taught literature at the University of Portland. When the mists had descended and consumed Portland, he'd survived. Like thousands of other survivors, he'd made his way here to Edmonton, the center of the largest Safe Zone in the world. After he was declared sane, the Office of Survivors Relations of the City of Edmonton had assigned him to us, to live in our home.

"Why weren't the Canadian Forces guardsmen watching?" Haywood wondered as he helped an elderly man up off the ground.

A woman came to stand by the old man. She laughed. She was middle-aged, stocky, and square-faced, with long black hair and feathers woven into her ponytail. An aboriginal, probably Cree, Ojibway, or Sioux. She didn't look Inuit but I wasn't good at discerning. She was wearing a Juicy Couture track suit under her North Face coat. "The guardsmen can't be everywhere. Not with rumors of the mists encroaching."

"What do you mean, mists encroaching?" I asked. "The mists never come near Edmonton."

She stared at me steadily. "They've been spotted north of Medicine Hat."

"They don't come north of Medicine Hat," I said.

"They're setting themselves free. That's the balance of it," she said.

I didn't have time to quiz her because Haywood was calling my name.

"Em, come here! There's a man down, and you can help him," Haywood yelled.

I threw a look over my shoulder at the woman—but she'd vanished. *Where'd she go that quickly?* I shook my head as I went to Haywood.

He was kneeling over a young guy who'd been shot, an acne-stubbled kid in his twenties who was probably out playing football in the snow. His buddies stood in a ring around us, staring at him in dismay. The kid clutched his gut, moaned, gurgled blood out of his lips, and writhed.

"Stomach wound. I hate those." I sighed as I peeled off my gloves. The air was so cold, a typical February minus five, that the skin on my fingers contracted around the bones. But I was needed. I knelt and put my hands on the young man's middle.

Two years and two months ago, the mists had come— roiling white miasmas, often the size of battleships, that consumed living beings for the metals in their bodies, and that imploded buildings and destroyed cities. Billions of people and whole cities vanished into the white cloud banks with their sickly sweet smell of lilacs and sulfur.

The mists didn't just destroy. They were bioactive; they changed people. They wreaked pain and bewilderment on the unmapped psychic regions of the human brain. People were left with strange gifts: clairvoyance, precognition, telepathy, astral projection. I was left with the ability to heal. I hadn't asked for it, and I didn't want it, but I used it when it was needed. Like so many others, I had learned to be ruthlessly practical.

My hands found their way to the ragged edges of his down coat where his red-slicked viscera protruded. I winced a little at the copper-and-defecation stink. Then, of itself, a calm descended. The shouting and screaming faded into nothing. It was just me and the man who was little more than a boy, really—a boy who was suffering. I felt sorry that he was in pain.

The quieter the world got, the more relief he felt. He

stopped moaning and gazed at me, his eyes open to slits of indigo and black.

A force rose and came through me. I wasn't its origin nor its destination, I was simply a conduit—a pipe of flesh and bone. The force was soft and strong and sweet and powerful all at once, and it flowed out my hands and into him. His eyes liquesced. I didn't do anything, I just kept the small egoic part of myself out of the way. The more 'I' stood out of the way, the more intense the force grew. The boy's head rolled off to the side and he passed into something like sleep.

Lately, in moments like these, when I was healing some-one (as I did every day at the Royal Alexandra Hospital), I experienced a presence with me. The healing current flowed through me and altered my state. I was expanded. I could feel things and see things that were normally veiled to me.

The presence was a man. He was black-haired and gray-eyed, with a perfection and symmetry of feature that thrilled me. I had once been an artist, and even still, in this failing and obliterated world, beauty made an impression on me. Arthur's beauty. Arthur who had loved me and hurt me in ways I couldn't have imagined Before.

I let the healing force pour out my hands into the wounded kid and looked at the vaporous presence that knelt on the ground opposite me. He was looking back at me; I could feel it. I could feel his heart beating, just as I'd felt it on my own chest a thousand times. It had been almost a year and a half since I'd last held him, and an ocean separated us. But I would never forget the feeling of being close to him. I ached for him. I hated myself for that. It wasn't fair to Haywood.

I owed it to Haywood to be true to him. We had children together, and they were what mattered. I looked down at my hands in the puddle of blood and torn flesh.

The presence remained.

"Let him go. You'll see him soon enough," whispered a voice at my ear.

I started.

It was the black-haired woman, leaning down close to me. The feather in her braid fluttered over my shoulder, tickling my cheek. She was looking over the injured young man— looking directly at Arthur.

I gasped. "You *see* him?"

She shrugged. "Everyone'll see him, soon enough. You've called him."

I started again. "I never call him. He just comes!"

The woman rolled her eyes, amused. "Soldiers are here."

All at once I was aware of the commotion around me: horses neighing and horns blowing, soldiers riding in on horseback and driving up in Jeeps with chains on their snow tires. A uniformed medic sprinted over to me, pushed me back, and leaned over the kid. I was sprawled out backward but didn't care. The medic began examining the kid. I rose and dusted the snow off my back and tush.

"Kangee," the black-haired woman said. "Sioux." She nodded and trudged off.

I watched her for a moment. Suddenly, just like before, she was gone. *A trick of the sunlight on the snow?* I blinked and shook my head, then looked for Haywood.

He was helping an elderly man whose arm was bent at an odd angle. Another medic ran to join them.

A soldier grabbed my shoulder with one hand, while his other arm cradled a rifle. "Are you all right, miss? Are you in need of medical assistance?" he barked.

"I'm okay," I said. "But they got my daughter! She's only nine!" I felt myself start to come unhinged. *We have to get Beth back! We have to save her!* A wild helpless feeling burned through my chest and throat.

The soldier's brusque military face went soft, just for a moment. He patted my arm. Then he was gone, querying the next person.

The uniformed medic was hollering at me. It took me a few moments to refocus on him. "Whatever you were doing, do it again! We need to get him stabilized!" the medic was saying. I blinked.

"Em, I'll see about going after her." Haywood draped his arm around me. "Thank God, Mandy was home with my mum. I don't know what I'd do if I lost her again."

"We have to get Beth back," I pleaded urgently. Haywood nodded and went to talk to the soldiers. The medic was yanking on my sleeve, dragging me back to a crouch on the crunchy ice.

I turned back to the boy, who was moaning again.

I will get you back, Beth. I promise. No matter what.

2 THE CITY FATHERS SAT IN A ROW AT A LONG
table on the stage. Their hands were clasped or
their arms were folded over their middles. Their
faces were hard, set, and very sorry, all at once.
I shivered in my coat, and not because the building wasn't
heated. More than five hundred people had come to the
meeting in the library theater at the Stanley Milner Library,
a scant three hours after the raid. They filled to overflow-
ing the small theater that was only designed for 247 people.
Heat wasn't needed in here, with all the warm bodies pressed
together. It was the calculation of the city government that
chilled me.

Haywood and I sat in the second row. Haywood was on his
feet, screaming at the council members. "If we do nothing,
they are all lost. We lose them all!"

The mayor himself cleared his throat. "I'm sorry, but we
must face the facts. Twenty-six people is an acceptable loss.
If we go after the raiders, all the way into the Wastelands,
we risk both manpower and valuable resources, with no cer-
tainty of retrieving any of our people. If we——"

He was cut off by the clamor that erupted in the library
theater.

Haywood leaned down, his face close to mine. "If we
mount an armed force now, we'll rescue more than twenty,
and Beth will be among them!"

"Don't say that," I cautioned. If people knew that

Haywood's precognitive sense was growing, he might be institutionalized. The Edmonton city government was leery of mist-given psychic gifts, which so often developed into insanity.

We couldn't really blame the city government. They had to be careful. Early in the After, when I was still at Arthur's camp in what was left of Europe, a group of the insane had banded together in Churchill Square outside this very library, and slaughtered thirty people with axes, butcher knives, rakes, and ice picks. Their bloody onslaught didn't stop until the soldiers shot them all. Beth had witnessed it. She was in a school group coming to the library and two of her classmates had their throats cut. *Beth.* My heart lurched.

The mayor rose and gestured with his palms, big sweeps through the air meant to quiet the hubbub. The noise dwindled. "We can't risk losing more. Our plan, effective immediately, is to strengthen the borders of the Safe Zone. The raiders are getting more daring. We have a responsibility, now more than ever, with so many gone and the world in shambles—"

"Now more than ever," Haywood chimed in, cutting him off, "there are no acceptable losses." His voice rang out clear and true, and the assembled masses murmured.

Next, someone applauded, and soon the whole theater rang with cheers. They gave Haywood a standing ovation.

The accolades didn't please the mayor and council, which was now comprised of thirteen representatives rather than the original twelve from Before. The last council position was from the Ward of the Safe Zone, which stretched from Medicine Hat north to Great Slave Lake, and from Kamloops in Thompson County east to Saskatoon. The councilor's duties encompassed the new reality since the mists' incursions. He was responsible, along with the mayor, for making the hard decisions. He and the mayor stared balefully at Haywood.

Finally, the new councilor, a Metis man named Peter

LaRocque, shuffled to his feet. "We can't mount an official rescue effort right now, in the heart of winter, with what we're doing to secure the borders. Much as we'd like to." He spoke in one of those voices that prided itself on being harsh with pragmatism. He nodded at the mayor and the whole council rose and filed offstage.

"They can't stop us from going after our own. It's our right and our duty," a woman next to me said, talking to her brother, whose wife had been taken in the raid.

Haywood and I exchanged a glance. We both knew what we would do. Abandoning Beth wasn't an option for us.

"I don't think it's a good idea," Brendan said, from his seat next to Haywood's. "'The gods had thought with some reason that there is no more dreadful punishment than futile and hopeless labor.' But I will support you all the way, no matter what you decide to do."

Peter Larocque came back out on stage, waving his hands to quiet everyone. "Edmontonians, I remind you that all horses are now the property of the City of Edmonton. That was one of the first pieces of legislation that was enacted After. Stealing a horse isn't just a misdemeanor. It's an executionable offense." Boos and cat-calls ricocheted off the rafters of the fifty year old building, but Larocque wasn't fazed. He just nodded grimly and walked offstage.

"That makes it harder," Brendan said. "Prometheus only had his liver eaten out every day. We're going to have to walk out in subzero weather."

HAYWOOD AND I were arguing. We sat at the kitchen banquette with Brendan, Sally, and Renee, Haywood's mother. Sally was the other refugee assigned to live with us. She was young and so blonde that her hair was platinum, and her features were tiny and exquisitely shaped. She was also mute. She understood everything but never uttered a single word. She was a great help to Renee, and she was sweet with the girls.

But she often just sat by the fireplace, her pretty face blank, her blue eyes staring into infinity. The OSR had assigned her to us after declaring her sane. I had my doubts, though.

"You can't go alone," Haywood said. "It's suicide." His lips were pressed tightly together. He glared at the candles flickering in their holders. Power was always shut off in the city at this time of day, in an effort to conserve—a futile effort to hold at bay the inevitable moment when the coal and gas reserves dwindled to nothing. Not enough solar panels had been installed Before to make a dent in the city's needs, and Edmonton wasn't powered by hydro-electric dams, like so many other, more fortunate cities in Canada.

"It's not fair to Mandy for us to put both her parents at risk," I said.

"I'll be with her," Renee promised.

"Not good enough. She made us promise that she'd never be without at least one parent. We promised. In the plane, on the way back to Canada from Le Havre. Remember? We have to keep our promise."

Haywood shook his head, though his eyes remembered. "For Beth, Mandy will understand—"

"No, she won't, not after what she's been through." I paused. "What do you see if we both go, Haywood?"

He shook his head, tore at his hair.

I repeated, "What do you see?"

He wouldn't answer and we all knew what that meant.

I nodded. "It's got to be me who goes after Beth. I'm experienced at trekking through hostile territory. I did it in France."

"I forbid it," Haywood barked. "Too dangerous. I'll go."

"A man will be shot on sight by raiders," Brendan interjected, for the tenth time. He scratched his beard thoughtfully. "A woman stands a chance. She won't necessarily be killed immediately. She'll be taken." His lean brown face crumpled with disgust.

"I'm good at defending myself, good with a gun," I said.

"There's got to be another way," Renee said softly. She was tall and slim like Haywood, and like him, she'd always looked younger than her years. Now in her seventies, she was finally beginning to show her age. Her auburn hair was streaked with white and her pale face was worn and tired. She rose and backed up against the sink.

"No one else will rescue Beth even if they go after the hostages. Mandy can't lose both of her parents, and Haywood doesn't see any good outcomes if we both go," I said. "One of us has to go. Me."

"No, no," Haywood growled. "This isn't France. This is Canada. It's minus ten outside on a good day. The raiders here are far more organized than they were over in Europe. I'll go."

A wry grin twisted my lips. "No gang was more organized than the Russian camp led by Alexei, and I made it out of there alive."

"You were *rescued*," Haywood said. He turned his face away and closed his eyes. He was thinking of Arthur, the invisible presence in our bed for the last sixteen months. He was thinking of Arthur who was always with me even though I would never see him again.

"I survived for weeks before he came for me," I said softly, not daring to say his name aloud. "And in the end, I saved Alexei from rogue soldiers."

"From what you've said, he was a sociopath, but he wasn't insane," Brendan said.

"Still, if I'm taken, I can work from within to save her," I said.

"Right. If you aren't killed right after being raped. If you don't go mad," Brendan parried.

Renee shuddered.

Sally's blue eyes filled with tears.

"Haywood, what do you see, if I go alone?" I asked again,

finally coming to the crucial point: *What does the future hold?*

Haywood dropped his face onto the table. He interlocked his fingers behind his head, squeezing until his knuckles went white and the tendons of his hands stood out like sticks, brittle and dark. His breathing grew ragged. We all held the silence. Finally, he said, "There are ten . . . branches. Nearly a dozen possibilities. Just at this moment, before you make any further decisions."

"And they are?" I prodded him.

"In two of the paths, you die. In four of them, you bring Beth back."

"The other four?" I asked.

Haywood shook his head.

"But you see no paths where we bring her back if we both go."

"I'll go with," Brendan said, as casually as if he was volunteering to walk me to a Sobeys grocery store.

I took a deep breath. "Brendan, your leg is still too weak. If you come with me, it may give out when we can't afford to slow down."

"I'm strong enough!" Brendan said. "Is this because I'm black?"

A reluctant giggle escaped me. I leaned over and kissed his forehead, which was a little warm, as if with fever. "Yes, of course."

"No, it isn't. It's because I'm a midget, you staturist bitch," he said. He puffed out his chest. "I'll have you know that we little people have God-given mystical abilities. . . ."

"Everyone has mystical abilities now," Haywood snapped. "It's because you have a bum leg. You'll be a hindrance and not an asset if she has to move quickly."

"I plan to steal a horse," I said.

"After what that despicable Larocque said?" Brendan cried. "Don't you dare!"

"That's another advantage to going alone. One person

moves quietly and can get in and out, while a group can't.
The other rescuers will go in groups, and the guards will be
on the lookout for that."

Haywood picked up his head and glared at me. "If anything
happens to you, Em, I'll never forgive you. You have to come
back to me. You owe me that."

"I'm going to throw up," Renee said.

I stood up, the matter decided. "I'm going now. It'll be
easier to steal a horse in the dark. Besides, the sooner I go
after Beth, the better chance I have of finding her. We've lost
hours already, waiting for the city council to mount a rescue
effort."

"This is not happening," Haywood said in a strangled
voice. "How has it come to this? No."

Renee touched his arm.

"We're not going to lose her," Brendan said fiercely.

"No, we're not," I said. I straightened myself, feeling
relieved to have made a decision. "I'm going to walk out, steal
a horse, ride after the raiders, get Beth, and bring her home.
That's the plan."

"You like this," Haywood growled, his eyes blazing at me.

"What I like doesn't matter. This is what must be done."
I shrugged.

Sally stood and gently gripped my arm. She wanted to
help me.

I said, "Sally, pack Beth's old green backpack for me. I'll
need water and food. See if we have any of those old protein
bars left. Extra socks and thermal underwear, one of Haywood's dad's old camping blankets, and a map; I've got a long
way to travel."

"Knife, gun?" Brendan asked. Haywood made a stricken
sound. He clenched his hands into fists and slammed them
down on the table, hard. The candles rattled in their sconces
and one of them flickered out.

I said, "I'll pack those myself."

UPSTAIRS, WITH CANDLES throwing shadows like dark confetti, I stripped down and put on fresh panties, along with two layers of thermal underwear: silk first, then the high performance layer, fabric woven with silicone. I added a fleece vest. I pulled on a pair of silk socks, a pair of wool socks, and then a pair of felt socks. I wanted to avoid frostbite. Finally, I put on bib-overall ski pants.

Downstairs, something crashed; it sounded like a chair being thrown. Haywood's cursing rang out like stones thrown through windows.

I stood on my tiptoes to reach the wooden box on the top shelf of our closet. The box was velvety with dust. I held it away from my body as I pulled it down. I opened the box. There it was: my handgun. The one I'd carried the whole time I was in France. The one with a bullet in it with Mandy's name on it, because I wasn't going to let my beloved daughter suffer if the mists got her.

I took the gun in hand and checked to see that it was loaded. It was.

Then, all at once, it all came back to me: all ten months I'd lived in France, how desperately I'd worked to survive and to keep seven children and Mandy alive; how I'd met Arthur and struck a bargain with him so he'd let me and the kids live in his camp, which was a Safe Zone. Newt had told me so.

Newt. I closed my eyes. Sadness and longing welled up inside me.

And the others. Genevra, the little French girl who'd regressed to an infantile state. Marco, the irrepressible Italian. Brave Shoshana, funny Felix, Dragomir whose mother had found him, sweet Caris who helped me care for the others. The people from the camp: James the doctor, Robert who married Jeannie from the women's camp. Theo who declared himself my brother because I healed his brother Pyotr. Cook who I bullied for better food for Arthur. Vasily who sang like an opera star and young Claude who couldn't remember his mother's gingerbread recipe. Nwokocha, the brilliant linguist, who had miraculously recovered from cancer. Torsten the big Swedish veterinarian who helped me and Laurette amputate a woman's foot.

Laurette, the herbalist—how did I go a single hour without remembering her? Didn't she become a sister of mine?

The cold steel in my hand made me miss them all fiercely.

There was no one I missed more than Arthur. But I didn't think of him. Rather, I thought of butterflies—the inheritors, taking over the green land in Europe once the mists had devoured buildings and cars and factories and highways.

Then I couldn't help but think of him, tall and warm, wanting me. I swallowed.

"Em, you'd better come down. Haywood's gone off the deep end." It was Brendan, standing at the bedroom door. He was rubbing his leg, in pain just from having climbed the stairs. His mouth was drawn up tightly.

"I'll work on your leg when I get back with Beth," I promised.

"'My fate cries out, and makes each petty artery in this body as hardy as the Nemean Lion's nerve.'" Brendan shook his head at me. "Come on. Your husband needs you."

"Let me kiss Mandy," I said. I tiptoed into her room, sat on the edge of her twin bed, and kissed her cheek.

She was sleeping soundly, snoring snuffily through parted lips. We'd been through so much together. Everything, really—the end of the world.

I'll bring your sister back, I promise. My heart felt a little better. Mandy would understand why I had to go. She would have faith in me. She'd already witnessed her mother doing the impossible. She would comfort her father. I brushed her auburn hair off her soft, round face and pressed my lips again to her smooth cheek.

Brendan coughed from the doorway.

More crashes and curses sounded downstairs. Haywood was in a bad way. He had a right to be. Our daughter was a prisoner of terrible, crazed raiders.

But I felt a surge of hope. My gun was at my side and I was setting out on a journey, setting forth to do something, to take action. Haywood claimed I liked it. Arthur had once accused me of the same thing.

"You like this."

"This what?" I sat astride a horse and steered it to walk circles.

"Getting ready to go. Leaving on an adventure."

"Having a little break from the usual routine of trying to avoid death, starvation, and attack?" I asked in a low voice, so the kids wouldn't hear. "I thought you wanted me to have fun."

"Have fun with me. You're at risk of death out there alone, alone," Arthur said grimly. *"Carry your gun. Be prepared to use it."*

"I'm always prepared to use it," I said.

I was still prepared.

I wondered what Arthur would say now, if he knew I was going out again. Alone, this time. To face the mists, raiders, and a force just as powerful as either of those: the cold.

3 A LIGHT SNOW SETTLED ON MY SHOUL-
ders, backpack, and hat. I wore a black uni-
piece hood and face mask under my hat so only
my eyes showed through a narrow slit. The air
was so frigid that it burned the sclera of my eyes.

My booted feet made soft crunching sounds in the snow.
It was one in the morning, well past curfew. The streets
were empty. Renee's big brick house lay far behind, and I had
walked past the western edge of Old Glenora Community. I
was headed toward Lois Hole Centennial Park, where a stable
had been set up with only a few soldiers to guard the horses.
I'd discovered this at the nurses station at the Royal Alexandra Hospital.

I'd been working in the coronary care unit, because my
strange, unasked-for healing gift was efficacious with heart
attacks, unstable angina, and cardiac disrhythmia. Within
a week of my arrival in Edmonton, I'd gone to the hospital and volunteered. I hadn't mentioned the healing gift. The
girls were in school and I wanted to be busy. Everyone was
expected to contribute to our survival as a species. Besides,
I wanted to help. I'd been put to work cleaning and running
errands, fetching things for patients, and bringing coffee to
nurses and doctors.

Then, unbeknownst to me, a nurse saw me laying my
hands on patients, and she started to take notice as most
of the patients I touched improved. The nurse reported my

gift, and I was summoned to an inquiry panel of doctors and administrators.

I confessed everything: how I'd discovered the healing gift by accident and used it extensively in Europe. I answered all their questions, and they were intrigued. While they'd have laughed me into a mental institute a few years ago, they were now desperate. There were too many sick and injured people, too few medical personnel, and rapidly dwindling supplies of medication. Besides, paranormal gifts had become commonplace; the mists influenced the part of the human brain in which extrasensory abilities reside.

I was suddenly a person of great interest.

For the next few months, I rotated through the hospital. Then some bean counter—amazing how, even now, After, bean counters still run hospitals—some bean counter realized that the cardiac care unit benefited most from my presence. So the cardiac care unit was my new posting.

There I started listening in on the gossip that flowed through the nurses station. Some part of me recorded all the news, facts and figures and speculation about the world. Some part of me was hungry for every scrap of information about life at the periphery of the Safe Zone and outside it, in the Wastelands.

Have I always known it would come to this, to my leaving the Safe Zone? Not with Haywood's prescience, but with my own intuition, have I known that I am not meant to remain within the four walls of a home in a protected area?

I sighed and my breath was a white plume against the inky air. I was just about to turn off Stony Plain Road onto Winterburn Road. There was a short cut to Winterburn via 199th Street, but a pack of wild dogs had taken up residence in an abandoned house there, so it wasn't safe. The city council kept promising to dispose of the dogs, but that was a low priority.

Edmonton now had a bumper crop of dangerous animals, including cougars, bears, and wolves. Whole animal populations had migrated into the Safe Zone in order to avoid the mists. I had to be alert for cougars in particular as I meant to stay close to the tree-line, which was still bare in places, thanks to a wildfire that had licked through a few years Before. But cougars were less of an impediment than guardsmen, who'd take me back to Renee's house in a heartbeat.

Distant headlights ripped across Winterburn and I dove behind an abandoned car. I crouched there for an hour, waiting for the Canadian Forces jeep to pass by. It was minus twenty out and the enforced stillness left me vulnerable to the piercing, frigid air.

Fatigue drifted over me like a cozy blanket. I didn't dare let myself sleep. If I drifted off into slumber, my mission to save Beth would be over before it began.

Desperate, purposeful, I thought about Arthur. I'd met him near the Lot River in Southern France, and ridden with him south to a camp near where the town of Valensole once stood. The last time I'd seen him, he'd sat astride a giant roan horse. A crazed Russian named Alexei pointed a gun at Arthur's head as Arthur watched me leave.

My younger daughter Mandy had been with me in Paris on The Day.

My mind drifted back to Arthur. *Is he still alive?*

I didn't know whether to pray that he was, or, because of what he'd done, to pray that he wasn't.

I only knew that it hurt to think about him. And the hurt kept me awake.

IT WAS FOUR A.M. and I could finally see the makeshift stable ahead, beside a cluster of fir trees. The stable had been built After and had a rudimentary look to it, with latched down prefab windows and aluminum doors, all lit by old-fashioned torches set in sconces. It was big, about forty meters long by twenty wide.

I got within a half-kilometer and dropped to my hands and

knees to crawl. Anyone looking out would see only a low dark shape, moving slowly. Could be any kind of animal. There was, in fact, a pair of glowing amber eyes tracking me from the distance. I hoped I could maneuver my way inside and escape with a horse before the animal got me.

Another half-hour and I was close enough to make out the round heads of two guards sitting by a lantern near the front left window. Were there two more at the other window? I couldn't see. The two I could see were still, as if they had dozed off.

A dog barked once, softly, and one of the heads roused.

I dropped flat onto the ground alongside an icy mound of horse manure.

The soldier stood at the window, looking out. Several minutes later, his figure left the dim glass.

I panted and got back up on my hands and knees, then crawled in a wide berth around the stable to its back. The ground turned to slick, glassy ice. Lois Hole Park was really a wetland preserve radiating out from Big Lake, with marsh-land surrounding the shallow lake. It was home to a multitude of bird species, along with deer, moose, and coyotes. It hadn't been developed Before other than a viewing platform at the mouth of the Sturgeon River.

The glowing yellow eyes got a little closer.

Smoke rose through chimneys and curled out along the eaves of the stable; it was probably heated by wood-burning stoves. The back of the building was dark.

I rose and walked quietly to feel it. I walked along the wall, feeling for another door. The walls, of concrete and wood and corrugated steel, only barely muffled the neighing and stomping of horses inside. I hoped that the noises I would make breaking into the stable would be taken as ambient ani-mal sounds.

My fingers found the door cut into the back. I pulled and then pushed a little. The door was unlocked. I kept working it, slowly back and forth, so it wouldn't make a big noise. Finally I managed to pull it ajar just enough for me to slip in. I was almost soundless.

A soldier waited for me with his rifle pointed, cocked and ready, at my head. He was stocky and of middling height, and he wore a thick woolen hoodie with the hood down, exposing his shiny black hair, smooth red skin, and intelligent dark eyes. He was young, in his early twenties. A big, alert malamute stood beside him. The young soldier didn't say anything but jerked his chin at me, his eyes flicking over my hood and face mask.

I lowered my hood and pulled off the mask. My blonde hair crackled with static electricity and clung to the mask before slowly dropping around my face.

He gave me a long, thoughtful look and his eyes narrowed, then brightened. He recognized me. I didn't recognize him. He lowered his gun and held his finger to his lips, shushing me. He pointed into a stall where a grizzled black horse stood, rocking a little on his feet.

I undid the latch and entered the stall. When the man pointed down, I slid down, my back against the wall of the stall.

The horse blinked at me sleepily.

The soldier held up two fingers, then pointed to himself and toward the front of the barn, where the other soldier sat by the lamp.

Two of them? I got it. I nodded.

He held his fingers to his lips again and then spread out his hands.

Wait? I nodded again.

I didn't know how long it was before he came back, but I was grateful for the warmth. It couldn't have been more than fifty degrees in the stable, but even that felt balmy. It made me almost punchy with heat. I peeled off my gloves and then unzipped my parka and laid everything on the ground beside me. I curled up into myself. The horse ignored me. My bones softened, and my mind dissolved. Arthur's face came back to me, as it always did in the hypnogogic state. I felt myself doze.

"You're lucky that big daddy cat didn't get you," the man murmured.

"What?" I mumbled. I shook myself awake. The vestiges of a dream of being held by Arthur fell away. The usual ache remained.

"You're that woman, the healer," he said in a low tone. He stood before me with a bundle of furs in his hand. "You saved my grandmother Aanak last month when she was admitted to the Royal Alexandra."

"Cardiac care?" I asked, rising slowly.

The old horse whuffled softly and the soldier patted his muzzle.

"Yep. One of the nurses said she'd have died but for you." He threw the bundle at my feet. "Put these on. Mike is sleeping now. We should have an hour, but maybe not, eh?"

I glanced at the fur and then back at him. "What are those? Why should I put them on?"

"Because you'll die in what you're wearing."

I shook my head. "This is high performance gear."

"Caribou is the best protection," he insisted.

"You're Inuit," I guessed.

He smiled.

"I'm well bundled," I assured him.

"Not well enough. I can't give you a horse, they'll shoot me if I do, and go after you anyway. But I can make sure you don't die of cold. There's a caribou parka here, and a proper atigi. Caribou trousers. Two pair kamiks and sealskin boot coverings. Mittens."

"I'll be fine in what I'm wearing."

He shook his head. "My grandmother made these the old way, with caribou sinew for thread. You could walk through a blizzard at forty below in these."

"I don't plan to walk through any blizzards," I said dryly, unconvinced.

"Sure you do, eh? You're walking to an outpost just north of Medicine Hat, where they're a little looser about guarding horses, mostly because the mounties there are usually drunk on home-made brew. But you didn't hear that from me." He smiled again, but this time without mirth.

"Medicine Hat?"

"Outpost City, where they know about the raiders who took the people today." The big malamute trotted into the stall and lay down, its white paws pointed directly at me.

"So you're expecting a blizzard between here and Medicine Hat?" I asked.

He nodded. "You'll need better supplies, too. Dried fish. I already put it in your backpack."

I shuddered slightly. I'd never developed a taste for dried fish. But then, that didn't matter. Starvation made taste a moot point. I bent and picked up the furs. "It's what, 500 kilometers to Medicine Hat?"

"I'd say 530, 540, on foot," he said. "Take you a week. You carrying a gun? You know how to use it? You're going to need it. Soon maybe. That big cat outside is going to track you for a while."

"Yes, and yes," I said. A multi-colored wool strap held the furs together; I undid it carefully. "I've been tracked by worse."

DAN ALIGNAK HELPED me shuck off my gear. I left on the two pairs of thermal underwear and the fleece vest, then pulled on an inner pair of trousers with the fur facing inward and an outer pair of trousers with the fur facing out. There was an inner parka, the atigi, soft and luscious, as the innermost layers always are.

"Never seen a cougar so big, 100 kilograms, a meter tall at the shoulder. He can jump, too. I saw him leap more than ten meters to take down a bison calf. You got a knife, carry it in your other hand, ready. You'll only have a few seconds if he decides to pounce.

"The snow will start in a few hours. Whopper of a storm, dumping lots of snow. Strong winds, the kind that'll pick you up off the road and hurl you into the trees. Wedge yourself in somewhere, but don't fall asleep. Better if you take cover. You'll find something—an abandoned store or house. Just watch for squatters and scavengers. There are more and more of them, and they can be as dangerous as anything else out there. Royal Forces can't get a handle on the problem.

"If you manage to clear Edmonton, there's some wolves along Highway 56. Real bold. Always hungry."

"You're full of good news," I said.

"Sit, I'll help you with your boots," he said. "The outpost is due north of The Hat, north of the river."

"Redcliff?" I asked, as he was lacing up an inner pair of kamiks.

He shook his head. "No. It's new, since After. Outpost City." He tugged hard on the lacings. The fur tightened up around my calf like a snake. I grunted. He said, "You don't want snow to get in. You'll recognize it. Group of buildings near some cliffs. Teepees and tents, prefab buildings, wooden shacks. There are all types lurking there—soldiers, hunters, traders, black marketeers, hookers, and other undesirables. Not everyone is friendly, eh?"

"I know, I know. Carry my gun and be prepared to use it," I said.

"And keep your knife in your other hand. Watch yourself. Outpost City brings out the worst in everyone." He finished with the other kamik and pulled on the second pair of boots over them. "Now, Emma—"

"Youknowalotaboutme.Ican'tbelieveyouevenremembermy name."

"I watched you one day at the hospital. I was happy you

saved my grandma. My parents and my sister were in Florida on vacation on The Day." His mouth made a small, sad quirk. I knew without him having to say the words that he'd never heard from them again. "Florida." He uttered a few words in Inuktitut that I guessed were not complimentary about the Sunshine State. Then he switched back to English. "They'll hang you at Outpost City if they catch you stealing a horse. You'll need to be smart and sly—and a little less noticeable than you were here."

"Sure. That'll get me past the cougar, the blizzard, the wolves, the Canadian Forces patrols, the ruffians, and the guards in Outpost City, all the way into the raiders' camp in the Wastelands to rescue my daughter, and back out again," I said, in a tone that was both serious and joking.

"You make it sound easy," Dan said. He winked at me. "You'll need divine intervention, too, I guess."

"If such a thing exists," I said. He slid sealskin coverings over my boots.

"It does, and I'll say a prayer that it will be on your side." He stood and helped me on with the fluffy caribou mittens, then pulled the caribou parka over everything. It was fringed at the bottom, to keep out the wind. He situated my backpack on my back, then scooped up my discarded gear. He tilted his head, gesturing for me to follow him.

In a moment, we stood outside the back door. He took a lit torch out of its sconce and walked a few meters out, threw my coat on the ground and set fire to it. He didn't look at me; he just watched my things burn. He said, "Goodbye, Emma. Good luck. I hope you find your daughter. Don't come back, hear?"

4

DAWN HAD BROKEN. THE SKY WAS MILKY, streaked with gray, and tremulous with precipitation. Snow coated everything; Dan was right, for there was going to be more.

The stable had dwindled into nothing a few kilometers behind me, when the hair on the back of my neck rose and sent chills along the sensitive peaks of my cervical vertebrae. I was being watched. I glanced around and caught sight of a lithe tan form some fifteen meters away, crouched behind a tree stump.

The cougar.

I had to take off the caribou mitten, leaving my hand covered only in a Thinsulate glove, but I got out my gun and carried it by my side at the ready, in case I had to shoot.

I walked southeast alongside Range Road, where there were no cars. Edmonton's gas reserves were almost depleted, and the only cars ever seen anymore were sporadic patrols or the occasional ambulance racing through the streets. The sound of a siren now was so rare that it made people stop what they were doing and gawk. Even ambulances drove less often; horse-drawn carriages and bicycle-drawn pallets took people from their homes to the hospital. The previous summer a teenage boy had ridden his skateboard to the Royal Alexandra, all while cradling a broken arm and clavicle.

We did what we had to do.

I helped myself to an old candy bar in my backpack. Sally

had given me our whole stash of Hershey's, Twix, and Power Bars, along with our flashlight and the last set of spare batteries, my toothbrush, and a tube of Crest. I noticed the dried fish wrapped in newspaper dated from the last November of Before; all newspapers in the world had stopped on December 24 of that year. I assumed it must have been Dan's own meal.

The chills wrapped along my shoulder blades, and I turned to check on the cougar. It had come in a little closer and was about twelve meters off to my left, and slightly behind me. I finished my candy bar and gripped the gun a little more tightly.

The sky grew even more fulsome and then broke open with thick, small fluffs of snow. They swirled down like ashy butterflies seeking petals on which to land. I felt myself start to come apart as the sky had, memories of Arthur swirling around in my head and heart like snowflakes in the frigid winds.

I couldn't think about him. I couldn't let myself.

The sky lowered closer to the top of my head, and the snow congealed, the way God's breath would, I imagined, if God breathed—or if there even was such a thing as a God. My breath crusted white along the wolverine fur that trimmed the caribou hood of my parka. Dan was right, I was incredibly warm. It had to be ten below, but I felt it very little. There was a slight chill against my cheeks, but the wolverine trim kept the wind off my face.

I crossed the Trans-Canada Highway, which was completely desolate. I swung out westward to avoid people and to stay in the empty areas between the range roads and the Queen Elizabeth Highway. I took a big loop around Edmonton. I saw no one all day.

If anyone had seen me, from behind curtained windows, they would have thought I was Inuit, and left me alone out of respect. We all assumed the Inuit knew how to survive before technology and would be able to do it again now, After. Next to armed soldiers and trained medical personnel, the Inuit were among the most respected members of what was left of civilization in the Safe Zone.

We all wanted to know what they knew: how to live with little or nothing.

What I wanted to know was, could we live with little or no hope? Because we were running out of the tangible objects from The Before that had filled our lives, and we hadn't yet replaced them. It left us, collectively, with a void we couldn't yet address because the mists were still attacking, wreaking devastation.

A pack of dogs at a deserted gas station watched me but didn't approach. I walked around back and used the toilet, which hadn't been flushed in months. The stench made me quail, but it was better than squatting in the snow.

I walked and walked and kept moving south. The snow fell in sprinkles and in swathes, alternating between the two. The wind Dan had warned me about picked up, sometimes rushing at me so hard that I had to bend forward at the waist to keep walking forward, like rolling a boulder uphill. The big tan form to my left kept pace with me from about ten meters out. Sometimes I thought I caught its gaze, when I looked sidelong.

I couldn't blame the creature. If I had a tasty dinner in my sights, I wouldn't just let it escape me, either. Nevertheless, I kept my caribou mitten untied at my wrist and my gun tucked in the drawstring of my outer trousers so I could reach it quickly. I carried my knife in my other hand.

Sometime in the evening, approaching the northwestern outskirts of Leduc by the airport, I saw a boarded-up clapboard house. It was off to itself, surrounded by fields of what had once been rich farmland. It looked as good as any place to stop for the night, and I was lucky to find the shelter from the wind and the cold. The doors were locked and the windows

were covered with plywood. A hand-written "NO ENTRY —
PROVINCIAL ORDER" sign was taped up on both front and
back doors.

Clearly, the home owners had not been seen since The
Day and the Royal Forces had pillaged the house for anything
of conceivable value: medicine, food, tools, weapons, and
even clothing, paper supplies, and cleaning products. Expro-
priation—what we in the United States had called *eminent
domain*—was established soon in The After, and everything a
citizen owned was subject to the state's needs.

After all, all citizens really needed was to live.

I found a rock and hammered at the edge of a piece of plywood on a side window. It took me a half-hour, but finally the
stubborn board creaked. I used my knife to pry the board off
the window pane along the bottom and one side. From there I
was able to break the window and climb in. Wasn't easy with
my caribou layers.

I landed on my bottom with a thump. I waited for a few
seconds, listening. Nothing. I felt in the dark for the zipper on
my backpack, groped inside for the flashlight, our precious
flashlight with the last few batteries. I turned it on and swung
the beam of light around me. An empty room. I got to my
feet and strolled from room to room. The fur boots threw up
swirling motes of dust into the beam of white light but they
made hardly any noise on the wooden floor.

No one and nothing was in the house. It had been picked
bare and sealed with almost bell-jar precision. I checked every
inch of pantry; there was not even a crumb remaining for the
taking. There was no furniture in the entire house. Even the
attic was empty. There was not even a footprint amidst the
dust, not a scrap of paper, nothing to indicate that the house
had ever been inhabited. The Royal Forces were nothing if
not thorough.

Good news: the kitchen faucet worked. I let the water run

a little bit to clear out the rust from the pipes, and then drank and drank and drank. I relieved myself in the toilet and drank some more. I intended to be well hydrated before I left here in the morning. It would mean I'd have to relieve myself in the cold somewhere, but it would also stave off death by dehydration. I ate a candy bar and forced myself to choke down a few bites of dried fish. Protein was necessary.

I took off the atigi and a layer of thermal underwear. Before curling up on the floor, I peeked out the window I'd come through. A pair of glowing orange eyes stared back at me from about five meters away.

At least I'm not alone. I have Death to accompany me.

I switched off the flashlight to conserve the batteries, and I lay down and slept.

THE NEXT MORNING, I took more water. I filled my thermos, and I brushed my teeth. I'd forgotten to do so last night. I couldn't help but smile at the oversight. The folks back at Arthur's camp would have teased me mercilessly for it. Robert, in his Irish lilt, would have razzed me until Theo told him, "Stop that or else," but then Theo would have taken me aside to continue the ribbing. Laurette would have sniffed and made a derogatory comment about Americans and their lackluster grooming habits. Arthur would have been amused, and smiled at me in his sardonic way, with one side of his mouth lifting.

Arthur.

When I'd first arrived at his camp, I'd found a barebones site patterned after the Roman legionary camps. The men were grungy, and the tents were worse. I'd been leading a group of seven children, along with my daughter Mandy, through mist-ravaged France, and since I thought we should make ourselves useful, I now led the kids in a cleaning foray.

The men were appalled at first.

"Lady, there's been an apocalypse. I've had other things on my mind than dental perfection," Arthur said.

But he got used to it.

And I got used to him.

I SAW NO sign of the cougar, though I wasn't naïve enough to hope he'd abandoned the hunt. I bundled back up and climbed back out the window. I placed the boards back over the broken window as best I could. Then I started walking again.

I hoped to make it to Wetaskiwin in a day's time, perhaps to Ponoka, avoiding populated areas by staying between the Queen Elizabeth highway and provincial highway 2A alt. The yellowed gas station map Renee had tucked into my backpack showed that I was traveling the old Calgary-Edmonton Trail, a natural footpath following a glacial corridor. I knew from Beth's school books that it had been used as a migratory path since ancient times, winding south between dense forest to the west and hilly prairie to the east.

There'd be railroad tracks and highways, but I felt optimistic about avoiding patrols who might ask too many questions and insist I return home. Gasoline supplies had dwindled, so military jeeps only drove out in emergencies, and mounted forces kept watch on the borders of the Safe Zone, where refugees and raiders snuck in. I'd have to watch for scavengers and bandits.

Bandits were a recent phenomenon. They were sane people—if any of us could be called sane in The After—who had lost faith in the backward-minded, barely responsive bureaucracy of the provincial government. Some folks had gathered into groups and started taking more drastic measures to take care of themselves and their families. A man had been brought in to the Royal Alexandra after having been stabbed in the chest while traveling to visit his cousins in Armena, a hamlet with so few inhabitants that a group of bandits had made it their base.

A platoon of soldiers had put down that group of bandits, but I thought that was a mistake. Not even the most docile Edmontonians approved of sane survivors being shot. I was sure the end result would be more discontent, more bandits.

We were all losing faith with the old structures. They just didn't fit the new reality.

But the tribal mentality starting to form new structures wasn't going to keep me safe, or support my mission to rescue Beth.

I made it almost to Ponoka that day. I slept in a shoe store within an abandoned strip mall. All the store shelves were empty. I found running water again in a small lunch kitchen, but I couldn't find any foodstuffs—not even a single leftover packet of sugar. There wasn't even a pod of long-soured half-and-half, which I would have eaten for the calories. I ate two candy bars and more dried fish. The urgency to find food would be grafted onto my mission.

THE NEXT DAY, I went from Ponoka almost to Penhold. I started at around six in the morning; at around nine that night, I found an empty church outside Tuttle, not far from the railroad tracks. The church wasn't boarded up but the Royal Forces had been through with their usual efficiency. There wasn't even communion bread to be found. But at least they'd left the cushions on the pews. For the first time I had a sort of mattress to sleep on.

At night I dreamt about the glowing amber eyes and sinuous tan form that forever lingered at the edges of my peripheral vision. Then I was standing on a beach and Arthur was there, but every time I approached him, he evaporated into a pulsing white mist.

THE SKY WAS vast and gaping, a pale void that alternately desiccated me of thought and stuffed me with it. For hours I walked—just walked—hollow, thoughtless, and vacant, one foot in front of another. I'd never been or felt so alone. Trek-king through France, there had been Mandy and the other children. We constantly bumped into other refugees. Then I met Arthur and I was surrounded by people.

Even when Alexei had kidnapped me and taken me to his camp to heal his son, I'd been constantly accompanied.

The aloneness now was devastating.

Then, suddenly, as the caribou boots shuffled forward, as if they had a mind of their own, I was filled to overflow-ing with images, with memories. Sometimes I drifted into a fugue state in which memory and projection intertwined indivisibly. Reason and reality stopped harassing me. All that was left was love with all of its demands. I felt less lonely dur-ing those times.

In one such episode, my youngest daughter, Mandy, walked with me. The sun glinted off her auburn hair. She was talking about the Nutella jars we found at a metro station in a suburb of Paris. "Yes," I say, and I stroke her hair. Beth came and gave me a look filled with grief. *"Do you promise, Mama?"* she asked.

"Yes, I promise, Beth. I promise," I said. *But what is the point of my promises, anyway? Haven't I broken most of them?* I was mar-ried to Haywood in name only. The bigger part of my being belonged now to someone else.

Beth walked off into the trees, leaving my eyes filled with tears. She left footprints, but the snow started again—thick, frigid whiteness that reached even inside the soft caribou parka to pinch me. The snow covered over her prints.

I stopped for lunch and sat on a rock to eat. It reminded me of another rock, one beside a stream in a lush and sunny stretch of land that had once been occupied by Valensole. On that rock, Arthur and I had often sat and talked. It was our place—that rock and his tent, where we shared our bodies and our conversation by the light of a flickering candle.

Arthur walked toward me as I nibbled more of the dried

fish. He shook his head and sat down next to me. *"Emma, how are you?"*

"Good," I said. I was so happy to see him. I didn't care what he'd done. I didn't care that he'd created the mists that had destroyed the world. That had killed billions. It just felt so good to look into his gray eyes while he sat near me. I leaned toward him. *"Good. Yeah, you betcha."*

"You're in danger, Em," he said in a soft voice.

"No, no, I'm okay," I said. *"I'm good at this. I like this, remember? You said that to me once."*

"You've got to get up, Emma."

"Let's just sit and talk. I feel warmer with you beside me. How is everyone? How are Robert and Jeannie, and Vasily, and Theo, and Pyotr? Laurette? And oh, Marco and Felix and Shoshanna? Any word about Caris and Ginny at the women's camp?"

"Everyone's okay. We've had some tough moments. Jeannie's pregnant. Caris came to help us build the new camp."

"She did? That's great!"

"We were all happy to see her, but now, Emma, it's time for you to get up."

"Tell me more," I begged.

"Get up." He reached his hands toward me. The next second, I lay on my back on the ground. The breath was gone from my lungs. I realized suddenly that my outer layers of clothing were crusted over with snow, and that my entire body tingled painfully with pins and needles. Shaking, I got to my feet. The candy bar lay unopened on the snow.

Did I fall asleep or fall into a fugue state?

Am I going mad?

I couldn't answer those questions, so I retrieved the candy bar, rubbed the snow off the wrapper, tore it open, and ate.

I couldn't shake the feeling of Arthur's strong, large hands gripping my shoulders, then pushing me off the rock.

5 THE SNOW LET UP AS THICK, PURPLE DUSK rolled in over the land. I was too far north of Crossfield, which had been my target. I had only reached Didsbury. I was following the rail tracks east of the town and by the light of a bright full moon, I could see the mansard roof of the Didsbury Railway Station up ahead.

Didsbury was a well-populated town. It had grown in The After, and pursued its own agenda. The citizens weren't about to become bandits, but neither were they knuckling under all of Edmonton's proclamations. Rumor had it that discontents from all over the Safe Zone gravitated to the town; they were welcome here, while the Royal Forces were not. Instead, Didsbury had established its own citizens militia.

That had been the subject of some tense meetings between the town councils of the two cities. So far, neither side was backing down.

Regardless, I still didn't want to encounter anyone. People here might be friendly, and some might actually sympathize with my plight. However, they could also send me back in an effort to placate Edmonton. Or, perhaps they wouldn't want me trekking through their town on my way south; people had become territorial in odd ways. On top of that, there was always the possibility of some other response I couldn't foresee.

Best to slip in and out without calling attention to myself.

I needed shelter for the night. The railway station was dark; trains didn't run any longer, so there was no need to light a station. Still, even a dark station could be in use as a home. It was all risky.

I stood still, deliberating. Probably shouldn't have stopped moving forward.

A soft growl sounded behind me.

I turned slowly while taking off my caribou mitten and reaching into the belt of my trousers, where I'd secured my gun.

Another soft growl sounded to my left. Two gray wolves, lean but powerfully built. One stood behind me, one to my side. Each had to weigh fifty kilos. They stood high up on their legs, their hackles raised. The one behind me raised its upper lip. They had me trapped.

Which should I shoot first? Its partner would be on me even as I fired the shot. I pulled out my gun, slowly. The wolves growled louder.

Something blurred in front of me and leapt atop the largest wolf. The other wolf lunged for it. Claws and fangs flashed in the brilliant white moonlight. Three powerful bodies intertwined. One was bigger than the other two: the cougar. Its paws swept out with deadly speed and accuracy. The wolves cried and then whined, and then they were silent.

The cougar lifted its head, blood dripping from its mouth, and stared at me. For a moment its eyes were blue—sky blue, like Sally's eyes, so much so that I could have sworn she was peering out of its face at me. Then the big cat dropped his head. Fur tore and a bone crunched.

I walked swiftly toward the railway station.

THE STATION WASN'T closed, nor was anyone in it. The men's bathroom had running water. I drank my fill and curled up in a corner. I called forth my internal alarm clock. It was an old trick I'd retained from my days in art college: I'd visualize a digital alarm clock set to a certain time in the morning. Invariably, without fail, I awoke within a few minutes of that precise time. I set my mental clock for five. As I dozed off, I wondered if digital clocks would still work in the mental realm in The After, where all that was digital was gone.

I SMELLED FOOD. Real food, hot food. Something like the aroma of freshly scrambled eggs. My eyes popped open. Sure enough, a steaming plate of food sat on the floor beside me. A fork was tucked into a mound of fluffy yellow scrambled eggs and fried potatoes. *Am I dreaming?* I pounced on the plate. My hand trembled as I lifted the fork to my mouth. The warm, salty food met my tongue and I groaned out loud. My eyes closed as I chewed and then swallowed.

It took me less than a minute to consume every bite. A chipped Corning Ware mug filled with milk completed the breakfast.

Then I hurriedly stood up. It was only about four thirty but I had to quickly use the bathroom and leave. It was imperative that I obey the handwritten sign that lay on the floor beside the plate: "Keep moving."

I WAS ONLY a few kilometers south of Didsbury when a crackle behind me drew my attention. I turned and saw the ever-present cougar about eight meters behind me. His mouth and chest were stained with dried crimson blood and his belly was distended. *He must have gorged on the wolves.* He froze in his tracks and stared at me with ordinary agate cat eyes.

I kept walking. After a while, he dropped back to fifteen meters. I would have liked a hundred meters between us.

It was three hours to Carstairs, and I stayed along the railroad tracks. Carstairs had forged a strong alliance with Didsbury, and it had reclaimed its heritage as an agricultural community. They grew grain and other crops with a vengeance, wooing Inuit families with promises of leadership roles. They'd also turned their 'community peace officers' into a citizens militia that trained with the Didsbury troops. Something else for Edmonton to worry about.

Initially, I meant to circle around Carstairs, though I was now traveling far enough south of Edmonton, in territory that wasn't particularly friendly to Edmonton, that I figured I could probably risk being seen by the inhabitants. They probably wouldn't ask too many questions.

Then again, they might want to hold me and interrogate me for hours.

The issue of food settled the question. With the cold and the walking, my body was beginning to consume itself. I was losing weight every day, and, since The Day, I'd not had any spare kilos to let go of. My food supplies had dwindled significantly. It was imperative that I restock.

I decided it was better to look for food in upstart Carstairs than in Calgary, which was sympathetic to Edmonton and remained subject to the Royal Forces.

THE TRAIN TRACKS took me to 9th Avenue, which I took south into the city center. For the first time, I saw people. Some were on horseback, some were walking, and some used cross-country skis or snow shoes. A couple with a small child drove past on a dog sled. The little one waved. So did other folks, but other than that, they all left me alone.

The town offices rose up on my left so I trudged into the parking lot. I went to the door and kicked my boots clean on the door jamb.

A gray-haired woman in trousers and a blue cardigan let me in. "Hello, friend," she said. Her mouth smiled but her eyes were alert. She parked herself in front of me so I couldn't move forward into the room. Behind her I could see a dozen people, some at desks and some ambling between offices.

"I'm just passing through. I won't be any trouble," I promised. I put down my hood and drank in the light and warmth
of the place.

"You need something, friend?" she asked. Her eyes went
to my hands and I realized for the first time that she held a
gun down at her side, her trigger finger ready. The safety was
off.

I held up my hands in a gesture of peace. "Food. I only
need food. And water."

"Weapons?" she asked. She didn't wait but patted my
waistband. She felt my gun and held out her hand.

Reluctantly I reached in and handed it to her, grip first.

She checked it thoroughly, turned on the safety. "Knife?"
she asked. But she hadn't felt it during my pat-down, so I
shook my head no. "Come in and sit, eh?" she said, stepping
to the side. "Our deputy mayor will talk to you." She ushered
me through the busy front room into an office in the back.

As I walked through, people scanned my caribou parka and
nodded at me. The woman led me into an office and pointed
to a wooden chair in front of a scarred metal office desk. A
few years ago, the office would have seemed pedestrian, perhaps even down-scale. Now, however, the overhead lighting
that shed a fluorescent glare on everything was a miracle all
its own.

I shrugged off my parka, sat down, and laid the parka with
my gloves in my lap.

The woman stayed just outside the door, watching me.

A man walked in. He had olive skin, jet-black hair, and
regular, well-formed Scotch-Irish features. Metis, probably.
He smiled and gripped my shoulder. "Nice togs," he said. He
seated himself and placed my gun on the desk in front of him.

"Inuit. Long story."

He nodded and seated himself at his desk. He had sharp
blue eyes the color of water under a bright sky. "Where are
you from, friend?"

"Edmonton."

"You *walked* that far through the storm?" he asked. He was staring at my face and my hair.

I nodded.

The crow's feet around his eyes tightened. "You're that woman, aren't you?"

"What woman?"

"The healer woman whose husband flew to France in a small plane and brought her back." He sat back in his chair and steepled his fingers in front of his chin.

"Emma Anderson," I said, properly introducing myself.

"Carl." He smiled. "I was a pilot. Knew Haywood from the Air Cadet League. I thought he was crazy when he decided to fly a small plane to Le Havre. Suicidal."

"Probably so," I said. "He was lucky." Haywood's precognition had told him the precise moment to make the attempt to rescue me and Mandy, but I wasn't about to disclose that to the Metis deputy mayor. Nothing good came of admitting to psychic abilities.

"Sure he was." The deputy mayor nodded slowly. "Why are you in Carstairs, Emma?"

"Just passing through."

"On your way to . . . ?"

I leaned forward. "Deputy Mayor, my daughter was among those taken in the raid on Edmonton a few days ago."

"Nasty business, that." He made a hand signal to the gray-haired woman, who tromped off. He turned back with a smile. "Lisa is protective."

"Good," I said, "but the raiders have my daughter. I'm going to get her back."

"The Edmonton town council handled that badly," he said. "They should have made an attempt. Bad faith to let it go. Bad for public morale. I heard they took twenty-six captives."

"Yes. Edmonton called that an acceptable loss," I said bitterly.

Carl stroked his face but didn't say anything.

Lisa trundled back in with a tray of food: a hunk of buttered bread, a baked potato, green pickles, and a slab of peppery meat. The scent assailed me and I couldn't refrain from salivating when she set the tray in front of me.

"Dig in," the deputy mayor said.

"Will I get my gun back?" I asked. I clasped my hands in my lap and twisted them together to keep them from tearing into the plate of food the way the cougar had torn into those wolves.

"You walking all the way to the raiders' camp in the Wastelands, or you planning to steal a horse along the way? I'd give you one, but we don't have any to spare," he said. He picked up my gun and examined it. "Kahr P90, stainless steel slide over black polymer frame. Nice."

"It's light," I acknowledged. "That matters when I'm carrying it all day."

He smiled crookedly and hefted the pistol in his hand. "Nice and tight, and the slide action is smooth. Good ergonomics, good accuracy."

"It came in handy in France." I twisted my hands harder because the savory aroma in my nostrils was making my gut churn with hunger. The bread smelled like it was warm, and the soft yellow scrims of melting butter attested to that.

"So you used it?" he said.

I knew what he was asking and I nodded.

His mouth puckered. He asked grimly, "Edmonton know you have it?"

"Hell, no!" I said. I was starting to get lightheaded with hunger. The room shimmered around me like the air above asphalt on a scorching-hot day.

"Good thing," he said. "You probably want to steer clear of Calgary. They'll take it off you. Unlike the people of Carstairs, they don't believe citizens should be armed. Here, we believe it's every man and woman's right to protect themselves and their family, especially in such desperate times." He slid the gun back toward my food tray.

I snatched it up and stuck it back in the drawstring belt. Then I grabbed up the bread and tore into it. After a few gulps, I said, "You have lights and electricity." I took a giant bite of meat.

"I wasn't deputy mayor in The Before. I was a business guy. I have a hardware store. Had one. Lot of hobbies and interests, like flying and singing. Also green energy. I lobbied to have the city changed over to solar power, and I convinced the town council to build back-up generators with solar panels, to get off the grid. They went along with it just to humor me and to prove that Carstairs was a hip small town. In the end, I came out looking like a fuckin' genius." He leaned back in his chair, placed his feet up on the desk, and tucked his hands behind his head. "When's the last time you ate?"

"Someone left me scrambled eggs in Didsbury this morning," I said through a mouthful of potato so delectable that it crumbled in my mouth.

Carl raised his eyebrows.

I added, "The Inuit who gave me this outfit gave me some dried fish in Edmonton."

"Delish," he mocked. "I hear the guards in Outpost City are always drunk." He wagged his head. "Drunks or not, they'll hang you if they catch you stealing a horse."

I didn't answer as he watched me eat every morsel of food off the plate.

Then he asked, "Would you mind stopping by our clinic? We have some folks there could really use a healer."

I SPENT A few hours in a brick building that had been converted to a hospital. Carstairs had a few nurses, a midwife, two veterinarians, and a chiropractor; the town doctor had been in the Caribbean on The Day. Two Didsbury doctors rotated through town, but neither was present. I got the

feeling that Carstairs residents preferred the vets, anyway. A
nurse tended the sick, and one of the vets handled emergent
care. He eyed me up and down and then pointed to an elderly
man in the corner of the room.

The man had an IV drip in his arm. It was shocking to
see. Even the Royal Alexandra had few such supplies left. I
opened up my mouth to comment on it, but what came out
was, "Parasites."

"What?" the vet asked, looking intrigued. "Parasites? Are
you sure?"

"I've seen it before," I said. I couldn't help but smile,
remembering the camp in France. William, Arthur's friend,
had finally been cured when Laurette came from the wom-
en's camp with her bag of herbs and concoctions. "I can work
on him, but you're better off finding an herbalist." I grabbed
a small, wooden tripod stool and pulled it next to the bed to
sit on.

"Yeah, all right," the vet said, rubbing his chin. "I have a
vetscan machine at the clinic. I can take some samples and
examine them there."

I didn't respond because the healing force was already
roused, already pouring through my hands and into the old
man's body. Would it help him? Probably. Would it cure him?
Probably not. But I couldn't be sure. I'd been using the gift
all along in The After but I still didn't know how or why it
worked. Sometimes it just didn't.

Kind of like God's grace, I figured: hit or miss. Unreliable.

A FEW HOURS and two more sick people later, and the
deputy mayor stood beside me outside the brick building.
"Nice work you did, with Eleanor and Charlie," Carl said.
He handed me my backpack, which was considerably heavier.
"Charlie finally has some color to him. He hasn't looked that
good in months."

"Thanks," I said, clutching the backpack in a grateful embrace.

"It'll get you to Outpost City," he said. "Here's something to help you with the raiders." He reached in his pocket and held out two magazines for my Kahr.

I gasped. "Thank you!" I said in utter disbelief. "Thank you, thank you." Tears sprang to my eyes as I held the magazines to my chest; in The After, ammo was just as valuable as the weapons that needed it.

"Here's a question for you," he said in a low voice. He took my elbow and walked me out toward the road, where no one could overhear. "Who's the big dark-haired guy?"

Arthur? I said, "What?"

"You know who I mean. I see it in your eyes."

"The mists have touched you. You must be seeing things," I said. It was unkind, but the best defense is a good offense.

He didn't flinch. "Sure I am. True things," he said, with a stubborn note in his voice. "Now, who is he?"

"A man I know," I said finally, wearily. "A man."

"Not Haywood."

"No."

"Is he still alive?"

"I don't know. I think so." I slipped the backpack over my shoulders. "I hope so."

"Why does he show up?"

Because he loves me. Because I love him. Because we'll never see each other again. But I just shook my head. "I didn't see him today."

Carl slit his eyes at me and then shrugged. "Think about coming back to Carstairs," he said. "Haywood's a good guy. Your family would be happy here. We're a nice town, and we'd take good care of a healer. We've got a few homes available for relocation. I'll make sure you get the best of them. We've still got schools, good schools. We have our own defenders, and we can hold the town against raiders. We take good care of our own. That's our commitment to our folks."

I stood and collected myself inside myself, into my core. I looked into his sharp blue eyes. "Fine offer, Deputy Mayor. I'm flattered."

"Just think about it, if you're still alive in a few weeks," he said with a wink. "Stay north of Trans-Canada One until Bantry. Two groups of bandits have bunkered in just south of the highway, one on the shore of San Francisco Lake and the other at Lake Newell. You leave them alone, they'll leave you alone."

6 THE NEXT STRETCH OF LAND WAS ALL about frigid air and open sky. I walked east into a mostly flat expanse that was dotted with grain elevators and fir trees, churches and lakes, playgrounds and cemeteries, and cattle and antelope. The winds around Calgary picked up, scouring the snow off the surface of the land. By late afternoon, the sky was irradiated with arching red and orange clouds. It had warmed, too. It was now five or ten degrees above freezing. I put down my hood, then shrugged off my parka and carried it. The inner layers more than sufficed.

I followed Highway 581 under an oppressively huge sky. It fell down around me, blanking me out as if I didn't exist.

After a while I had company. "He's coming for you," said a voice. It was Kangee, the Sioux woman.

"You're not really here," I said.

"You think I am," she said, smiling in that funny way of hers. "Isn't that what matters?"

"I'm going mad."

Kangee shook her head, sending her feather flying around her head, a strange etheric shape against the unnaturally warm air. "I'm here to keep you from going mad." She sang to me as we walked.

I asked what she was singing.

"This part of the universe," she said, and returned to her song.

I wondered what would happen if she stopped singing.

I broke the window of an abandoned gas station and crawled through to find a spot to sleep.

Kangee could walk through the wall because, of course, she wasn't really there. She was still singing when I dozed off.

THE NEXT MORNING, Kangee was gone, which relieved me, but it also left me dispirited. The deputy mayor of Carstairs had packed my backpack with cans of tuna fish, wax paper-wrapped leaves of beef jerky, a jar of pickles, and dried apples. I ate an entire can of tuna and was so protein drunk that it would have been sufficient fuel for a walk of 500 kilometers.

The wind was blowing and the temperature had dropped again. I was still walking east, and I still saw no one. I kept looking around for Kangee. I would have welcomed her because the figments of my own mind would ease the aloneness of this snowy, desolate landscape, but she didn't return. The cougar was back, though, five meters off to my left, coated with more dried blood.

There was so much cold, pale, empty space everywhere that it opened up all the voids within me. I thought of The Day. I was in Paris with Mandy when giant white mists rolled down the avenues like lethal tumbleweeds, gorging on buildings, automobiles, people, and any unfortunate thing or being that got in their path. We were sitting inside a brasserie, enjoying breakfast. It was supposed to be our last meal in Paris before flying home. Then the screaming started, the death roars of millions of people in the city and environs. People bolted out without their coats, but I pulled mine on and made Mandy shrug on her coat, hat, and mittens.

In the days that followed, we were both thankful for my forethought.

For almost five months we wandered, taking on one child after another, running from the mists and the brutal bands of crazed survivors. Then I met Arthur and struck a deal with him: my company for his protection.

Arthur.

And then there was Newt, precious Newt, the little girl who was like a daughter to me. She'd died in pain, ingested by a mist—one of Arthur's mists, since he'd created them. In some horrifying transitive property of causality, Arthur had caused the deaths of billions, including those whom I had loved, like Newt.

The ache started again. I huddled into myself. Snow was falling again, blowing around in frigid, angry swirls. I kept walking, walking, robotically placing one foot in front of the other. I was grateful for the deep caribou hood, which shielded my face from the blowing wind and ice.

The weather worsened. The snow blew against me so roughly that I was pushed into a grove of iced-over trees. I wrapped my arms around a glistening black tree trunk and clung to it, shivering as the Chinook wind slammed into me. I slowly sank to my knees, curling into myself for warmth, leaning into the tree for stability. The wind's cold breath was vicious. I felt myself drowse. I wriggled and writhed to stay conscious. Fifteen minutes later—maybe it was an hour—I was exhausted. The wriggling slowed.

Just as my eyes closed and sweet numbness smoothed out my brain, something bumped against me. I turned my face and struggled to slit open my eyes. A sleek tan form stood nose to nose with me, its tail twitching back and forth. I thought I would be a poor meal for it, impossible to chew, as frozen as I was.

But instead of gnawing on me, the big cat wound itself around and around me like a house kitten, curling into a furry, warm ball with me in the center. Its face stayed near mine. Its breath was meaty and foul. But its body was warm—warm with the life it consumed to live. The chill eased out of my bones.

The last time such warmth had enveloped me, it had been Arthur's body curled around me, both of us satiated.

I pried my eyes open all the way, and once again, Sally's blue gaze peered at me out of the tawny, triangular face. I laid my head against the animal's shoulder and passed into a fitful sleep.

BY THE TIME the snow ended, we were almost buried in a snowdrift. The cat made paddling motions to free itself and I set to work alongside it, digging us out. We climbed out and the world was covered in fractal patterns of white. The cat bounded off without a backward glance. I set out eastward.

OUTPOST CITY WASN'T a sustainably designed collection of environmentally conscious, high-concept architected build-ings. It was a grotty collection of mismatched lumps and bumps against the ground. I'd never before seen such an ugly expanse of town, but then I'd never before been so happy to see any kind of town at all.

A high barbed wire fence, reminiscent of a gulag, encom-passed the huge area, hundreds of square acres. I hadn't real-ized there was so much barbed wire left in the world. Three gates opened into the city: smaller ones to the east and west, and a big one on the north side that let out into a field with a gallows and barrels where trash was burning. Two men swung from the wooden frame, their bodies encased in ice. *The storm must have hit here, too.*

Five guards stood at the north gate, and five rifles trained on me as I advanced toward it. One of the soldiers barked, "Who are you?"

I let down my hood and pulled out my hair, then combed it down around my shoulders. They could see for themselves that I was a woman, and I wasn't waving a gun at them.

Four rifles snapped up off me. The guy on the far left kept me in his sights.

"I'm a refugee," I said. "I just need some food and water."

"Nice gear," said the soldier who'd challenged me.

"Yes. It got me through the storm," I replied. I walked a few steps closer to the spokesman.

The soldier with the rifle readied his finger on the trigger.

I kept walking so the guards could see my eyes and my face, so they could see that I wasn't crazy. I stopped two feet in front of the questioner.

He stared for a moment, then finally decided he liked what he saw. He grinned and waved, and the rifle released its focus on me.

I breathed a little more deeply and walked forward to pass through the gate.

The questioner grabbed my arm. "Three laws."

"And they are?"

"One, no freebies. Everybody trades. You got nothing tangible, you work for food. There's plenty to do in Outpost City."

"No hand-outs, you betcha," I said. I pulled my arm from his grasp.

"Two, you try to steal a horse or a gun, you get hanged." He had green eyes and they flicked over toward the gallows.

I nodded.

"Them's the only laws I know!" one of the soldiers called. "What's your third, Rolf?"

Rolf, the questioner, touched his gloved hand to my hair. He leaned close to me so I could smell his breath, which reeked of gin or something less civilized. "Third law is, I get off at seven, which is only two hours from now . . . and I like blondes."

"That's an ugly law. I'd rather hang," I said.

The other soldiers hooted and howled as I shook Rolf off and continued onward.

After the aloneness of the last several days, I was shocked by the insistent stares that came my way. All kinds of people moved around the misshapen structures of Outpost City: young and old, men and women, aboriginals, whites, Africans, Asians, and any mixture of the aforementioned. Most openly carried guns, even a boy who could have been no older than seven. Everyone had a knife at their waist. They moved about purposefully but stopped to scan me balefully. Dogs, goats, and chickens roamed freely, and even they paused to eye me. It was a lot of energy to absorb.

The sun was still high enough on the horizon that the purple haze of dusk hadn't yet settled in to obscure details, so I turned my attention to the city itself. *Can they even call this place a city?* It was a splay of all kinds of buildings: tents, shanties, trailers, sheds, teepees, and domes made of cut earth. There were several larger structures built of prefab panels of fiberglass and plastic, all slapped together on frames of corrugated steel. There was no order to the buildings; they were muddled up together haphazardly, backing almost into one another with patches of manure and snow-covered yard showing. The 'streets' were a labyrinth of dirt walkways.

The entire eastern end of town was a kind of horse ranch, with three giant stables built of aluminum, wood, and concrete—by far, the nicest buildings. South of the stables wandered cattle, sheep, and pigs, and there were smaller, home-made-looking barns for them.

I surveyed the city. *I've arrived. Now what?* I needed food and rest—real rest, in a real bed. I needed information: had they heard, here in Outpost City, where the raiders had taken their hostages? Where was Beth, or at least, where was I likely to find her? And I needed a plan for stealing a horse and getting away with it.

"Get yourself a drink and a meal at the tavern," said a woman, walking past.

I whirled to ask where the tavern was. The long black braid with a feather in it, the pink Juicy Couture track suit under a parka: Kangee! I leapt toward her, grabbed for her shoulders.

I had to know, was she real? My hands closed around solid flesh.

She laughed, a big wet roar from her belly.

"Kangee, what are you doing here?" I cried.

"Did you like my song?" she asked, jerking her shoulders out of my grasp.

"How did you get here?" I asked. "When did you come?"

"Six months ago, by dog sled," she said. "Me and my man. He's busing tables at the Borealis Tavern. He'll take care of you."

"So you weren't really there in Edmonton that day, the day the raiders took Beth?" I clarified.

Kangee grinned. "Sure I was. What's *really there* mean anyway? Now, follow that road over there that runs east. It's gonna curve around in a big C. When it bumps into a grocery store, take a hard right. You can't miss it. Follow that road past five lefts and take the next one. There's a medical clinic. Two doors down is the Borealis."

"Let me guess . . . I can't miss it?" I said. "I'm glad to see you, whether you're really here now or not."

"You need all the friends you can find, this suicide mission you're on," she said. She rolled her eyes at me. Then she stepped closer and ran her dark eyes over my fur outerwear. Her plump face puckered thoughtfully. "Don't trade the gear. Trade anything else, even your knife. Fair market, that'll get you a week of food and lodging."

I crossed my arms over my chest, patting the caribou parka. "I'm not letting go of this. They'll have to strip it off my cold, dead body."

"Let's avoid that," she said, laughing again. "See Donny. He'll help you. For now, I've got work to do."

"What kind of work?" I asked.

"Picking up trash off the streets," she said. She held up two bulging sacks made of stretched animal skin. "Mostly shit. But people toss out all kinds of stuff. I collect it, sort it, and burn what can't be reclaimed." She winked at me and trudged away toward the gate I'd come through.

What she'd called a 'road' was little more than a curving dirt alley, but I walked it for about a hundred meters, all the way to the big supply tent that boasted a carved wooden sign, "Groceries Here." I peeked in and spied shelves full of eggs, loaves of bread, milk in reused cartons and in screw-top jars, dried foods like pasta and jerky, and of course, canned goods and other items left over from Before—all the things that were rapidly diminishing.

Someone bumped into me, and the backpack tugged slightly, as if to float off my back. My hand grabbed out reflexively, quick as a snake, before my conscious mind even knew what I was doing, and I caught a slim wrist. I squeezed, hard, and my flashlight dropped into my other hand.

"Well, if you're gonna be that way about it," said the boy in a whining voice. He was probably fifteen years old, small and wiry, with hyper-alert hazel eyes and a shock of dirty blond hair poking out from a leather cap. "I guess you can have it back."

"What do they do to thieves here in Outpost City?" I asked, meeting his gaze steadily.

His eyes dropped, and his feet shuffled. He wore black army boots that were at least three sizes too big for him. "They hang 'em."

"I want the dried fish back, too," I said.

He shuffled his feet again, tried to pull his wrist from my hand.

I didn't let go.

He reached his other hand around into his pocket and pulled out the last of my newspaper-wrapped fish.

I took it. "What's your name, boy?"

"Gaffney," he said. "Everyone calls me Gaff."

"Are you the only pickpocket around?" I asked.

"Nah, but I'm the best." He brightened a little and yanked

his arm again, harder this time. When I didn't let go, he gave me a sour look. "No one but you's caught me."

"Maybe your luck is changing. You don't want to hang, do you?" I asked softly.

"Man's gotta earn a living," he said. He jerked his arm again ferociously, and I let go. He teetered on his feet but righted himself immediately, nimble as a cat.

Impressive, I thought, as he sprinted off.

I took the hard right turn and stepped into a big, soft pile of poop that I suspected to be goat droppings. I scraped my boot off on a wooden plank lying athwart the path, then kept going. It was another 150 meters winding along the path, counting lefts, before I took one to get to the clinic. I'd learned my lesson from Gaff; now, as people passed me, I pulled into myself and didn't let them brush against me. I knew better.

The clinic was a three-story prefab building. I glanced in the window. The sun had dropped over the horizon and the light had changed; shadows oozed like a plum tide in over the streets. People lit torches that were mounted in sconces on walls or atop poles. The clinic was cozy bright with candles and hurricane lamps and a huge roaring fire in a brick fireplace. Beds, most filled, lined the floor. I figured I could find work there.

A few doors down stood another scrofulous prefab structure with music pouring out of cracked yellow polyurethane windows. I pushed open the door, a corroded aluminum thing, and saw a piano in the corner of a big room with a bar in back. Thirty people sat at scattered tables and they all looked up; the piano player kept on pounding out Led Zeppelin's "Stairway to Heaven."

I walked to a small, empty table facing the door from the edge of the room. Two fireplaces, one at each end of the room, blazed red and orange, and a big wood stove in the center radiated warmth. The room was toasty. My blood was thick from the cold. Sweat broke out on my face and back. I peeled off layers—parka, atigi, fleece vest—and draped them over the other chair at the little table.

"Hey, Blondie. I'll buy you a drink!" hollered a hearty voice behind me.

I pulled my gun from my pants and whipped around to aim it directly at his face.

He was a tall, dark haired, rough-hewn fellow, obviously tipsy. He held up his hands over his head and backed away with a goofy smile, his eyebrows raised up into his hairline.

I kept the gun trained on him until he sat down with two other guys who were laughing at him.

An older, burly black man with a pock-marked face and a tray under his arm came up to me. "You must be Emma."

"Donny?" I asked. He smiled and stretched out his hand. I shook it, looking him over, liking what I saw. I'd expected a Sioux, but of course, the aboriginals weren't prejudiced and intermarried freely. Then it hit me: I'd seen him before. A year ago. He was in the cardiac care unit at the Royal Alexandra, and barely scraped through. My face lit up with recognition.

He laughed. "That's right. I met you at the hospital. I'm feeling good now, too."

"Glad to hear it," I told him.

"First drink's free, comes with a meal. After that, you trade or work for credit." He smiled in friendly fashion, but his eyes looked serious.

I wondered what he was trying to communicate, but the mists had given me the gift of healing instead of mind-reading, so I had no clue. "I don't have much to trade," I started. "But for work, I could—"

He shook his head, a warning, not a conversational gambit. "You'll figure it out." He went off quickly before I could tell him what I wanted.

I sat down.

The guys at the table over yonder were still laughing. One of them caught my gaze and made a gun out of his fingers, pointed it at the big guy and pretended to shoot him. Laughs of hilarity sprang up at nearby tables.

I was still flushed and chafing with heat. I loosened my boots and slipped off the caribou pants. I was basically down to my silk thermals now, but so were most of the other patrons, women as well as men.

Donny brought back a tray with a huge mug of brown liquid, a glass of water, and a plate filled with meat stew and fried potatoes and onions. To the side was a large bowl of cottage cheese and a hunk of bread. I couldn't imagine a meal looking more appetizing. He put down a folded, butterfly-patterned square of cotton, then laid an aluminum fork and a sterling spoon atop it. "Lamb stew and Outpost ale. Enjoy."

I took a big gulp of beer and nearly gagged. *Is this a joke?* It wasn't what I expected. It was sour, thick, meaty, and nearly as strong as vodka. My throat burned and closed up around the liquid. I didn't know what to do. I wondered if there were any innocuous place to spit it out.

"You get used to it," sang Gaff as he slid into the chair beside me. He had to perch on the edge, sharing the seat with my bulky Inuit gear.

"Go away," I said when I finally managed to swallow the beer.

"Give me some potatoes and I'll tell you what you need to know about Outpost City." His eyes gleamed as he leaned toward me.

"Not happening." I chewed a bite of the potatoes, maybe the best thing I'd ever eaten in my life: crispy and oily and salty and hot on my tongue. I shuddered with delight.

Gaff's eyes were glued to my fork. "Really, it's a good bargain for you. I've been here over a year and watched it grow. I know everything and everyone."

"Get lost," I said.

"Come on. It's only fair. You kept me from eating for a week."

"By not letting you take my flashlight?" I asked skeptically. I took a spoonful of the stew. It was fantastic: rich and savory, hints of thyme and rosemary, with lumps of parsnip and carrot. I groaned with pleasure.

Gaff actually slurped, he was drooling so copiously.

Obscene curses scrolled across my brain. *How can I deny a starving kid food?* I snarled, "Get a plate."

His narrow face brightened. He was away like quicksilver and returned with a bowl even before I lifted the second spoon of stew to my mouth.

I took the bite and then split my food nearly in half, giving him a big portion of stew and potatoes and a piece of my bread.

"Jesus! Thank you, lady," he breathed. He laid his leather cap on the table beside his bowl, and it was a moment of reverence for the food.

"I own you," I said, in not the kindest tone of voice I'd ever used.

"Sure, yeah, anything," he said, inhaling his food just as I was inhaling my portion. He finished before me and sat back, his eyes half-closed in appreciation. "Okay, listen up. They're real serious about hanging horse thieves around here. All horses are property of Edmonton Royal Forces. Don't even try." He lifted his face to make sure I understood.

Of course I understood. I was going to steal one anyway. I said, "What else?"

"There are 20,000 people in Outpost City, and everyone wants something—food, shelter, privacy, opportunity...you name it." Gaff spoke up to be heard over the strains of the Allman Brothers, piano-bar-style. "Anything you can imagine. The key to getting along in Outpost City is figuring out what other people want and how you can either give it to them or help them get it."

"What else could they want, besides food or shelter?" I wondered.

He tipped his head and smirked. "That's the thing. People here are from all over, from inside the Zone and outside it. Some of them just recently passed the sanity test, but that don't mean they're really sane, you know? There are a lot of refugees from the Wastelands. They want to build a life. They want to find their loved ones or friends in the Zone. Sometimes they're stocking up to go back out into the Wastelands to look for family or friends."

That was me, more or less. "Everyone has an agenda."

"Exactly," he said. "Plenty of people here are hiding abilities."

"Mist-given abilities, psychic powers?" I clarified.

He nodded.

"They don't want to be institutionalized, right?"

"Right. So they come here—the iffy ones, the scared ones, the misfits. Outpost City is a good place to hide. We get sick and injured people too. The Hat shut down six months ago."

"What? I didn't hear that!" I exclaimed.

"You couldn't have," he said. "Royal Forces came through and threatened to shoot everyone if word got out. They don't want a panic in Edmonton. They want citizens up there to stay happy, safe, and stupid." His spoon crept over toward my cottage cheese.

I paused mid-slurp to give Gaff a hard stare.

He retracted his hand with a pout.

"The mists went through the Hat, breaching the boundary of the Safe Zone," I said.

"Yep. Lotta people died. No one's supposed to know, though. Survivors came here."

"Where did the mists stop?" I asked.

"Broadway Avenue in the north part of the city." He paused as a sad expression flickered over his face. Then he resumed. "No one knows if or when the mists'll be back, or if the Zone will stay safe."

"Keep talking." I was done with my cottage cheese and took another gulp of beer. It was a bit more palatable this time and merely tasted like lighter fluid.

He grinned. "Outpost City isn't a charitable organization. You got to trade or to work. You want to trade sex, there's a lot of competition." He pointed at my hair. "You got that nice blonde hair and all, and you're real pretty. You might do okay."

"I'm not a prostitute," I said dryly.

"Lady, I never said you are, and I ain't judging. There're men here who like boys. I'm not that way either, but don't think I ain't been tempted." He gave me a frank look; it was probably the truest thing he'd said. "People do what they have to do to survive."

His words cut close enough that I flinched. Wasn't that exactly what I'd done with Arthur? Trade him the comforts of my embrace for safety for the children in my charge in France? At the time, I'd had no idea how I'd end up feeling about Arthur, or he about me. I would never have guessed that we'd share something tender and fierce, something binding, something that neither of us wanted to live without. I'd never foreseen being back in Canada with Haywood, feeling only half alive because I missed Arthur so ferociously.

I took a long, long draught of Outpost ale. That lighter fluid taste grew on you, after a while. Sort of. It certainly took the edge off the clarity of pain.

Donny trotted to the table, took a chair from another table and turned it around to sit on it backward. He laid his tray on the table. "What lies is this little creep telling you?"

"Donny, my man!" Gaff said, wearing a wounded expression. "I'm giving her intel, clean intel."

Donny grimaced and looked at me. His eyes flicked to the mug of beer. "You better drink some water, Emma. Outpost ale can be hard on folks who aren't used to it."

I nodded and drained my water glass.

Gaff took my glass and left the table.

"Filter what he tells you," Donny said in a sotto voce. "If that boy ain't lying, he ain't talking at all."

"Well, a lot of people are like that, since The Day," I responded.

Donny grinned, shrugged, and nodded.

I said, "I still don't know what I'm trading."

He leaned close to whisper. "You do that thing with your hands, right?"

I nodded.

"You got anything else you can do?"

I shook my head.

He shrugged and whispered again. "Go about it quietly, then. Talk to the doc tomorrow on the sly. Otherwise, you'll be mobbed by people with sick family."

"I was kidnapped once before for the same reason," I said.

Gaff came back to the table with my water glass filled. His canny eyes moved, lightning fast, back and forth between me and Donny. He knew we'd said something private, and he wanted to know what it was.

Donny caught my eyes with his, then rose.

I realized I wasn't supposed to tell Gaff about 'that thing with my hands.' Donny was worried that Gaff would sell me out. Gaff wasn't to be trusted.

"Shift changes in an hour or so. Talk to the next barkeep about a room, we got one empty upstairs. Last tenant was hanged yesterday, and this barkeep's in a foul mood." Donny picked up the tray and piled the dishes and silverware on it.

"So you're Emma," Gaff said. He sat back down, crossed his arms on the table and leaned toward me as if I were the most fascinating person he'd ever met.

"Maybe it's time for you to go," I suggested.

Gaff looked like he wanted to argue.

I took out my gun and checked the magazine.

Gaff sprang to his feet. "Well, it's good to meet you, Emma. I'll be seeing you around," he said.

"I still own you." I picked up the cloth napkin and wiped my Kahr pistol clean.

Gaff snapped off a salute and sauntered out of the tavern. Some of the guys yelled things at him, but Gaff didn't turn around.

I cleaned my gun and drank my water. From time to time I sipped ale. My body was adapting to the heat in the room, albeit slowly, and the ale made me more vulnerable to the temperature. I was flushed, soggy, slow, and loose-limbed with perspiration.

An hour rolled by, and a tight group of people walked into the bar. Out of the corner of my eye, I noted a very tall, broad-shouldered man, a stout gentleman, a man with a guitar, a tall black woman, and a gangly youth with dark curly hair. The pianist stopped playing when the guitarist went to him. Greetings and laughter drifted out, and the fellow with the guitar shrugged off his coat and hat, revealing short, gingery hair. The thick gentleman picked up drumsticks and seated himself beside the guitarist.

The black woman went behind the bar, gave the departing bartender a high five, and then tied an apron over a large, round belly. She was six, maybe seven months along. She went to work, tallying drinks and greeting customers. The gangly kid went to a back room. All of this I noticed on the periphery of my vision without decoding it.

Donny came back with another ale on his tray. "This is for you."

"I thought only one was free?"

"Big guy sent it over." He jerked his chin toward the bar.

"Is this going to be a problem?" I sighed, stood, picked up my gun, and turned, aiming where Donny indicated. I looked into a pair of gray eyes I never thought I'd see again.

Arthur.

7 I TURNED AWAY, TURNED MY BACK TO HIM. I replaced my gun in the waistband of my thermal bottoms. I was shaking, trembling fiercely. Everything inside me had gone soft and hard, boiling and icy all at once. My mind skittered away from order and reason like a small animal evading a trap. I slipped into my caribou pants without bothering to fix my boots.

A few guitar chords sounded; of course it was Robert, greeting the crowd with friendly words spoken in his customary Irish lilt. He was unaware of my presence. Robert, my friend from the camp in France. Robert whom I'd eaten with and fought beside, who'd helped me with the children in my care. It was the sweetest joy just to behold him again. I wanted to hug him and hear how he'd been. I wanted to reminisce with him and have him tease me like he had back then, back in Arthur's camp, when life had an elegant simplicity: stay alive, stay together. We'd been one family there, all of us survivors.

But the cool, calculating part of me, the part of me that could walk from Edmonton to Outpost City in sub-zero weather to rescue my daughter, didn't want him to see me. I didn't want to drag him into my problems, into what Kangee had, probably correctly, called 'a suicide mission.' I knew that wouldn't be fair to him.

This was my problem, my mission. We didn't belong to the same camp anymore. I belonged to Edmonton, to Haywood, to a different family. Life had become more complicated.

Loving Arthur, loving all my old mates, couldn't change that.

I glanced at Robert's face. He wore a short, shaped gingery beard and mustache, like a goatee, the same shade of red as his hair. He had a few more laugh lines around his eyes than I remembered, but he retained all his old skill at the guitar and then some. I'd listened to his music a hundred times.

Theo sat beside him. Theo's round face was bare of beard, but his black hair was long and gathered into a ponytail at the back of his head. Theo had claimed I was his sister because I'd saved the life of his brother. My heart felt full just seeing him again.

Theo hadn't spotted me, and that was a good thing. If he had known I was here, he'd have insisted on going with me to rescue Beth. He would never accept 'no' from me. He would be glued to my shoulder as a few of us faced a large, armed band of mist-crazed raiders, and he'd likely die in the process.

I could not let that happen.

I could risk myself for my daughter, but I could not risk the lives of others.

The woman bartender could only be Jeannie—pregnant, just as Arthur had told me she was, that day that I'd hallucinated him beside me in the snow. How was that possible, how had my unconscious known? Was it just a piece of information transferred to me by the mists' action on the human biomind, that unmapped psychic region of the brain?

Had Arthur somehow sent himself to me, to save me that day?

I tossed a glance at the tall black woman pouring Outpost ale from a jug into two mugs. Yes, the long neck and high cheek-bones, the astonishing Nefertiti-like beauty and the strains of a Liverpool accent: Jeannie. I wondered if anyone else in the tavern, besides me and Arthur, Theo and Robert, knew what an expert sniper she was. She and Robert had to be so happy and excited about a child, their child, coming into their lives.

Jeannie's pregnancy resolved me further: *I will not involve*

*them in my quest. It wouldn't be right. I love them all too much to
expose them to the danger I face.*

Arthur strode over to stand beside me.

I shrugged into the fleece vest and then the atigi, ignoring him. But I couldn't ignore the felt sense of his presence:
his long limbs and large hands, his heart beating, the blood
coursing through his veins, the thrum of life emanating from
his flesh. I could even smell him: he smelled like every time
he'd ever lain atop me and held me.

Arthur didn't speak.

I wondered if I could shoot him, if I had the nerve. *Outpost
City wouldn't hang me if I told them what he'd done. They'd celebrate
me. I'd be a world hero if I could just. . . . Survivors everywhere would
thank me for serving justice.*

I wondered how he felt, seeing me. I wondered how he'd
got here from France. I wondered how he'd escaped the gun
held to his head by Alexei the Russian sociopath. Most of all,
I wondered how I'd survive another minute without being in
his arms. My body twanged with the old hungry longing for
him, which had grown more acute after all the months apart.

People nearby had fallen quiet, sensing something, but my
old friends still hadn't noticed me.

Arthur didn't speak. He just stood there, alert and poised,
beside me.

I felt his breathing deepen, roughen. He was struggling,
too. I slipped on the caribou parka and pulled up the hood
to obscure my face. I slung my backpack over my shoulder,
tucked my mittens under my arm, and walked out.

Arthur followed me.

I felt bereft. I missed them all more now, having seen them
in the flesh. I missed them far more than I had before, when
all I had were fond memories.

Arthur put his hand on my shoulder and swung me around
to face him. "Emma," he said hoarsely.

I held up my left hand so he could see the wedding band.

I'd traded away my old one in France, when Mandy and Shoshana and I had first left the rubble of Paris, but Renee had given me hers to wear when I'd arrived in Edmonton.

Light flickering from a torch glinted on the gold band. Arthur recoiled. I took a moment to look at him. He wore a black beard, close cropped like Robert's. Other than that, Arthur looked exactly as he had the last time I'd seen him: short black hair, perfectly symmetrical, harmonious features like a god or an angel might boast. He was still the most beautiful man I'd ever laid eyes on.

He straightened and reached for my hand.

"Don't," I said, in barely a whisper. "I can't . . . I don't want you."

He answered, "Liar." His eyes gleamed.

It hurt to look at him. I turned away.

Arthur didn't pursue me. He was breathing raggedly into his chest.

I took the first few turns, randomly turning right and left, to make it harder for him to see where I'd gone.

I SPENT THE night at a shelter for newcomers in the southwest corner of town. I was lent a blanket, which I inspected for lice and bedbugs. Other than a few crusty smudges of something smelly and purple, it seemed okay. I found a spot in the corner of the room, curled up, and slept fitfully, trying not to think about what might be happening to Beth. I had to focus on my plan to rescue her; I couldn't dwell on the horrors she might be facing. Controlling my thoughts was hard. Sound sleep eluded me while people coughed, talked, and snored and babies cried. Besides, I was prey to my own terrors.

I'd have to find a room of my own.

I was given water and milk the next morning, but the shelter staff asked me to trade something if I wanted a full breakfast. I declined and finished my last can of tuna. I used the restroom and brushed my teeth, then headed out for the medical clinic.

I was about to emerge from the dirt walkway to the clearing in front of the clinic when I spied Arthur leaning against the building diagonally across from the clinic, watching. I darted back into the alley from whence I'd come, nearly knocking over a woman and a little girl. The woman exclaimed and gave me a dirty look but the girl just giggled. I made apologetic hand motions but didn't speak.

Arthur had keen senses, and his ears were sharp.

I flattened myself against the side of a structure that seemed to be a place for trading and obtaining clothing. *Of course Arthur would be waiting for me at the clinic. He knows all about my healing abilities.*

"Your hands feel wonderful. Now I see what all the fuss is about." That was what he'd said when I'd put my hands on him to heal a cut on his chest.

Arthur knew I'd come here. What now? I wanted to avoid him.

Because I couldn't help myself, though, I peeked around the corner. Arthur wore a dark green pea coat over a woolen turtleneck, a gray woolen cap, black gloves, brown lace-up work boots, and black synthetic snow pants, the high-performance kind. His face was pale, and his eyes were raccooned with dark circles. He'd had a restless night.

I knew that look from when I'd woken up next to him. Often I was the cause of his restlessness; he didn't want to sleep when he could be making love with me. He used to laugh at my concern and say that a little fatigue was a small price to pay for what we shared.

Suddenly, unexpectedly, anger spurted up inside my chest, a crimson wave of feeling. I slammed back against the wall. I had been unable to respond physically to Haywood since coming to Edmonton.

But was that Arthur's fault or my own?

There were no answers. There never were anymore. All that was left was devotion to my mission: to save my daughter, to rescue Beth. I needed information, and I needed a horse.

Three soldiers came around the corner and narrowly missed bumping into me. It was about eight in the morning but they already reeked of Outpost ale. The one who'd brushed past me gave me a woozy salute and a leer. I ignored him. When they were well past, I tiptoed out to peer around again at Arthur.

He was still waiting, his stance stationary but his eyes moving over the passing pedestrians. He was looking for me. I could sense it, and that made me hungry for him all over again.

But I didn't need the encumbrance, the distraction, of those feelings, of those people, of Arthur and my old, beloved mates from his camp. I had something to do, something urgent. Beth was in hell, a captive of crazed raiders, while I tarried in Outpost City. There was no telling what they would do to my daughter, and every hour I delayed getting to her was an hour she suffered.

I turned and walked swiftly back into the southwestern part of town, losing myself in the swarms of people and animals and the chaotic sprawl of buildings. Gaff had told me that Outpost City was a good place to hide. I would test that out for myself, hiding from Arthur and the others.

OUTPOST CITY WAS dense and compact. Gaff had told me it was home to 20,000 people, but it wouldn't have surprised me if the actual number was twice that. How could anyone count or take a census here? People were constantly coming and going, a relentless human flux like a rapacious sea tide. Every sodden mud path—or 'road,' as they liked to call them—was constantly crowded with pedestrians, and buildings were always full. There were few single rooms. Entire families bunked with strangers. The free shelters were always so crowded that people slept back to back, sitting upright.

The city was oblong, covering roughly twelve kilometers east-west by six kilometers north-south, much larger than I'd originally perceived when I'd first traversed the north gate. It was surrounded by fields that were planted with crops in the spring, and it was completely enclosed by high barbed wire fencing, some of which, I was told, was reclaimed from prisons outside the Safe Zone in The After. Every time new barbed wire was found, it was brought to the city to expand it. Barbed wire was the second highest form of currency, twenty credits a square meter. Only guns and bullets were worth more.

Royal Forces barracks were scattered throughout the city and also situated by the stables on the eastern edge and by the three gates. Soldiers, both on foot and on horseback, kept peace through simple means: hanging people or shooting them. I saw two men killed when they fought over a half-credit for a loaf of bread. It was drastic, but it kept the city at a low simmer.

I used up the last of my food supplies over the next two days while I looked for work. Water was freely given, and I moved between shelters, but I knew I wouldn't be able to secure regular meals or a room until I purchased credit, either by trading or working. The credit system was simple: One meal cost one credit, one night in a private room cost three, and to eat for a day and sleep alone in a room for a night cost six credits. It went on from there. Men and women wearing orange coats with reflective stripes went around recording credits, and the Royal Forces settled disputes—usually by shooting both parties in their kneecaps, discouraging disputes altogether.

I was looking for work that wouldn't call attention to myself but would give me access to information and perhaps even the stables. I asked about caring for the animals and was brusquely informed that only Royal Forces soldiers were allowed near the stables and barn. I mostly kept to the south-western section of town, which was fondly called the Bad-lands and was even grungier than the rest of Outpost City. I didn't run into Kangee or Donny or Arthur and the others there.

During the early evening of the second day, I wandered into a tavern where a lithe, gray-haired man was describing his wife to the crowd, asking if anyone had seen her.

"She's got red hair down to here," he said, indicating his own collarbone. "She's got big eyes, nice shaped eyes. Beau-tiful eyes." He had drawn a crude picture, little more than a stick figure, and was waving it around helplessly, looking terrified and desperate.

Everyone was shaking their heads, both in pity and in scorn.

He made frustrated noises.

In The Before, I'd been an artist, primarily a painter and illustrator. I was skilled and had earned some renown. It felt like a million years ago. It wasn't even three. I went up to the man and tapped him on the shoulder.

"You've seen her, lady?" he asked eagerly.

I shook my head. "No, but maybe I can improve your drawing so people will know who it is you're looking for."

His eyes lit up. He slapped the paper and a nubby pencil into my hands.

I led him to a table, and we sat down together. "You're going to describe her—"

"She's so pretty! I don't know what's happened to her. I have to find her. She needs me!" He started eagerly. He was in his fifties, lively and concerned. He wore good quality gear and carried a Glock at his waist; clearly, he was doing well in Outpost City. He repeated, "She needs me. I take care of her. I'm all she's got. I've got to find her!"

"Hold your horses, stud muffin. Let me ask the questions. How old is she?" I asked, erasing the thick graphite lines on the paper, white notebook stock with blue lines—a precious commodity in and of itself.

"She's twenty-two. Her birthday is March 10." He made a face as I glanced up at him. "I know, I know. She's a lot younger than me. But we're happy together. I know she hasn't run off. She loves me too much for that, and I take good care of her."

"Okay. You said red hair, this long." I held my hand to my collarbone. "Is it straight or wavy?"

"Curly—real curly. She has me brush it every night because she likes how gentle I am." He seemed proud, as if it was his greatest accomplishment.

I had a flash of memory: Arthur combing out my hair. *Now he's on the same continent as me, just a few kilometers away. Arthur, here. If I go to him. . . . No!* It was impossible. I blinked and refocused.

"Good. And how would you describe her face? Square? Heart-shaped, oval, round?" I forced myself to listen to his answers, to question him ever more thoroughly as I sketched.

After a half-hour, he yelped. "That's her! That's my Amy!" He snatched the paper away, even though I wasn't done drawing, and would have highlighted the forms at the side of her mouth for greater accuracy. He was yelling, "This is her! This is Amy! Has anyone seen her? She's been gone two days!"

The bartender stood at my shoulder, having watched in fascination as I worked. He said, "Norman, I haven't seen Amy, but maybe you want to give this lady a meal for her good work?"

Norman turned around and gripped my shoulder. "Of course! Sure. Right. How many credits for this sketch? It's perfect, really."

I thought fast, wondering how much could I get away with charging. "Four?" It was a question.

Norman looked at the drawing, then back at me. "Three credits," he said. "I run the two bakeries here in the Badlands, the only two bakeries in this section. You can charge your three credits to my bakeries."

I'd passed by the bakeries and looked in hungrily. I knew exactly where they were. I opened my mouth to thank Norman, but he went out of the tavern almost at a canter, waving his drawing and calling out to see if anyone knew the woman, his woman.

The bartender smiled at me, exposing all his teeth. He wanted my bakery credits. "So, lady, you want a meal?"

"It's Emma . . . and you betcha," I said.

"Jean-Pierre." The bartender grinned and shuffled off.

A petite woman took Norman's place at the table. "I'm looking for my husband and two sons," she said. "I got a can opener worth nine credits."

Nine credits would get me a place to sleep for three nights, and by then, I'd have found out about the raiders and stolen a horse to get to them. Or I'd be hanging out by the north gate because I'd failed in the attempt. "I don't have any paper."

"Neither do I," she said softly. She had glassy brown eyes that quickly filled with tears. "I don't know how I'm going to find out about my family. We all came up from Great Falls a year ago, in a big caravan with other survivors. We made it to Medicine Hat, but we got separated when the mists surprised us there."

The bartender was back with a big plate of lamb chops and stewed greens, pickles and roast potatoes, a slice of wheat bread and a pot of honey. "Paper? You need paper? I can help with that too."

"How much?" I asked automatically.

Jean-Pierre smiled that shiny-toothed grin of his and wagged his finger back and forth at me. "No credits. You just have to work here, at the Big Sky Café, until the notebook's used up."

"Big Sky Café?" I struggled not to laugh at the grandiose

name for a dingy hole-in-the-wall in the scruffiest part of an already grimy town.

Jean-Pierre nodded excitedly. "People will hear that you're here, and that will bring in customers."

I thought for a moment. I didn't want to promise him that I'd be here for long. "I'll work in this tavern while I'm in Outpost City. I can't say how long that will be."

"Agreed." He shook my hand and lumbered off.

I turned to my plate of food, which was steaming and savory, and took a bite.

The woman was still sitting across from me.

I sighed. "Okay. I'll take your can opener for three sketches. Meantime, you want some?"

She dimpled at me so I tore the bread in half and pushed the honey pot toward her. Eagerly she dipped the honey onto her bread.

"Ma'am, have you heard anything about the raiders who went through Edmonton about eleven days ago?"

THAT NIGHT, WITH a full tummy, I slept in a cubicle-sized room of my own, which had a narrow bed and a closet with a toilet. I finally had some concrete information, having heard the same things several times: The raiders had ridden out of Bismarck, where the group who'd hit Edmonton was based. It was in the Wastelands, but rumor had it that the mists hadn't been through the city in several months.

Now all I need is a horse.

8 I HAD JUST FINISHED WITH ONE CUSTOMER when the next slid into the chair across from me. "Three credits for a sketch," I said, tearing a clean sheet of paper out of the notebook and licking my pencil. It was mid-day, and business was good. People came to the Big Sky Café to eat, and many wanted a sketch for whatever reason; either that, or they came here for a sketch and stayed for a meal. Our little arrangement benefited both me and Jean-Pierre, who owned the place. He considered himself my new best friend, and I considered him a decent man.

"Where did you learn how to draw?" asked a nasal young voice.

I looked up. The shock of blond hair poking through a leather cap, the narrow face with its expression of sly greed: Gaff.

"How'd you find me?"

"It wasn't easy," he admitted. He stretched, clasping his hands overhead and cracking his knuckles. "How 'bout a meal for my efforts?"

"How about you go right now and I don't shoot you?" I asked with a tight smile.

"Such a mean look for such a pretty woman. I thought we were friends." He smiled ingratiatingly, but the smile didn't encompass his eyes.

"What do you want?"

"I want to know what a good-looking woman like you is doing alone in this sketchy part of Outpost City, when there are credit-rich folks looking for her in the nicer part of town," he said quietly.

He was here to trade information.

I swiveled in my seat and gestured for Jean-Pierre to bring us both a plate of food. I was flush; I'd drawn twelve portraits in two days for a total of thirty-six credits, and I'd spent only eight. I needed ten more to eat and sleep on. I was working now for supplies for my journey to Bismarck. I was going to need food and more bullets, if I could earn enough to buy some.

Jean-Pierre walked over with a tray and two mugs of Outpost ale.

I waited for Gaff to take a deep drink and chew on his chicken leg before I asked, "How much will it cost me to keep you quiet?"

"Why don't you want them to find you? Arthur and Robert and the rest?" he asked, chewing.

"Didn't your mother teach you not to talk with your mouth full?" I asked. I took a drink of ale, aware that my cheeks were burning. The ale, even more noxious than usual, fizzed along my tonsils as if to dissolve them. I had to gulp it down quickly and hope it didn't blister holes in my stomach.

"My mom survived the mists in Boise. We joined up with a caravan coming north to the Safe Zone. One day the raiders tore through our group. Then she was gone," he said. He took another bite of chicken but peeked to see if I was affected by his sad tale.

I was and I wasn't, both at the same time. Since The Day, we all had hard luck stories. His was really no different. Nevertheless, he was still a kid, skinnier and littler than he ought to be at his age, his temerity matched only by his determination to stay alive. He was alone in the world, except for his wits. I had to cut him some slack. I shrugged and looked away.

"It's that big guy, Arthur. He's something. What's his story?" Gaff asked.

"Ask him yourself if you want to know."

"He's looking for you, but you're married." Gaff leaned over and touched my wedding band with his index finger.

I didn't say anything but dug into my chicken breast, which was stewed in prunes and raisins, impossibly delicious over a bed of home made noodles from Norman's new pasta shop.

Unfortunately, even with my drawing, poor Norman still hadn't found Amy. And I wasn't going to let Arthur find me.

"Most women I know would be happy for Arthur to find them," Gaff said slyly. "He gets a dozen invitations a night. There're women who offer him credits—"

"Gaff!" I snapped. "Eat your meal. Tell me what it'll take to keep you quiet about my whereabouts. Then leave."

He shrugged while taking a giant bite of bread. "I'm just saying, Arthur and the others—especially Robert and Jeannie—they're real nice. Why don't you want them to find you? What could you have to gain by staying hidden in the Badlands?"

I sighed and templed my fingers over my plate, for once unable to eat. "Gaff, what do you know about them? How did they get to Outpost City?"

"Now *you* want information," he smirked. I reached across and grabbed his collar, pulling the fabric tight enough that he choked.

He held up both hands. "Easy, Emma!"

"You've eaten two meals on my dime."

"Okay, okay! I heard Theo talking with Jeannie about a boat crossing."

"You've been eavesdropping." I returned to my meal, forcing myself to take in sustenance, though food could not have been farther from my interest.

"You know how it is. Man's gotta earn a living." Gaff wagged his head at me. "Arthur found a fancy yacht. He thought he was going alone, but the rest of the gang surprised him. They came across the ocean and landed in Quebec. They came on horseback and made it all the way here."

"That's the abbreviated version," I said dryly.

"Sure. That's what you get for a meal and a half." He smirked. He had me on the hook and he knew it.

"How much?" I could splurge a little.

Two tables behind Gaff sat an older lady, twisting the leather straps of her Coach purse and staring at me anxiously. She was a customer. She'd offer me a hammer or a necklace, a book or a matching fork and knife, or three credits backed by the clothing store or the grocery store or the butcher, and I'd draw for her some missing relative—maybe a son she hadn't seen in a while, a husband, or a sister. She'd cry a little when I finished. I'd have three more credits toward what I had to do.

"Eight credits!" he sang.

I gave him an incredulous look. "Three, and you forget you saw me here."

"Six, and I don't even remember your name."

"Four, and if you ever come near me again or mention my name to anyone, I'll hurt you—or worse," I threatened grimly.

He tilted his head, considering. "Okay. Four, and this meal doesn't count." He stared expectantly.

I sighed.

He sopped up the last of the chicken sauce with his bread, pushed the plate away, and leaned toward me. "Arthur found a twenty meter schooner in Le Havre, mint condition. He stocked it while he was recuperating."

Dizziness rushed through me. "Recuperating?"

"He was shot, but I don't have those details," Gaff said. "I think his shoulder's still stiff. I seen him rub it. He sailed the yacht down through the inland waterways of France, rivers and canals. It was rainy, and that helped him. He went south, to where his people were building a town."

"A camp," I murmured. "They were building a new camp."

"Sure. Some guys named Vasily, Will, and Shinji were in charge there, taking care of people and setting up the town. Camp."

"Some guys," I said. My heart filled with poignant nostalgia. *Some guys, indeed. Will I ever meet their like again?* The ache of the last year and a half began again.

"Arthur and his crew set off last October, sailing north and west. They stopped by Iceland. It took them thirty-six days to sail to Quebec. They dodged a few icebergs. I don't know how they made it past all the mists. The oceans are the worst for mists." Gaff paused and stared again.

I didn't answer. I knew how they made it past the mists: Arthur had created the mists, and they obeyed his will. But I would never say that aloud in front of Gaff or anyone else here in Outpost City. To do so would be to cost Arthur his life.

Gaff shrugged and continued. "They got off the boat there and helped some Quebecois fend off raiders, then started making their way west on horseback. They've been here about three weeks." He sat back, looking pleased with himself.

"So Arthur, Robert, Jeannie, and Theo are all?" I asked.

"Well, also a really smart guy named Charles, and a hot little number named Laurette." Gaff waggled his eyebrows in approval. "She was in charge with Vasily, but she refused to stay behind when Arthur left for Canada."

"Laurette." The name wrung a wry smile from me. *Of course she'd come along. She probably wanted to captain the expedition.* I would not have been surprised to hear that she was issuing orders to Arthur himself.

"They've got rooms up by the Borealis Tavern," Gaff said. "Jeannie's been bartending, and Robert and Theo provide music. Charles Nwokocha got work at Outpost City mayor's office—"

"There's a mayor's office here?" I interrupted him.

"Yeah, course. This is a real town. You know, sorta.

Charles is some kind of special writer guy or lawyer or something."

"He's a linguist, one of the greatest linguists in the world."

"Yeah, well, now he's writing down the laws and regulations for Outpost City."

"Laws and regulations? What laws and regulations? There are only two that I've heard of," I said.

Gaff shrugged. "That was what I thought. Hey, how 'bout a glass of milk or some dessert? All this talking is making me thirsty . . . and hungry again."

I shook my head. "What is Arthur doing?"

Gaff scrunched his young face thoughtfully. "I can't rightly say. He was pretty mad when Royal Forces took his horses away from him."

That would make him angry, implacably so—almost as angry as if someone took me away from him. Arthur had never been good at sharing. Aloud I said, "What did you see when you followed him?"

Gaff smiled a little sheepishly and leaned back in his chair. "How do you know I followed him?"

"Gaff, do I look like an idiot?"

"Really."

"You follow him—and others—because you're always hoping to find out something that you can sell to someone. Information is what you trade."

"Hmm," Gaff said. "Well, what do you expect? I'm not a national charity foundation. Anyway, I ain't seen him working or heard him talking about it to his friends, but he always has credits somehow."

"So . . . ?"

"So when I followed him, I lost him. First time that's ever happened. Someone that big . . . well, you don't expect him to be so quick and light on his feet. One minute he's there, next he's not. He can move like lightning. I saw him take down a guy who was about to shoot him. Only took him maybe four seconds to disarm the guy and leave him writhing on the ground. Arthur had his gun and was out of sight, just like that." Gaff looked at me, expecting me to comment. I didn't.

I was well acquainted with Arthur's extraordinary physical prowess. *What else could be expected from a man who had once been an Olympic athlete?*

Gaff sort of chortled. "I expect Arthur's doing the same thing as you—well, besides looking for you. He's figuring out how to get to the horses." Gaff gave me a cool glance. "That kind of intel deserves a piece of pie or something, don't it, Emma?"

AFTER I GOT rid of Gaff, I went to see Norman at his bakery. I opened the door and was instantly ambushed by the rich smell of magical yeasty baking things, enveloping me in sweet warmth. Open shelves were laden with rolls and loaves, buns and baguettes. People milled about, sniffing the air and waiting to be helped by one of two apron-wearing girls employed by Norman.

Norman himself stood behind the counter, chatting with some customers. He acknowledged me with a nod and finished his conversation. When the people went out, two rolls of Scotch tape traded for two big boules of bread, Norman tossed me a small white dinner roll.

I held it. "I need something from you," I said, offering it back to him.

He gave the roll a cavalier glance.

I took a big bite. "Thanks," I told him. "Any word from Amy?"

"Naw, and it's real strange. No one's seen or heard anything. It's like she just vanished." He shook his head dolefully. His eyes strayed to the wall, to the second portrait I'd drawn of her for him, which was emblazoned with the words "REWARD 30 cr. for information as to the whereabouts of this woman." This sketch was more detailed; I had drawn it more carefully, taking longer and asking better questions. Norman said it was more accurate than a photograph. It showed a lovely young woman with poetry in her eyes and mirth in her smile.

Truly, I hoped he'd eventually find her. "Maybe she'll turn up," I said sympathetically.

He gave me a bleak look. "What can I do you for, Em?"

I leaned over the counter and said in a low voice, "I need a wig and some clothes that make me look different. A disguise."

Norman stroked his chin, thinking. His gray brows drew together. Then he smiled and shrugged. "Do you care who it comes from?"

"No, but I prefer not to get lice," I said.

"That won't be a problem, and you can't get the clap from borrowing clothes." He winked. "I've got a friend who owes me a favor or two—or a dozen. Meet me around five, and we'll go see him at his boarding house."

SHORTLY AFTER FIVE, I found myself at the jazzy suite of rooms belonging to Norman's friend Lailani Delacroix, aka Larry Jones. Lailani was a tranny who had a number of male 'friends' in Outpost City—so many, in fact, that her rooms were dazzlingly well appointed: matching teak furniture, luxurious silk curtains and bed coverlet, and paintings hanging on the walls, including a Hudson Valley plein air number I was pretty sure was an original Thomas Cole; I remembered seeing it at the Wadsworth Atheneum in Hartford, Connecticut.

A list of Lailani's services was posted outside her door, indicating the number of credits required for each. I read with interest until I realized that I didn't know what most of the items meant.

Arthur would have relished finding out with me, once upon a time.

It was not the kind of thing I'd ever shared with Haywood, much as I loved him.

Lailani had mocha-colored skin and a chocolate afro that she kept shaved to within a few millimeters of her scalp. When Norman knocked, she opened the door and threw her long, elegant arms around him, cooing about Amy. She was bare-headed but in full panoply of make-up, and she wore a ruffled fuchsia silk dress, of the kind girls used to wear to high school proms. "Who is this darling vixen with the long blonde locks?" Lailani purred, fingering my hair jealously. "Girl, you bringing some competition?"

"I'm just passing through," I said, swatting at her hands, which were sylphan-fingered and soft, like some confection-ary shepherdess girl painted by the French academicians of the nineteenth century.

"This is Emma, and she needs to borrow a wig," Norman said. He rubbed Lailani's shoulders. "Come on, Lani. You know that after Amy, you're the prettiest one around. Don't be jealous. Help us out."

"Mirror, mirror on the wall," Lailani said, with a sulk on her mouth. She wasn't done checking me out; she circled me, poking and prodding in my intimate places.

"You want to lose a finger?" I snarled. "I'm carrying a gun!"

"So am I, sweet cheeks," Lailani hissed. But then, all at once, her pique was over. She kissed me on the cheek. "You're a friend of Norman's, doll, so you're a friend of mine. You need a wig, I can hook you up. You've come to the right place. I'm all girl, all the time."

AN HOUR LATER, I was a brunette with long black eye-lashes, black eyebrows, blood red lips, a mole next to my nose à la Marilyn Monroe, and a light-weight gray wool dress that pretended to be librarian worthy in front, only to drop down below the crack of my ass in back. Intricately tooled, high-heeled, bright red, buffalo skin cowboy boots completed the ensemble.

I couldn't remember the last time I'd worn make-up.

"These don't look like anything that ever saw a stirrup," I said, staring down at the boots.

"Honey pie, those are all about getting you back in the saddle," Lailani said. She walked her fingers down my back suggestively.

I gave her a wry look and stepped away.

"Just keep the coat on," Norman advised, with some skepticism. He held up a green plaid wool coat, a demure thing like a school girl in a convent school would wear. He caught another glimpse of my back and his eyebrows rode up along his hairline.

I struggled to get the back of the dress to lie correctly and cover my buttocks before shrugging on the coat.

"Good Lord, no! Remove it at the first opportunity," Lailani said, giggling. "Doll, with assets like that, you ought to drop the coat accidentally, turn around," she pivoted on her stilettos, demonstrating, "and bend over to pick it up!" She waved her behind in the air.

Norman rolled his eyes.

Lailani set a bonnet-like felt hat on my head. It seemed designed to call attention to itself, but it did obscure my face.

"Look at her! All we see is those red lips. Then if she takes off the coat, Jesus, all hell will break loose. We want her back in one piece, Lani," Norman drawled.

"But she'll have more fun in many pieces," Lailani joked, "or maybe with one piece many times!" She made her fingers into a gun, punning on the word 'piece,' and then made a lewd back-and-forth motion. The play with her hand was soon mirrored by her hips, and in a moment she was bopping around the hall of her boarding house, dancing burlesque and singing a song whose raunchy lyrics made me laugh and blush.

Norman shook his head. "Lani, she's going to get herself in trouble in that dress."

"The luscious kind of trouble," Lailani said, winking broadly. Then she straightened and put her fists on her hips, arms akimbo. "Now, Dollface, do you have the gun in your garter, like I showed you?"

"Yes, but I'm going to show everyone more than my garter if I try to reach for it," I said. I was wearing thigh highs, and, at Lailani's insistence, nothing else. She claimed panties would ruin the dress line.

"You cocktease," she said in a sibilant tone of voice. "Norman, isn't she just a delicious, sweet ol' cocktease?" Lailani stroked Norman's crotch.

Norman slapped her hand away. He was starting to look haggard. "I really don't think anyone will recognize you," he said to me. "Like I said, keep your backside covered, and you'll be okay."

"I can blot the lipstick," I said. "That'll draw less attention to me."

"No it won't!" Lailani shrieked. "Fool, calling attention to yourself is the way to disguise yourself. It's the way to hide right out in plain sight. Boring ol' Emma would never wear that color on her mouth. She'd never wear that dress or those boots. But some other smokin' hot brunette would. You be *that woman*, not halfway."

"I am not boring," I said, rather archly. "Boring people don't have multiple orgasms." Arthur's face flashed across my mind's eye.

Lailani put her rouged brown face next to mine. "When's the last time you had even one big O?" She chortled, an unlovely, unfeminine sound.

I bared my teeth at her, as my friend the cougar might have.

Norman covered his face. "Aren't we done here?"

"Not yet," Lailani said. She turned to me. "Now, say something."

"Why?"

Lailani put her arms akimbo again and clucked her tongue, as if I was Outpost City's resident idiot. "Because men are gonna be talking to you."

"No, no. I'll just sit quietly, nurse one drink, and then sneak out."

Lailani whooped, and even Norman shook his head. "You'll be talking, Em," Norman said. "You won't be able to avoid it."

"Buy me a drink, sailor?" I asked, winking broadly.

"You're getting into the spirit of things," Lailani said, "but you need to drop your voice back into your throat, with your throat open, and also into your chest. Pretend you're British, only without the accent. It'll give your voice more resonance. And know your intention—who it is you're playing, and why. Like this." She brought her hands in front of her chest and closed her eyes, curling into herself like a bud, and then unfurled quickly. "Well, he acts like an animal, has an animal's habits! Eats like one, moves like one, talks like one! There's even something—sub-human—something not quite to the stage of humanity yet! Yes, something—ape-like about him, like one of those pictures I've seen in anthropological studies." Lailani moved about the hallway, her hands making dismissive motions. Her voice and affect were different, as if she truly was a different woman than the woman she usually played with such panache. "Thousands and thousands of years have passed him by, and there he is, a survivor of the Stone Age!"

"There we all are, falling back into the Stone Age," I said dryly.

Lailani shook her finger at me.

I took a deep breath and tried to position my voice as she'd advised. I tried to imagine the sexy dark-haired femme I'd suddenly become. That woman would give those women who offered Arthur credits for his companionship a run for their money. I felt my throat work differently. "Buy me a drink, sailor?"

Lailani rolled her hands at me, demanding more.

"What's a nice boy like you doing in a place like this? Are you looking for trouble? Because if you are, you've found it."

"Not bad," Norman said. He gave me a half-impressed, half-scared look.

"Just don't forget what you're doing mid-sentence," Lailani said. "You don't want your voice to suddenly change back. If it does, cough to cover it up."

"I've got to be getting back to the pasta shop before my chefs steal the flour bags," Norman said. "Two walked away last week."

I touched Lailani's shoulder. "Thanks, Lailani. This is all great."

"Voice!" she commanded.

I took another deep breath, and imagined myself into the dark-haired bombshell who would coax men into chasing her instead of the blonde chasing an impossible rescue mission. It was a relief to take a break from who I had become, this mother and wife of lonely, steely resolve. It was fun, and it had been far too long since I'd had any of that.

"Fun . . . it refers to enjoyable experiences that human beings are hard-wired to have," Arthur had once told me.

I lowered my pitch and let my eyelids flutter. "How can I ever show my gratitude to such a beautiful thing as yourself? What would I do to express my thanks? Whatever would you like?"

"Nice," Lailani said, her face wreathed in smiles. "One last detail." She slipped a bangle on my wrist, silver and engraved with butterflies. "Now, I want to hear all about it! You tell me everything. Do your old friends recognize you? I have to know if my handiwork holds up. It usually does. When my hand works someone, they stay worked," she said, with sly innuendo. She wouldn't let us leave until I promised to tell her how it all went down when I returned the dress.

I didn't know I wouldn't be returning the dress.

9 I SET OUT FOR THE BOREALIS TAVERN. Hearing about Arthur and the others had engendered a longing that was impossible for me to resist, a longing to see them and hear them and be near them. I couldn't let myself get distracted from my rescue mission, and I couldn't let them follow me on an impossible mission. Still, I could spend an hour near them, without them knowing, while I hid in plain sight.

I tried to think of myself as the bold vamp whose clothes I wore. Her hips would swing a little, and her shoulders would be back to thrust out her chest. Just like that, my walk changed. It was subtle, but it changed the very air around me. Men turned to look and then stopped to stare as I passed by. There was nothing to see because of the convent school coat and the bonnet, but my vibe was suddenly juicy with promise. That was all it took.

Robert was mid song when I stepped in, singing a lively rendition of the Rolling Stones song "Angie." He missed a note when I stepped toward the bar. Jeannie relaxed in a wooden chair near him, her feet propped up on a tripod stool; she leaned forward to see why her man's attention had stuttered. Theo, totally absorbed in the rhythm, wailed away on the drums. *Funny. All those hours we'd spent together in France, and he never told me he was a drummer.*

"What can I get *you?*" asked Donny, who was tending the bar. He leaned across the counter toward me.

I tilted my head slightly downward, just enough to keep him from looking into my eyes and recognizing me.

"Anything she'd like is on me," said a young guy, offering an admiring glance as he positioned himself directly in front of me. Three of his friends crowded eagerly behind him. A few guys seated at nearby tables jumped up and joined the mob.

"Get lost," said Arthur, stepping through them as if they were so much detritus.

The men stepped back, muttering and snarling. I saw a few of them reach for their guns.

"Gentlemen," I said, in that other woman's voice, "no violence, if you please."

They backed up and dispersed.

Arthur gestured to Donny, who set down two of Outpost's finest ales, one for me and one for him. Arthur turned toward me, and even through the lowered brim of my hat, I saw him shamelessly surveying me up and down, appreciating what he saw. I took a deep gulp of the ale; like sulfuric acid, it bubbled away the lining of my throat. That would help disguise my voice.

"May I help you with your coat?" Arthur asked. He moved around behind me.

I lifted my arms a bit and arched my back to aid him, and the coat skimmed off my shoulders.

He sucked his breath in. His whole body froze a few inches behind me, and he seemed paralyzed as the coat hung from his hands and his gaze traveled down the length of my bare back.

Victory.

And with victory, surrender. Everything in me that could soften and open did.

"That's . . . quite the insolent frock," Arthur said finally, his voice ragged.

"Pshaw," I said lightly. "It's just what a girl needs on a cold, lonely day in February in Outpost City."

Arthur laid the plaid coat over a barstool. He wore a gray wool sweater over a black turtleneck and dark pants. He moved to the barstool on the other side of me and sipped his ale. He smiled at me, searching for my eyes under the brim of the bonnet. "In a dress like that, a girl's going to get whatever she needs—on a day in Outpost City that doesn't have to be cold and lonely."

I smiled and stretched up on my tiptoes to seat myself as gracefully as possible on the barstool.

A male cheer went up in the bar, followed by applause: The back of my dress had been pulled lower.

"Maybe we should move to a table," Arthur said, his voice still unsteady.

I nodded and slithered down from the stool, which set off another masculine chorus of whistles and cheers. Every woman in the tavern glared at me as if she wanted to kill me.

Arthur ignored the outcry and laid his hand on my back to steer me to a table.

My skin burned at his touch. I felt a little breathless myself.

Donny brought over the ales on a tray.

Arthur laid my coat, which he'd been carrying with his other hand, on the back of an extra chair. He turned his chair to face me instead of the table. "May I order you some dinner?" he asked.

"No, thank you, handsome. Just the ale." I took a sip and smiled, and his eyes smoldered as they watched my mouth.

"What are you doing here in the Borealis, Miss . . . ?"

"Angie," I said.

He smiled. "Of course. Nice boots, Angie."

"I just came in to get out of the cold." I crossed my legs. "These boots remind me of being back in the saddle."

Arthur straightened in his chair, and a particular light shone in his eyes.

"Of a horse," I added in a drawl.

Arthur seemed to want to say something, then he shook his head.

I let the silence play out.

A red stain crept up over his cheekbones. "Another drink?" he asked finally.

"I haven't finished this one," I said in coy Angie's voice.

"Do you have to? It's a nice night for a walk." He leaned toward me and reached over to tilt up the brim of my bonnet. His eyes on my face were lush and intoxicating, like black wine.

I would sell my soul for a single sip.

"All right, Sugar. That sounds delightful," I said, letting my lashes flutter down demurely. I rose again, to another smattering of applause and a few calls of "Don't leave!"

Arthur helped me on with my coat.

As we walked across the room, Robert unleashed the strains of Santana's "Black Magic Woman."

I paused to listen, and when I looked up at Arthur, he was smiling with one half of his mouth. I had seen that ironic expression on his face a thousand times, back in France. It nearly undid me now.

We continued out the door. I took Arthur's arm confidently, as if I'd never before touched him. I didn't know where we were going. I didn't care. He led me past the clinic and around the corner, and I was about to ask where we were going, when he picked me up bodily and pushed me against the side of the building and kissed me. Not gently.

After a few moments I needed air, so I moved my head to the side, gasping. Arthur kissed my neck. He pinned me up higher against the wall with one arm and his hips and reached around with the other hand to unbutton my coat. He kissed my throat and my collarbone.

I thought if he kept going, I might burst. *How much more can I take?* I moaned. "Maybe we should——"

Then his tongue was in my mouth, as hungry and demanding as I remembered. I groaned. My thighs clutched his waist. A few moments later, his hand traveled along my black-silk-stockinged thigh, past the garter and the metal bulge of my gun, to meet soft flesh. It kept moving to find the warmth and wetness he could always so easily elicit from me. There was no impediment to his fingers. He kind of bucked against me. He was moaning, too.

"Find a room," he said, finishing the sentence I'd started. He stepped back, releasing me gently.

We stood facing each other, completely entwined though physically separate. My lipstick was smeared all over his face and probably all over mine. We were oblivious to that and to the many passersby; they'd surely seen similar scenes and worse many times before in Outpost City, town of only two laws, neither of which concerned public decency.

"I can smell you," he said. He undid the bonnet from my head in quick, agile jerks. He pulled me roughly against him and kissed me again, more softly this time, and all the lightness of the cosmos sparkled through my veins. "I want you," he murmured against my cheek.

"I want you, too," I answered. I shivered.

"I've got a room somewhere. Fuck, where's my room?" He lifted his head to look around, as if his room were some missing object, like a dropped keychain. He squeezed me a little harder in the process.

"Boarding house on the next block, few rooms open," said a passing soldier. He winked and then laughed.

Arthur took me by my upper arm and half-dragged me, double quick, along the path to the next block.

Three credits vouchsafed by him and we set forth up a staircase for a third-floor room, me in the lead.

Near the first landing, Arthur grabbed my waist from behind. I turned and bent to kiss him, though he was so tall

I didn't really have to bend. I just wove my arms around him and kissed him with all the unhinged desperation in my being, which was a lot.

Arthur groaned in his throat and eased me down onto my bottom on the landing. He pushed me down onto my back. My coat flopped open, and he grasped the collar of the gray dress and tore straight down in a neat, razor-cut line so that it flopped open, also. He kissed my navel, and then his knee jammed in between my thighs, parting them. My long wait was over.

IT WAS ONLY a few moments before Arthur rolled off me. Despite the short time, we were both gasping and covered with sweat.

A woman called into the stairwell, whether from above or below, I couldn't tell. "Could y'all go do that in your room please?"

"I should go now," I said, panting.

"I'm not done with you," Arthur stated crisply. He rose fluidly, fixed his pants, and then helped me onto my feet.

Wobbling, I clutched the edges of my dress together.

Arthur grinned wolfishly and swept me up in his arms. Off the next landing was a room. He opened the door with a key and then closed it with a quick backward kick, all while holding me. He didn't release me until he was laying me gently on the bed. "Let's do this properly, shall we?"

But it was another hour before we got all our clothes off. And another hour after that before we both consented to cry "uncle," and that was only because the human body does have limitations to which it must occasionally submit.

Then again, maybe we were trying to kill each other.

"IT'LL BE MARCH soon," Arthur said. He was lying on his side, stroking the soft rise of my belly under my naval.

I lay on my back, an uncongealed puddle of satiated bliss.

Every bone, every muscle, and every synapse had melted and spent itself. Even the pores of my skin, where it hadn't been rubbed raw by our thrashing against each other, felt as if they'd been raptured and left to dissolve. I struggled to sit upright so I could fix the wig, which sat askew on my head.

"Allow me," Arthur said. I thought he was going to straighten the wig but he slipped his fingers under the lip of the hairline and pulled it off. Then he pulled off the net that Lailani had so carefully affixed. He flung the net aside and then used his fingers to comb out my blond mane.

"How did you know?" I wondered.

Arthur grinned lazily. "I know every cubic angstrom of your being, woman. How could I not know?"

"I'm not staying."

"Doesn't matter. I'll find you again." He pulled a handful of my hair against his face. "You make a fetching brunette."

"I like the beard." I rolled over on top of him so I could cup his scruffy chin with my hands.

He smiled and kissed my palms. "What are you doing here? Why aren't you in Edmonton?" The unspoken words at the end of his question were *"with Haywood,"* and his eyes narrowed to gray slits as he waited for my response.

But I offered him no answer or explanation. Instead, I kissed his mouth, and thrust my hips against him a little.

His eyes glowed and he wrapped his arms around me, cupping my buttocks.

I slipped my tongue into his mouth and he became very interested. His interest stirred me. Maybe the body's limitations weren't absolute.

Maybe we're just making up for a year and a half of lost lovemaking.

"You'll answer questions later," he murmured. "So will I. We have a lot to talk about, plans to make." He lifted my hips and positioned me just so. "Now where are those cowboy boots?"

Some hours later, well past midnight, the red boots were

back on my feet. I had just finished healing Arthur's left shoulder, which bore the puckered pink scar of a bullet hole—a 'through and through,' he'd called it. He'd flexed his arm and moved his humerus around inside the socket formed by the glenoid fossa of his lateral scapula, all of which I could visualize perfectly, thanks to hours spent in anatomical drawing class in art school.

He claimed he had full range of mobility but admitted that it hurt sometimes.

I put my hands on him, hoping the mysterious healing gift would come forth and help him. It did. I was grateful. I hated to think of Arthur in pain.

I pulled the coat on over my nude body; the dress and the stockings were so much confetti on the floor. I tucked my gun in my pocket.

I kissed Arthur's forehead gently. His soft snores accompanied me as I slipped out the door.

10

I WAS SORE AND EXHAUSTED. I didn't even lift my head when a customer sat down beside me. "Three credits for a sketch," I muttered.

"For you, Emma, a million credits," said a merry young voice with an Italian accent.

I looked up into the face of a dark-haired youth with sparkling, expressive eyes.

"Marco!" I yelled.

Then we were both on our feet, hugging each other, dancing and squeezing and squeezing as if we'd never let go. The hang-over evaporated as if it had never been present.

"Emma! Oh, Emma!" he said.

"I didn't know you were here," I said. Gaff hadn't told me, and I had to wonder why.

"I dreamt that you needed me," he said, laughing, but when we finally released each other and stepped back, he was crying.

"When did you get so tall?" I wondered, wiping and patting his face. When we were walking south through France after The Day, he'd only come up to my shoulder.

He caught my hand. "*Basta*, stop that! You're embarrassing me." He held my hand to his cheek briefly. "Wipe your own face."

So I was crying too. It had been over a year since I'd seen Marco, who'd been as dear as a son to me.

"I wouldn't be embarrassed," said a deep voice from behind me.

I turned slowly, still clinging to Marco. "Arthur."

"Emma." He nodded, the skin across his cheekbones looking as if it were stretched tight. But his eyes were mirthful. They dropped to my collarbone, where a big red hickey crept up past my shirt.

Pulling up my shirt, I turned back to Marco. "I'm so glad to see you! Are you hungry? Would you like something?"

"We've just eaten," Marco said.

"We'll eat," Arthur said. He sat down at the table, stretching his long legs out to the side.

"*Si, in fatto*, I am always hungry," Marco confessed. He squeezed my hand and gestured for me to sit.

I did, and then he did. I turned and waved for Jean-Pierre to bring them plates of food. "How did you find me?" I asked. I couldn't refrain from patting Marco again, even though he blushed and pushed my hand away.

Arthur reached out and touched my hand. Just the night before, his hands had been all over me. "A kid told us where to find you. Cost us a bullet."

"Gaff." I sighed and drew back my hand.

Arthur's index finger chased my wrist, and he raised an eyebrow at me.

Last night, my hands had been all over him, too. I blushed and murmured, "You were ripped off."

"I'd have paid two," he said. "I'd have paid ten. Ten bullets, ten years of my life." He took my hand firmly in his.

"He'd have taken half a piece of bread." I gave up trying to get my hand back and looked away. Of course Gaff had sold me out.

"I wasn't looking for a bargain," Arthur said. "I was looking for you."

Jean-Pierre brought two plates of food and three glasses

of water on a tray. Marco dug in as if he hadn't eaten in days, though it had probably been less than an hour. Arthur released my hand, then ate while looking at me intently.

"I heard you guys sailed a schooner to Quebec," I said.

Arthur raised an eyebrow.

I smiled. "Your little informant has lots of information for sale."

Arthur shrugged. "A man's got to make a life."

"Arthur is a very good sailor," Marco said. "It was fun, except for a storm we encountered. The waves were so tall, they took out the sky." He held both hands above his head, illustrating.

Of course Arthur was a good sailor. He was good at everything. He was eating and watching me carefully.

"Emma, why are you here, in this bad part of town? Why did you run away from us?" Marco asked reproachfully. His young face, usually so merry, wore an expression of deep sadness.

I sighed. "I wasn't running away from you."

"*Magari*, when you came into the tavern, you did not even say hello to us—not one word. You just pulled up your hood, turned around, and left. How could you do that to us after all we went through together? For shame!"

Only Arthur had recognized me as the brunette. I explained, "There's something I have to do. It's personal . . . and dangerous."

"We will help you," Marco said.

I shook my head and looked away. "It's my responsibility. I can't involve any of you. I will not put you at risk."

"Where's your husband?" Arthur asked. "Why isn't he here, by your side, helping you with this treacherous mission of yours?"

"Edmonton."

"Great." Arthur sneered.

"It's not like that," I said. "One of us had to stay behind. He wanted to come."

"So he should have, and not let you bully him out of it," Arthur said. "I take it you're headed out of the Safe Zone?"

I nodded.

He asked, "Mandy or Beth?"

I closed my eyes but didn't answer.

"You're not going alone," Arthur said tightly. He reached around his plate and gripped my hand again.

"It's too dangerous, and I don't want any of you hurt—or worse."

"I came for you, Emma. We came for you. I won't leave without you. I sure as hell won't let you roam the Wastelands unprotected." Arthur paused and set his jaw. "I don't care about your husband."

"You can not pretend we are not here," Marco added. "We are your family."

I took a deep breath. "I . . . I care about my husband. This is something I have to do on my own."

"You haven't been on your own since the day you gave yourself to me in France," Arthur said, his voice low but fierce.

"You have not been on your own since the day you took me with you," Marco said, his voice reproachful. "Remember? You found me not far from Paris, hiding in a Fiat. You got me out just before a mist ate the car."

"Yes, and we ran like crazy," I said, recalling those terrifying days before we'd run into Arthur, who, alone of all people on Earth, could control the mists and disperse or call them as he wished.

Marco nodded. "It was you, me, Mandy, and Shoshana then. Before Caris, even."

"Caris came to help set up the new camp. How is she?" I asked.

Arthur picked his head up and his eyes gleamed. He didn't

say anything because Marco launched into a fast recitation about how the kids were doing, his monologue laced with both Italian and French.

I leaned forward to listen, and couldn't restrain the tears that welled up. All my beloved children were well, healthy, and cared for and, most importantly, safe—all except dear, sweet Newt, who was beyond the reach of mists or hunger, because she was dead. Killed by the mists Arthur had created.

AN HOUR LATER, two men were waiting for me to draw for them. They sat in the next table over and moved about impatiently, scuffing their boots against the floor and clearing their throats loudly.

Marco excused himself and got up to use the bathroom, leaving Arthur and me alone.

The waiting men murmured to get my attention.

"Some business you've got here," Arthur said, eying them coolly. "Drawing portraits? I should have guessed."

"I went to the clinic, but you were waiting for me," I said quietly.

He grinned, a sour thing without humor. "You can elude me so easily? After I crossed an ocean for you?"

"I can't go with you, Arthur. This isn't your problem. It doesn't concern you or the others."

"Anything to do with you concerns me, and the others feel that way, too," he said. He paused and eyed me quizzically. "Meet me at the boardinghouse tonight?"

My face flamed over with emotion: embarrassment, longing, sadness, and desire. The need to hold him again, and to be held by him, was so powerful that it was like a sucker punch in my gut. Had I not been sitting already, my knees would have given out. "I shouldn't have done that. It was a mistake."

"Make the same mistake again tonight," he said. "You know you want to."

"I'm . . . married."

"Not for much longer."

"I have two children with Haywood, and—"

"You're going to have to make a decision about Haywood and about your life. Ultimately, that decision will be about your children too. I'm sorry." His face was solemn.

I continued as if he hadn't spoken. "And one of them is in trouble."

"Beth," Arthur guessed. "Something happened to Beth. Haywood stayed home with Mandy and sent you out on an impossible journey—alone. Jesus priest! That man sent you, his wife, out alone, to face God knows what."

"It's complicated," I said, not meeting his eyes. I was reluctant to tell him about Haywood's prescience.

Marco came back to the table and shrugged on his coat. "I know the others will want to know what happened to us. Emma, *carissima mia*, you're coming."

I stood, and Arthur slowly rose to his feet. I shook my head. "No, I'm not. I have work to do here." I tilted my head toward the waiting customers. "Tell the others I love them. Tell Jeannie and Robert congratulations on the baby."

"Tell them yourself," Marco muttered, scowling. "They don't want to hear it from me."

I shook my head at him.

"*Merde!* Are you joking, Emma? You will not come? After everything we have been through together? After everything?"

"I have to do this alone, Marco. I'm sorry."

"Bullshit!" he exclaimed, glaring at me.

I shook my head again.

His young face tightened with anger. He turned on his heel and stomped out of the bar, muttering ugly things in fast, florid Italian.

Arthur came to stand directly in front of me, two inches from me.

I tried to move back but the table prevented me.

He grasped both my shoulders. "You knew about Caris because I told you. I felt you dying, and I sent myself to you. You were in a bad way."

"You saved me," I acknowledged. "Thank you."

"You belong to me."

I shook my head slowly. "Not anymore, even if I wish I did."

"And I belong to you," he said, as if I hadn't spoken. "Tonight at the boarding house," he reminded me. His lips grazed my forehead, and everything in me quivered, feeling his heat. He released me and stepped back, zipped his coat, and pulled on his hat.

"Not tonight," I whispered. "Tonight I have something to do."

Arthur gave me a sharp look.

I gulped. "Tomorrow night," I said, but it was a lie; there would be no tomorrow for me in Outpost City. Tonight I'd steal a horse. Tomorrow I'd be out riding in the Wastelands or hanging from the scaffolding north of town.

A FEW HOURS and three sketches later, I went back to my room. I packed my belongings into my backpack.

A knock sounded at my door.

Gun ready, I opened it a crack at first, and then threw open the door. "Brendan!" I yelled. We embraced each other. I kissed the top of his head.

"I couldn't let you have all the fun without me," he said. "'One thing is certain, no party is any fun unless seasoned with folly.'"

"How on Earth did you get here?" I asked. I squeezed him again, so glad to see him.

"Dog sled," he said. "Belongs to one of my students. Do you believe, even in The After, some kids will do anything for a good grade? I gave him an A-plus and left a note for the dean to that extent."

"I believe anything happening in The After," I assured him. I wiped at my eyes with the back of my hand. "But how'd you find me here?"

"First person I saw when I came through the gates was that Sioux woman from the day the raiders took Beth," Brendan said.

"Kangee," I murmured.

He nodded. "She told me where to find you."

"Really? I didn't know she knew. I can't believe you're here. How are Mandy and Haywood?"

"Mandy seems serene. Haywood has been in a foul mood, but Mandy keeps telling him you know what you're doing."

"That sounds like Mandy. And Renee and Sally?"

Brendan shook his head. "'Dispute not with her, she is lunatic.'"

"Maybe not," I said. "I think Sally has a psychic gift. She can control animals."

Brendan gave me a long, thoughtful stare. "You have a reason to believe this? She's been unreachable since you left. Sits in the rocking chair all day, rocking back and forth, her eyes blank."

"She may be the reason I'm still alive," I said softly. "You know, my friend, you came at the worst possible time for your own safety. I'm going out in a few hours to steal a horse."

"What did I just tell you about fun and folly?" Brendan asked. He winked and tramped over to climb up my bed. "I didn't come to be with you for simplicity's sake. Say, anything to eat around here?"

"I'll take you for dinner as soon as I've finished packing," I promised. I was checking my gun, making sure it was clean and loaded. I paused and gave him an unhappy look. "Brendan, I haven't figured out how I'm going to do this."

"How we're going to do this," he said.

We exchanged a smile.

"You know I love you, Em."

I leaned over to pat his shoulder. "I love you, too, Brendan."

He shook his head, the beautiful, normal-sized head that sat atop a tiny, awkward body with a lame leg. His dark eyes were sad and liquid. "Not the way I love you. I love you *that* way—the way you can never reciprocate because of Haywood and the girls. Mostly because of Arthur."

I didn't know how to respond. I'd never suspected that Brendan felt that way about me. "Brendan, I—"

He smiled at me crookedly. "'Reason does not enter into it. In many ways, unwise love is the truest love. Anyone can love a thing because. That's as easy as putting a penny in your pocket. But to love something despite. To know the flaws and love them too. That is rare and pure and perfect.' What can I say? I have a weakness for lost causes."

I couldn't speak in the face of his kindness, his vulnerability. I was glad, grateful, and relieved that I wouldn't have to go out alone tonight. It was a weakness, but I wanted company. Nevertheless, I was terrified that Brendan's support would get him killed alongside me. He was worth so much more than the price he'd have to pay for his loyalty to an unfulfilled love.

I was also struck to humility by his graceful declaration of love. There was nothing rare, pure, or perfect about me. My actions the other night, going after Arthur in a brunette wig and high-heeled red cowboy boots, had proven that to me. I knew Haywood was waiting for me, and he deserved my fidelity. I'd called it a mistake, but I was glad to have done it. If I died at sunrise with a noose around my neck, I would rejoice in having spent that night with Arthur. Those would be my last thoughts.

I took Brendan's hand and squeezed. *At least I'm not alone in my mission.*

11

IT WAS THREE-THIRTY IN THE MORNING, THE witching hour in Outpost City. Even the miscreants were asleep, and miscreants made up the largest segment of the population. Brendan and I crept along the twisty streets, which were mostly dark, as the torches had sputtered out over the last hour. A sliver of moon shed not enough waxen light by which to see the piles of excrement, so it was like walking a smelly, sticky minefield. Only a few drunk and drowsy souls wandered the cold, inky town. Brendan and I clutched each other as if we were tipsy. The pair of inebriated soldiers on patrol who passed us didn't look twice.

We'd come up with a plan: We'd start a fire near the stables. I would approach the stables with a large bottle of whiskey, for which I'd paid eight credits. I would tease the soldiers into drinking, which would be easy, because here in Outpost City, everyone drank all the time, especially soldiers.

While I was intoxicating the soldiers, Brendan would get our fire blazing. When he gave the signal, a birdcall, I would alert the guards. The guards would run to put out the fire, and I'd ride out with a horse, pick up Brendan, and ride for the fence. Brendan had a set of heavy wire cutters, the object on which I'd spent my last twenty credits. We'd cut the barbed wire and slip out the eastern side of town.

Arson, alcohol, and brazen theft. Lame, but the best we could do. We only hoped that our sobriety and a just cause would be our saving graces—that and divine providence, something I hated to trust, because it had been in short supply since Arthur's mists had unleashed terror and havoc on the world.

We had a bag of manure and kindling. Brendan had matches. We wound our way through the labyrinth, whispering to each other about our plan, refining as we went. We passed not far from the Borealis Tavern, its lights still aglow.

I wondered if Arthur was asleep and where. My heart wrung in on itself. He would be upset to find me gone the next day, be it far or forever.

We found a small shack that served as a grocery stand on the outskirts of town, near where the pasture land started. The lights were off and it was boarded up tight for the night. We couldn't even look in the windows.

"Too bad about the food in there," I said, with genuine regret. I glanced around carefully. "There could be someone watching to make sure thieves don't break in. Norman pays some kids to watch his stores at night. They do a pretty good job of it."

"Great deeds are usually wrought at great risks," Brendan said. He took the bag of crap from me and waved me on. "This is my cue. Go on, Em . . . and good luck."

"If you're going to get caught, run. Hide. We can try again another day."

"Right back at ya, lady."

"See you on the other side," I said.

We clasped hands and looked into each other's eyes. I could feel him thinking about Beth, as I was. He nodded slowly.

FOUR SOLDIERS MANNED the front of the stable. It didn't take much to induce them to drink the whiskey: All I had to do was extend my arm with the bottle in it. Four rifles dropped out of ready position, and four thirsty men crowded around me.

"What are you doing here at the stables?" demanded one soldier as he waited his turn. He was swarthy and pock marked and watched me with narrowed eyes. He seemed a little smarter than the others. I figured I'd have to get him a little drunker than the others. I also figured I might have to give him more than whiskey to allay his doubts.

"Oh, a girl just wants a little fun sometimes," I said in the musky Angie voice with which I'd approached Arthur. Angie's blithe suggestiveness provoked whistles and hoots from the other men, and even Mr. Suspicious grinned.

"A girl like you must be having all the fun she can handle in Outpost City," he said. His eyes went to my hair. "Outpost City's all about fun."

"No sirree. It's been a lonely apocalypse," I drawled. That elicited more hollers and some filthy suggestions. I pretended to be amused. A few of the suggestions brought Arthur to mind; we'd explored those positions with gusto, just the night before.

Mr. Suspicious got hold of the whiskey and gulped for a long time, his eyes never leaving my face.

I smiled back at him.

The other guys thumped him on the back and he finally passed the bottle. "I'll make sure you ain't lonely," he said. He didn't wait; he grabbed me roughly and encircled me with his arms, then shoved his tongue down my throat.

I had to work not to gag. I had to force myself not to jump back when he ground his hips into me. I was suited up in my Inuit gear so I couldn't feel his erection, but I knew he had one. I was prepared to go as far as necessary to attain my goal.

But in the next instant, his head exploded.

I screamed and jumped back, covered with blood and brain tissue. I couldn't think for a moment, but then my brain asked, *Why, Brendan? This wasn't part of our plan.* I had hoped not to have to kill anyone. Even for Beth, I didn't want murder on my conscience.

The other three soldiers jumped to alert, their rifles up and their backs together.

Nothing moved in the darkness. The only sound came from the horses, softly nickering and snorting in the stable. Yellow and orange flared nearby.

I pointed. "There!" I said.

The grocery shack was going up in flames. The three soldiers ran towards it.

I waited for a split second, then I threw open the stable door and ran inside. I dropped to my hands and knees, scrambling along as swiftly and quietly as possible. It was utterly black, so I went by feel and sound. I groped my way up to open a stall door and felt for the horse. It didn't spook as my blind hands felt along its nose, which was a good start. It whuffled and swayed, but it didn't stamp or snap at me. *Bingo! We're made for each other.*

I found a lead, which I clipped on, and led the horse out of the stall. As I did, I groped along the walls, hoping to find reins, a saddle, and a pad. My eyes were adapting to the intense black of the stable and I could just barely make out lumps of darker dark. *Is that . . . ? Yes, a saddle!* Then reins and a pad. As best I could tell with my fingers, I had an English saddle and Western forked-cheek reins. They'd have to do.

I blessed Arthur for all the times he'd made me tack my good-hearted horse Rosie back at his camp. He'd drilled me in the proper way, insisting that I do it almost as expertly as he did, the Olympic equestrian. His strict instruction came back to me now.

Pad, saddle. I cinched up the girth, waited for the horse to release some air, and then cinched it a little bit tighter. I measured out the stirrups against my arm, remembering the length that had made me most comfortable in my seat. It had been more than a year since I'd sat on a horse, but my body remembered.

I eased the horse out toward the open door. The horse was

responsive but slow, a perfect combination for me. I could conceive of riding it to the rogue camp in Bismarck without falling off and killing myself.

A few more soft steps and we stood outside the stable. Brendan was supposed to be waiting for me near the sheep and cow barn. I touched my calves to the horse's sides.

A *click* rang out in the night: Someone was pointing a gun at me. I froze. In the dim moonlight, I made out a form sprinting toward me from around the side of the barn. He didn't say anything and I wondered if I could get away with only a small wound. I squeezed the horse's sides to get it to move, and the horse stepped forward obligingly.

Another dark shape hurtled after the first. There were two guns pointed at me.

"Get off the horse, miss," said a steely voice.

A flashlight irradiated my face, and I instinctively blinked and jerked my head to the side. Slowly, trembling, I dismounted. The soldier kicked the flexion fold on the back of my knee. Grunting, I lurched forward to my knees.

"Shoulda kept that date with me," breathed the soldier with the flashlight.

I looked up. He moved the beam of light back a little so I could make out his face. It was Rolf, the soldier who had informed me of the town laws when I first arrived.

He smirked. "Looks like you got your wish. You'll hang instead."

THEY MARCHED ME out the north gate, to the field with the gallows. I was tied to a stake. The air was bitter, so frigid that the buildings and even the barbed wire fence seemed to be outlined with a thin violet-blue radiance. I was glad to have worn my Inuit gear, and I remained glad even when another soldier joined the two who had captured me, and the three of them bickered about who would get to strip the gear off my dead body. They decided to settle it by a wager: how long it would take me to die.

Would my neck snap and kill me quickly, or would I die more slowly, by strangulation? The latter would take between ten and twenty minutes. Apparently the drop from the execution platform was only three feet, so as to maximize the impossibility of predicting how the condemned prisoner would die. Outpost City soldiers liked placing bets as much as they liked drinking.

Not even twenty minutes later, Brendan was brought to the stake. He looked bad; they'd roughed him up. In Outpost City, arson was grimly regarded—perhaps more so than murder. I was also being held responsible for Mr. Suspicious's death, though I hadn't shot him.

Rolf said, "You'll hang at first light, sweetheart."

"Let the little guy go," I said. "He isn't involved in this. He didn't do anything."

"'The first mover of the cause above, when he first made the fair chain of love, great was the effect, and high was his intent,'" Brendan muttered. His right eye was closed, swollen, and bloodied. His nose had been broken, and blood crusted his mouth and chin.

I glanced at his face with sorrow and anger. I wanted to kill the men who had done that to my friend.

Rolf stroked my cheek. "You're right, Blondie. Technically, arson isn't illegal."

"Neither is murder . . . technically," one of the other soldiers said.

There were six of them, and they all laughed. Two of the night guards trotted over from their positions at the gate to join the crowd.

"Technically, only horse theft is illegal in Outpost City," joked one of the night guards. "Shooting a soldier the way your little friend did isn't illegal, per se."

"What? I didn't shoot anybody," Brendan said.

"Sure, his head went off like a grenade all on its own,"

said another soldier, sarcastically. He was one of the guys who had been drinking with me and had witnessed the explosion of his comrade's head firsthand. He threw back his arm and punched Brendan again.

Blood and a tooth swirled through the air like red lace. I cried out. Brendan made not a sound.

"Not illegal, but we frown upon murder and arson," Rolf said. He winked at me. "It's a big, mean, *ugly* frown."

That provoked the soldiers into gales of hilarity.

"We could have a little fun with her before she swings," suggested the soldier who had hit Brendan.

The world went very cold and still and my stomach clenched up.

"I thought about that, but the captain don't approve," said Rolf. "He shot two guys in the kneecaps for that shit last month."

"What a waste," said another soldier.

The soldiers went to stand by a trashcan with flames erupting from its mouth. They were joking and laughing, too far away for us to make out their words, but close enough for us to hear their jovial tones.

"I'm sorry," I said to Brendan, my eyes filling with tears. "I'm so sorry." My heart ached. I was sorry for Brendan and sorry for Beth. *Who would rescue her now? My sweet Beth, serious and gentle, full of questions and insights wiser than her years.* The keenest regret and frustration enveloped my being. I prayed that Haywood would go for her. *Maybe his prescience will show him a way where I've failed.*

"'Whan that aprill with his shoures soote, the droghte of march hath perced to the roote, and bathed every veyne in swich licour of which vertu engendred is the flour; What zephirus eek with his sweete breeth...'" Brendan said.

"Brendan, I'm sorry, truly," I said. "I would give anything for you not to be here. Anything." Tears ran down my face in cold rivers.

Brendan lifted his voice into the night air. "'Inspired hath in every hold and heeth Tendre croppes, and the yonge sonne hath in the ram his halve cours yronne, and smale foweles maken melodye . . .'"

I thought of Arthur, who would see my corpse swinging from the gallows in the morning. He would be sorrowful and furious. I remembered our night together. It made my heart ache, but it was also some comfort. At least I'd been able to hold him again before I died. At least I'd felt his warm body against mine one last time. It would have been too much to die without having accomplished that much, at the very least.

I only wished I had told Arthur with words what my body had told him freely and without reservation: that I forgave him, that I loved him, that I could not live without him.

Brendan kept reciting as I wept and the deep veil of night lifted.

THE MEAGEREST, MILKIEST scrims of light broke out over the eastern horizon, and the soldiers were already untying us from the stake. They were full of good humor and keen appreciation for the moment. I vomited all over the one who stood in front of me, which sent the others into hysterics.

Brendan was still reciting poetry. His lips moved with small sounds, his limpid eyes were fiercely focused within. I was overcome with anguish for him: He'd come to help me rescue my daughter, and now he was going to die for it, as I had feared any who got involved would.

They marched us up onto the platform. Two soldiers brought up a smaller, struggling form. They knocked off his leather cap as they settled the noose around his neck.

Gaff? But he's just a kid!

I wanted to say something to him but my heart was too full, too terrified. As the soldiers settled the noose around my neck, my bladder betrayed me. I had wanted to die with dignity, but clearly, that wasn't going to be possible.

"'For certes, as saith St. Jerome, the earth shall cast him out of him and the sea also, and the air also, that shall be full of thunderclaps and lightnings. Now soothly, who-so well remembreth him of these tidings, I guess his sin shall not turn him to delight but to great sorrow, for dread of the pain of hell,'" Brendan sang out, as if triumphant. He gave me a small smirk, his bruised and bloodied mouth twisting proudly.

My whole being ached with his courage as my urine soaked my clothes.

A small crowd was gathering to watch the dawn's entertainment. Jokes were tossed back and forth between the onlookers and the soldiers; they'd witnessed the cruel spectacle many times before, and they enjoyed every moment of it. After another twenty minutes, the soldiers started down off the platform.

I closed my eyes and prayed. I'd had little use for prayer over the last few years, so vicious had God's hand been upon the Earth. But in that moment, it was all I had left.

Screams sounded. My eyes popped open. In the city center, yellow flames fanned into the air, and explosions crackled and boomed. The soldiers paused on the platform steps. The soldier nearest me went down in a smog of blood and vaporized skull shrapnel. The other soldiers ran to no avail, for bullets found them too.

Gaff jumped up and down, trying to get his bound hands under his feet so he could move them forward to the front of his body. Brendan and I looked around in awe and confusion.

The ground vibrated and shivered like a tympanum. Then came a wild, rumbling noise. It reached a crescendo, and out through the city gates thundered a stampede of horses and cows. At first glance, it seemed there were hundreds of galloping animals, frenzied and directionless, knocking down sections of barbed wire and trampling over other animals and unlucky citizens who couldn't get out of the way.

With a burst of incredulous hope, I recognized the big

frame on a tall horse near the front: *Arthur!* It was almost as if he was surfing the swell of crazed animals. He aimed an Uzi at the soldiers. They scrambled to return fire, but he mowed them down accurately and without mercy.

From the corner of my eye, I saw two soldiers on the ground near the platform crawling toward the lever that would slide back the platform under our feet, so Brendan and Gaff and I would still hang.

Is Arthur too late to save us?

My heart pounded furiously. My eyes picked out other figures on horseback, including a tall figure with a round belly who pointed her rifle at us. "Gaff, hold still!" I yelled, urgently. I knew Jeannie wouldn't be able to shoot him down if he was bobbing around like that.

Unfortunately, one of the fallen soldiers, trailing black blood in his wake, had dragged himself to the lever. It was Rolf, and he snarled up at me. "Fuck you, you blonde bitch!" he said as he threw himself over the lever.

Empty space opened up beneath my feet, and I fell with a nauseating lurch, my body jerking like a fish being gutted. It was the longest millisecond of my life. But the noose never closed on my throat. I dropped all the way to the ground: a bullet had found the rope above my head. I couldn't hear gun-fire over the roar of the stampede, but my life was proof of it.

Brendan fell with a *crunch* next to me, and then Gaff hit the ground too. I crawled over to check on Brendan and he was still breathing. I staggered to my feet, screaming at Brendan and Gaff to run out of the path of the stampede. They couldn't hear but had gotten the idea themselves. The three of us bolted eastward, since the stampede was still moving north.

Arthur's arm swept down and snatched me up by the ropes around my wrists.

I wondered how he'd gotten free of the herd. I felt my left shoulder snap loose from its socket, and the world hazed

out around me. The pain was sickening. So was the unex-
pected relief: I was atop a horse. Alive. Gasping, I twisted to
see what had happened to Brendan: Robert had pulled him
onto his horse, and Theo had Gaff. I caught a quick look at
Laurette's set face before the pain unfurled like a black sail
blotting out the sun. I passed out.

12

I CAME TO AS I WAS BEING STOOD ON my feet. My Inuit parka had been stripped off, as had the atigi. Moaning sounded in my ears, and I realized it was my own, much to my dismay. I opened my eyes, and the undulant pain in my shoulder and arm caused my head to loll backward. My wrists were untied. Arthur held me on my left side, and Donny on the right. *Donny?* I picked my head up and tried to focus my eyes on him.

"This is going to hurt," Arthur warned. He looked at someone behind me, who came close and cradled me from behind, supporting my back. Arthur held my upper arm still, then flexed my arm at my elbow to ninety degrees.

I screamed.

He shook his head sympathetically and made some sort of rotation movement, pulling my arm and shoulder inward toward my chest while pressing my arm.

Agony. The world fizzled out like a firecracker dying. My legs succumbed, and I sank, but Donny and the person at my back held me up.

Slowly and steadily, Arthur rotated my arm and shoulder outward, keeping my upper arm stationary. Every motion elicited the spasmodic, radiating pain I had thought was reserved for childbirth. Arthur kept pressing my arm and shoulder back, seemingly oblivious to my screams. At just

past ninety degrees to my chest, my shoulder slipped back
into its joint. I passed out again.

WHEN I AWOKE, I was lying back against a boulder, my atigi
and parka snugged around me like a blanket. Jeannie sat next
to me, and on her other side sat Laurette. I struggled to an
upright seated position, cold, sore, and confused. *Where am I?*
Who's here? What's . . . happening?

"You're an ardfaced git, didn't even say arite," Jeannie
said. She didn't look at me but rose and strode away. Even her
long back, still slim during pregnancy, shut out inquiry.

My left arm was ensconced in a sling, bound close to my
body. It required tremendous effort, but I managed to shrug
on the atigi, leaving the left sleeve empty. I wrestled as best I
could with the parka. After several minutes, I got it on too. I
pulled the hood up with my right arm, then sat back, sweaty
and exhausted.

We were in a snow-covered clearing surrounded by trees.
A wan, cream-colored sun was high overhead in a vast leaden
sky. A campfire burned nearby. Theo and Marco hovered by
it, cooking meat on a spit. Robert squatted close, eying me
balefully.

"Robert," I said, smiling at him.

He shook his head and then rose and went to the fire. He
stood with his back to me. When Jeannie trudged over to
him, he draped his arm around her shoulders.

I turned to Laurette.

"Do not start with me, Emma. You ride off without saying
adieu and then fail to greet us in Outpost City. You are on my
shit list," Laurette said, her idiom only slightly spoiled by her
French pronunciation of 'shit' as 'sheet.' She waved her hand
imperiously.

They were angry. I figured they had a right to be.

I looked around to find the others. On the far side of the
campfire, Arthur stood in rapt conversation with Donny,

Nwokocha, and Brendan. Kneeling, Kangee was wiping the blood off Brendan's face. She must have felt my eyes on her, because she cocked her head at me and laughed. Arthur and the others turned to find the source of her mirth. I shrugged and made a rueful gesture with my good arm.

I stumbled to my feet and walked to the group. "Any of you still talking to me?"

"I am," Brendan said. He tried to smile, but it was clear his face hurt. "I like your friends. They have a knack for a timely arrival. Words can never express my gratitude for helping me escape the hangman's noose."

"Give them some time. They'll come around," Arthur said. He touched my cheek gently. "How are you feeling?"

"Like I've been run over by a truck," I said, "which feels pretty damn good, considering I was a few seconds from being dead."

"I wouldn't let that happen to you," Arthur said softly. His eyes on me were intense, brooding, troubled and determined, all at once.

"Emma! You're awake," sang Gaff, who came around a tree toward us. "Ain't this great? We ain't dead. How 'bout that stampede? Never saw nothin' like it."

"Yeah, a clever distraction," I said to Arthur.

"Donny's idea. I can't take credit for it." Arthur exchanged an amused glance with Donny.

Kangee laughed again.

"Kangee, what's so funny?" I demanded.

"Arthur," she said. She stood up, done with her ministrations to Brendan. She looked at Arthur and burst into gales of laughter. She walked off toward the treeline, still laughing, and Arthur scratched his neck.

I grabbed Donny's sleeve. "Is she . . . ?"

He nodded. "She's here."

"And where is here, exactly?"

"Not far from Woolchester," Gaff said. At my blank

expression, he added, "A teeny tiny crap farm district south of The Hat."

"We're outside the Safe Zone," I said. But not really, because Arthur was always at the center of a safe zone. He could control the mists and summon or dismiss them at will. As if reading my mind, he looked away. I asked, "Can you spare a horse?"

"We brought a few extra with us," Donny said. "Of course, you'll be riding one."

"I have to get to Bismarck."

Arthur put a hand lightly on my good shoulder. "I'd forgotten how bull-headed you can be. Don't you get it, woman?"

I must have looked confused, because Brendan spoke up. "We're all going to Bismarck."

"I can't involve . . ." I started, but when Arthur's mouth tightened in an ugly way, I shut up fast.

"Don't, or I won't talk to you, either," he said. That settled things.

OVER A DELICIOUS meal of charred roasted beef, carved out of a cow that had fallen during the stampede, we discussed the route to Bismarck.

"It's about a thousand kilometers," Arthur said, peering at a fold-out travel map, the kind that used to be found in every gas station, but had dwindled in the last few years of The Before, thanks to the almighty Internet.

"We ride fifty or fifty five klicks a day, and we'll get there in eighteen, nineteen days," Robert said.

"That's a significant push every day," Nwokocha said.

Laurette, sitting beside him, nodded vigorously.

"The horses are in good condition," Arthur said, not looking up from the map. "But, yes, it's ambitious."

Robert looked in my general direction, but his eyes didn't meet mine. "When you rode north through France with that fucking wanker, Emma, how far did you ride each day?"

"About forty kilometers, I think," I said. I was going to say that I wasn't sane for much of the ride, but I decided that the less said, the better. My old mates weren't in the mood to hear much from me. I found their anger irritating.

"Wanker?" Brendan asked from beside me. He tilted his head as he chewed, avoiding pain in his jaw where he'd lost teeth. His eye was still swollen shut, though Laurette had bathed it with an herbal concoction and then bound it lightly.

"The Russian sociopath," I said. I shuddered internally, remembering Alexei. I was glad to be far from him, but I did wonder what had become of him. The last thing I saw, leaving France, was Alexei holding a gun to Arthur's head. But Arthur was here with me, alive. *Is Alexei dead?*

"What will the people who took Beth do to her?" Arthur asked.

"The usual," I said.

Laurette and Jeannie gave me sharp looks, before concentrating again on their meat.

"What do you know about them?" Arthur asked.

"Not much. They rode up the park system in Edmonton, grabbed a bunch of women and children in the park, shot the men who tried to stop them, and then rode off," I said. "They rode in formation and maintained ranks. They seemed . . . organized."

"They are," Gaff said. He'd eaten several helpings of beef and was eying the haunch as if he'd go back for more. "They ain't as crazy as some of the other fuckers, but they're mean, and they've got a nasty agenda. They want to invade Edmonton and take it over for themselves."

"You're a clever boyo," Robert said. "How do we know you're not a brick shy of a load, talkin' a lot of shite?"

Gaff smirked. "One thing about me, mister, is that my intel is so clean you can brush your teeth with it. It's simple arithmetic, really. In Outpost City, if I gave bad intel for good credits, someone was going to come back and clobber me. That don't add up to smart. No thanks to pain."

"So why'd we find you in the gallows, then, if you're so sharp and all?" Robert persisted.

"Some people got no sense of humor about the, uh, redistribution of wealth," Gaff said. As he spoke, he looked more than just disgruntled; he looked dispirited, and I felt a flash of sympathy for him. He knew what I knew now: Standing inside a noose, waiting to die miserably, refreshed one's perspective.

"If they're as organized as you say, with a plan, someone's leading them," Arthur surmised.

Gaff perked up. "Yep. It's some guy they call The One."

"The One?" Arthur raised his eyebrows. "So we're dealing with a charismatic leader."

"He came about a year ago," Gaff said. "He killed the guys who didn't agree and took over, then started attracting new guys."

"That's what he would do," Arthur said, wearing a pensive look. "Consolidate his power over his soldiers."

"Not soldiers—just half-crazy raiders," Gaff corrected him, a little smugly. "They ain't totally crazy, but they ain't exactly sane, either. They'll hear 'bout you, too, now."

Everyone looked at him.

Arthur asked quietly, "How is that?"

"Spies," Donny offered.

Gaff nodded. "They got spies in Outpost City that tell them everything. They'll be hearin' about the stampede and the rescue."

"Will they guess we're coming for 'em?" Jeannie asked tightly.

Gaff shrugged and then went back to the roast beef. He tore himself another piece with his dirty fingers.

WE MOUNTED THE horses after lunch. Arthur helped me up onto a leggy golden palomino, then stroked the horse's neck affectionately. "This big handsome fella carried me 3,500 kilometers from Quebec to Outpost City, through storms and raiders and bandits. He's got the courage of ten warhorses."

"How'd you get him?" I asked.

Arthur swung himself up onto the saddle behind me. "Well, when we got to Quebec, the city was largely intact, but under attack. We helped the Quebecois defend themselves. They were grateful." He settled himself in and put his hands on either side of my hips, scooting me into position, and then circling me with his arms to hold the reins.

I noticed Brendan watching us with his one good eye, a hooded expression on his face. "What did you talk to Brendan about?" I asked in a low voice.

"Haywood and your girls." Arthur steered the horse away from the extinguished campfire.

The others were mounting their horses too. Donny helped Brendan up and then climbed up behind him. It felt like old times, like my months in Arthur's camp. We'd mount up as a group and ride out on some mission. The women's camp, a deer- or boar-hunting expedition, an intel gather; we did it regularly. Some subliminal part of my brain felt good, felt comfortable, and despite the pulsing ache, my body relaxed.

Arthur felt the change in my posture. He kissed the crown of my head. Brendan was watching and his eye receded. I wondered guiltily if he was thinking about Haywood.

We were twelve people and fourteen horses, though four horses carried only packs and weapons. Brendan and I were too dinged up to ride solo. We rode south and east, through pine forests and small, clear lakes and over flat-topped plateaus, keeping up a brisk, punishing pace. We stopped only once for a bathroom and water break. I wondered how the pregnant Jeannie was faring on such a physically demanding journey, but I didn't dare ask. She dismounted fluidly enough, and she never complained. Still, I knew it couldn't have been easy for her.

During the break, Robert stood close to her, watching as she drank water and took a few mouthfuls of something. I didn't get close enough to her to see what she was eating, but I could tell from the tension in his body and from his gestures that Robert wanted her to eat more.

Theo, like the others, wouldn't speak to me; even Marco was brusque. I gave up trying to engage them and went about my business as best I could, though pulling down the caribou pants with only one arm required ingenuity. I trudged back to the circle of horses, and Kangee came to stand next to me. I was breathing hard with ache and exertion, not looking forward to climbing back up on Arthur's horse. Every molecule of my flesh cried out for rest, for relief. Still, the cold, hard truth was that pain meant I was alive.

"I have something that will help you with the pain," she said.

"Really?" I asked gratefully.

"Do you trust me?" she asked.

I nodded.

She smiled beatifically and went to her horse, pulled something from her saddlebag. She crooked her finger and glided out of the stand of ice-laden pines, up a hill that looked out over undulating, snow-covered land.

Kangee unscrewed her jar. Inside was a dark, tarry substance. A vile scent wafted to my nose, causing me to recoil. She laughed. "Yes, but it will take the pain away. Dip your little finger in and lick it off."

I looked askance at her.

She nodded encouragingly.

I dipped my little finger in, coating the tip of my pinkie.

"Too much," Kangee said. "Scrape most of it off."

I rubbed my fingertip off on the lip of the jar until Kangee nodded. Then I sucked my finger clean.

Kangee said, "Too much is poisonous."

"*Now* you tell me?" I asked.

"Doesn't kill you right away," she said casually, as if that meant I didn't need to worry.

The sky split open as if a giant hand had peeled it back. Then the sky turned purple. At the same time, a wave of peace crashed over my body. I had never before understood how exquisite was the cessation of pain. I gurgled. "Wow!"

"Works good," Kangee said, with satisfaction.

"Thank you," I said. I wanted to cry, so deep was my gratitude and relief.

"You're welcome." She turned and walked away, her black braid drawing concentric circles in the air.

I watched in utter fascination. Then I turned back to the sky, which was putting on a sumptuous aurora borealis for my benefit. I felt the deep peace of the universe seeping in through my pores. It was hot so I took off my parka, which was easy now that my body felt so loose. It felt so good that I took off my atigi too.

"Emma!" Arthur barked.

I looked at him and he was bathed in radiance: gold, scarlet, and indigo.

He strode close to me.

I threw my arms around him. "You're so pretty!" I said. "All of your lights are . . . beautiful!"

"Kangee!" Arthur called, in a voice that seemed much too harsh for the moment, causing me to recoil. Arthur picked up my atigi and parka off the ground and slipped them back over my head.

I watched the rainbows whirling around him and wondered how I had been able to bear being apart from him for even one day. "I missed you," I said to him.

"What did she do to you?" he demanded.

"Kangee is my friend," I said. "Sometimes she isn't there, but sometimes she is."

Arthur shook his head and took my hand to lead me back to the horses. I felt rooted to the ground, like a tree. I was a tree, with sap from the earth circulating through my veins rather than hurtful old blood. My hair was tree branches. I didn't move. I just experienced the cold, clean air flowing through my twigs.

"Jesus priest," Arthur muttered. He picked me up in his arms and cradled me close to his chest, carefully arranging my hurt arm so that it wasn't pressing into him. His face looked dark and worried.

Why was he worried? "You can't carry a tree," I said. But it felt so good to be close to him that I snuggled into him. It was sweet like a Schubert melody, so I told him that, and then I hummed it for him.

Then we were back at the horses. Most everyone had already gotten into their saddles.

I said, "I wore red cowboy boots! Arthur likes them."

"Kangee, what did you do to her?" Arthur asked in a steely voice that made me flinch.

"None of you would help her, so I did," Kangee answered. She seemed to be staring at Laurette, who looked away, as if annoyed.

Laurette had big gray wings like a turtledove, and they flapped about in the air, making noises of fluster and irritation. I sang some bird calls, figuring that would soothe Laurette.

"Undo this," Arthur said. "She's off her rocker."

"I don't have a rocker. I have roots," I corrected him.

Kangee smiled and shrugged and led her horse out of the pack.

Arthur swore and settled me on his saddle.

All of my bones had melted, which gave me a fit of giggles. I couldn't sit upright. I kept sliding down like a noodle woman.

Arthur spoke many curse words and climbed up in the saddle with an extra set of reins, which he wound around us both, lashing me to him. Theo dismounted and came over to help. Theo radiated Mozart like a high-end speaker in The Before.

"Theo," I said, "you're the andante in C major for flute and orchestra."

"Oh, Emmy," he sighed. "So pissed with you. Such trouble and you ignore us."

"Not the time for that," Arthur said. He checked the knots and then nodded at Theo.

Theo shook his head and went back to his horse.

"You should be happy for me. It doesn't hurt anymore, you know," I told Arthur.

"Pain's not always a bad thing," Arthur said. He wheeled the horse around to follow Kangee, who was singing.

I watched the land spring forth like flowering seeds from her beautiful melody.

IT WAS DARK, and I was still free of pain. The stars were flashing at me like cabaret dancers, but they'd grown tamer. We had reached tall woods of spruce and pine, balsam and aspens, with stretches of snowy prairie. I listened in on a conversation about Cypress Hills Park, and then we arrived at a small wooden cabin.

". . . what's left of Elkwood lodge. . . ." Gaff was saying to Nwokocha, or maybe to the three spheres of light that floated near him.

Arthur untied me and handed me down to Donny.

"I can walk," I said.

Donny set me on my feet.

My feet skidded out from underneath, and I plopped down onto the ground.

"I thought you said you could walk," Donny said.

"Mighta overestimated things." I giggled. It felt so nice to be sitting on flat, unmoving earth that I lay back and looked up through the trees at the stars, those rosy flirts.

"I got this," Arthur said. He scooped me up and carried me into the cabin.

Jeannie and Laurette were lighting candles and hurricane lamps. The soft yellow lucence danced across Arthur's face, revealing the symmetry and grace that had always taken my breath away.

"You're a beautiful man. If we made love right now, it would be really, really good," I told Arthur.

Arthur smiled. "It's always good with us."

"Yes, but I read a list on a tranny's door—all this exotic stuff. I could do really fun things to you, things we have to try. Have you ever done rimming? Should we try it?" I must have spoken louder than I meant to, because Jeannie and Laurette hurried over and stood on either side of us.

"We will take her from here," Laurette said.

"I was going to—" Arthur started.

"She's ten pence to the shillun right now. You can't have her," Jeannie said.

"Around the world? COF? What does that stand for?" I asked.

"I think she needs me," Arthur said solicitously.

"Don't be a bloody perve. Give her to us," Jeannie said firmly, motioning with her hands.

"Pegging?" I wondered aloud.

Arthur set me on my feet. I would have slid down but Jeannie grabbed my good arm and hoisted it around her shoulders, and Laurette slipped her arm around my back to support me. I said, "Arthur?"

"See you in the morning," he said.

My head lolled on my shoulders as Jeannie and Laurette maneuvered me up a set of steps into a dark loft bedroom.

They helped me shuck off my Inuit gear. I was asleep before my head reached the pillow.

I awoke in the middle of the night with a bladder full to soreness. I was squeezed in between two sleeping forms: Laurette on one side and Jeannie on the other, both of them snoring peacefully. I crawled as unobtrusively as possible down and off the bed, then wandered in the dark through the hall. A lantern from downstairs shed some very faint light, but it was good enough for me to find a bathroom. I made my way back into the bedroom and gingerly clambered back into bed. Jeannie and Laurette kept snoring.

13

I AWOKE THE NEXT DAY WITH A RAG-
ing headache. I was alone in the bed which
was a good thing, because I suffered
through some dry heaves when I swung my
legs out over the bed. Bed? What a treat. My mouth was desiccated as if I'd eaten hot sand, and when I stood up, I realized
that I was dehydrated. Other than that, my body felt better.
I didn't have that bruised, stiff feeling when I moved about,
and even the ache in my shoulder was tolerable. My arm was
still slung and wrapped, but the bindings were looser. The
additional range of movement didn't cause pain.

Downstairs, Robert stood at the fireplace cooking something, and it smelled divine. Donny, Brendan, Laurette,
Nwokocha, Gaff, and Marco sat in the living room on scattered chairs and the couch. Gaff and Marco played a slap-
ping game with their hands; Laurette and Nwokocha sat close
together, talking softly, their hands laced together. Kangee,
Jeannie, and Arthur were nowhere to be seen. Theo bustled
back and forth between the fireplace in the living room and
the kitchen area, bringing spices to Robert.

A pot of something hot steamed on the dining room table,
so I poured myself a cup: tea, strong and dark. There was
even a cup filled with sugar packets and a bowl of crackers in
cellophane wrappers. I dumped four packets of sugar into my
tea, then seated myself in a chair next to the table and sipped.
It helped, but not enough. Still, the caffeine was wonderful.

I went to the faucet and tested it: *Water!* I filled a glass three times, slurping down every delicious drop. I went back to the table and sat with my tea.

The cabin was a little miracle in and of itself. Three years earlier, it might have aspired to rustic, settling for tired and cheap, but now it was exquisite. It seemed completely untouched in The After, like a tiny island of civilization in the woods. There must have been other buildings surrounding it in the Before.

How had no one found it before now?

Brendan wandered over to sit across from me. "How are you this morning?"

"Better," I said. "You?"

He raised the eye patch above his eyebrow. The swelling had gone down, though his eye sat at the bottom of a well of black and purple striae, his eyelid was still closed. I wondered if he would ever see out of that eye again. I wondered if I could heal one-handed, and resolved to try later. He shrugged. "Better, I think. Laurette is going to bathe it again, after breakfast."

"Venison?" I guessed.

"Elk," he said. He had a mug and refilled it with tea. "That was some trip you were on last night. 'We derive our vitality from our store of madness.'"

"You betcha, but there's a lot less ache today." I took another sip of the tea, which was cooling.

Arthur and Jeannie banged open the door and came through laughing.

"Guess who shot another elk with a single arrow from her bow?" Arthur called, with great good humor.

"That would be the one with a puddin' in ther oven," Jeannie said, pleased. She carried a crossbow on a strap slung over her shoulder.

"I dress and quarter nice dead elk," Theo said. He went to his outwear, which hung on a wooden hook by the door. He shrugged on a few warm layers and then paused at the open door. "Call for breakfast!"

Arthur came and kissed my forehead as if he'd been doing it every morning for forever, as if we hadn't spent more than a year apart. He leaned close to my ear. "Shall we try rimming and around the world today?"

I slapped his arm and didn't dignify the question with a response.

He poured himself a cup of tea, then sat down in the chair next to me, his long legs stretched out alongside the table. "How are you feeling?" he asked, scanning my face intently. "You're not as pale."

"I feel okay," I said. "I can ride."

"Sure?" he asked, his expression troubled. "We can wait another day, let you get your sea legs back."

"I'm slowing us down," I said.

"You will if you fall and hurt yourself."

Donny walked over to pour himself another cup of tea. "We're aiming for Battle Creek, Saskatchewan today—about fifty kilometers."

"Any intel on it?" I asked. "Raiders, bandits, soldiers, roguers, anyone?"

"We went through it on our way to Outpost City," Arthur told me. "Should be just fine. There're some good folks there." He turned and looked over at Marco, who blushed furiously.

"Marco has a girlfriend?" I asked in a low voice. I still hadn't caught up on all the gossip, and their gambit of not talking to Emma was seriously starting to annoy me.

"Meat's ready," Robert said. Donny hurried to the kitchen and returned with a stack of melamine plates and a handful of stainless steel forks.

Marco opened the front door and called for Theo.

I took a plate from Donny. "Where's Kangee?" I asked Donny.

He shrugged.

I took another plate, intending to bring Kangee's meal to her, and stood in line.

Arthur stood behind me. He slipped his arms around my waist. "So, about that tranny's list of pleasures," he said in a low voice. He nuzzled my neck playfully. It felt natural for him to do so, as if we'd been sparring with each other continually, the way we had back at his camp. Yet we'd shared only the one extraordinary night after a long, hard separation. He nipped my neck. "I think we should go over the list together, in detail."

"You wish, you perve," I retorted. I tried to push him away with my good shoulder but he was a big fella, not to be easily shoved around.

"You'll beg for it later. You know you will," he teased.

"Seems to me you're the one begging."

"Well, you'll be the one moaning," he said.

I pushed him a little harder, and when I couldn't move him, I kicked his shin, which only made him laugh and tickle my ear.

Brendan, standing in front of me, turned entirely around. With his one good eye, he gave me an earnest look.

I fell still, the horseplay forgotten as my mission and my guilt returned.

In a few minutes, I held two heaping plates of steaming, succulent elk meat, salted and peppered perfectly and smelling divine. My stomach rumbled and clawed inwardly at the scent. I piled some crackers on the plates, then went to the line of wooden pegs by the front door and found my Inuit gear. I set the plates on an end table and bundled up. As I was slipping on my atigi, I spied my backpack hanging among the coats and snow pants.

"My backpack!" I cried out happily, embracing the stupid thing, unaccountably glad to have it. I peeked inside and then poked around. Everything seemed intact. The magazines were there, but there was no gun. I'd have to obtain a new one.

"Kangee grabbed it off a dead soldier," Donny called.

I flashed him a grateful smile, then went outside with the plates. I didn't know why I thought I could find Kangee, but I knew I would. Sure enough, she wasn't far.

She stood in the center of a wide flat clearing, her footsteps the only marks on the white breast of the snow. "The lodge was here, in The Before," she said, as I approached her with the food. She took a plate and smiled. "Under the snow is the sand." She meant the dusty yellow grit that was excreted after the mists devoured buildings.

"Thanks for getting my backpack," I said, "and thanks for the magic potion yesterday. I don't know what that stinky stuff was, but it sure took away the pain. Made me a bit loopy, but it was worth it, though I'm really dry today."

"If it doesn't kill you, it makes you stronger," she said. "Drink a lot of water."

We stood and ate in silence, surrounded by a brilliant cerulean sky and deep green pine trees whose cones and tendrils ended in crystalline loops of ice.

After a while, I asked, "Why? Kangee, why are you helping me? Why'd you come with us?"

"You'll need us."

I chewed and ruminated. "That's not an answer."

"When we needed you, you were there—you and your hands. I still have my husband." She peered over her plate at me, her round moon face stricken with rare sobriety. "I don't want to live without Donny."

"I understand," I murmured.

"No, you don't—not yet—but you will after you make a choice. Choosing something makes it yours. That's what makes it more precious than anything else." She looked up into the sky, her black braid dragging over her arm. "The world is going to change again. I want to see that. I want Donny to see it."

"Change how?" I asked her.

But she had finished eating and handed over the plate, laughing.

ARTHUR INSISTED THAT I ride with him again, because of my injuries.

"You just like rubbing up against my bottom," I said, with some indignation.

"Oh, yeah, I do." He laughed and touched the tip of my nose with his finger.

I couldn't help but smile at him. Then we were standing by his palomino, grinning at each other like a couple of fools. Warmth enveloped us both. His gray eyes lit up in a way I remembered well. He reached out and stroked my hair where it fell over my shoulder, his face going soft and somber all at once. I could feel his strength inside the core of my being. There was something else, something new inside him: gentleness. It washed over me, holding me. I knew, without him having to voice it, that he was thinking about how he'd lost me and how he'd found me again. He was thinking about our wild night of passion. He was wondering how to hold me forever.

"Do you doddering twits intend to stand there all day?" Robert called, breaking the spell.

The others had mounted and were waiting impatiently for us, their horses whinnying and restless to get underway.

Arthur and I exchanged a rueful smile and he helped me up into the saddle. After he got settled behind me, I mashed back into him, pressing my buttocks into his groin.

He knew immediately what I was up to, and he laughed.

"Just you wait," he said, in a juicy tone, half a threat and half a promise.

"You talk big," I teased back.

"Big trouble," he said, shaking his head. "Big trouble."

But I knew the trouble didn't wait for us in bed. It lurked in our daily lives.

IT WAS LATE and dark, maybe eight at night, and we hadn't yet reached Battle Creek. We broke for dinner, part of Jeannie's elk, quartered earlier by Theo, frozen solid in the cold, and now roasting on a spit over a camp fire, thanks to Robert and Donny. Theo opened cans of green peas and heated them in a big cast-iron pot. Laurette and Jeannie sat near the fire next to each other and drank water. Kangee wandered off. Marco and Gaff held a spitting contest, despite my discouraging comments. Nwokocha and Arthur rode off to explore the area, in case we decided to stay for the night.

I took Brendan aside, apart from the fire. "Sit here," I commanded, indicating a low rock.

He scrambled up painfully. "All this riding is killing my leg," he admitted. He rubbed his thigh and squinted at me with his one good eye.

"I'll try to do some healing," I told him. "I want to work on your eye, then I'll see about your leg."

"But you're injured yourself. Can you heal with only one hand?" Brendan said in a doubtful voice.

"I didn't say it would work for sure, but it can't hurt," I said, with some asperity.

He shrugged and stopped moving, sat quietly.

I closed my eyes and felt my heartbeat. I let myself breathe deeply. I let myself yield to the moment. I was courting peace, and it finally eased into me. It was soft and sweet, like a daisy in a ray of sunlight. I put my good hand on Brendan's shoulder, hoping the healing tingles would come through me into him. I kept breathing and sinking deeper and deeper into the unmitigated repose that existed on the other side.

Then the healing energy burst forth. It poured out through my hand into Brendan's shoulder. I let the shoulder and torso fill and then, when the tingles tried to come back toward me like the tide ebbing back against the land, I moved my hand to tent his hurt eye. The tingles flowed ferociously into his damaged eyeball.

"Ow," he moaned. "I feel that!"

I inhaled deeper into my heart, the place where my love lived—love for Beth and Mandy and Haywood and Arthur, and even Brendan himself. At the same time, I held my intent to soften the healing current. It melted a little. Brendan sighed.

"I forgot how good that could feel," he said.

I smiled.

BRENDAN WAS TIRED and wanted to rest. I'd seen it many times: A healing would relax the person receiving it. He or she would let down his or her defenses so that the body and mind relaxed. Fatigue often lay beneath the outer endurance. I told Brendan to rest and I'd fetch him when the meal was being served. I got a blanket for him off one of the pack horses, and he curled into it atop the flat rock where we'd done the healing.

I went to sit by the fire. As the healing current often did, it had left me energized and expanded. I looked at my old friends and their comfortable camaraderie and wanted to chat. They didn't look at me. Marco and Gaff were now tossing rocks into the trees, trying to see who could hit what—pine cones, squirrels, or whatever they could knock down. I curled my hands inside my caribou mittens and waited for dinner.

WE SAT IN a circle around the fire, eating. Laurette was telling a story about the new camp in the south of France, not far from where Toulon had once been located. My old friend Torsten, the Swedish veterinarian, had built a veterinary hospital that James the doctor felt was superior to his people hospital, and the two men had begun feuding.

"Why didn't James just ask Torsten to help him upgrade the people hospital?" I asked, a reasonable question, in my opinion.

Laurette didn't answer. She turned to Jeannie and asked how she was feeling.

Something inside me slammed shut. I jumped to my feet. "That's it!" I said. I went to Gaff and dumped my last few bites of elk onto his plate. I picked up a handful of snow and scraped it over the plate to clean it. "I've had enough of this crap!" I marched over to stand next to the fire. From there I could look at each of them in turn, and I did, glaring into their eyes. "Laurette, Theo, Jeannie, Robert, Marco, Nwokocha, I'm sorry that you're pissed at me. I'm sorry if you were hurt when I left. I'm sorry if you were angry when I didn't greet you in Outpost City. But I didn't ask you to go there looking for me. I didn't ask you to follow me to Canada. I didn't ask you to, and I didn't expect you to."

"Emma——" Theo started.

"No, you listen to me! I'm grateful to you guys for saving my life at Outpost City, but I didn't ask you to do it, I didn't expect you to do it, and I'm sick of being judged by you. None of you were married on The Day. None of you have children. None of you understand. Jeannie, you're going to be a mother in a few months." I scowled at her. "Do you think you're going to love him? More than you love yourself? What do you think you'll be willing to do for your baby boy? Will you take a bullet for him?" I pointed at her stomach. "Would you walk hundreds of kilometers in the cold for him, risk starvation and freezing and hanging just for the tiniest possibility of saving his life?"

Jeannie's eyes filled with tears. "It's a boy?"

"What do you think you'd do for your son? Would you leave the love of your life, the other half of your soul, in Europe, get in a small plane, and play hide-and-seek with death, just to get back to the continent he was on? Because that's what I feel for Beth, and now she's a prisoner of some very bad people who aren't much better than those red-caped bastards who were killing and eating women in France, the ones who attacked us and killed Claude and left most of you with bullet wounds!" I was breathing hard now, and I was pretty sure the vein on my temple was throbbing.

Everyone else remained very quiet.

"I need a gun," I said, facing Arthur.

He reached inside his coat and handed his to me, grip first. I stuck it in the belt of my pants. "Fuck you all. I've had enough. This is it for me. Sayonara, goodbye, good luck, have good lives. I'm going after my daughter, and I'm not going to stop until she's safe in my arms again." I stomped over to the pile of leather saddle bags, found the one holding the plates we'd taken from the cabin, and shoved mine inside it. I went to the horses and looked for one small enough for me to control. There was a chestnut gelding who seemed good-tempered, I'd noted him earlier. *Now where are the damned saddles and bridles?* I turned around to ask and saw everyone standing up and wiping off their plates with snow. I barked, "What the hell do you all think you're doing?"

"We're coming with you, Emma," Jeannie said, her voice gentle.

"You think you can get rid of us so easily? We are your family. You are stuck to us," Laurette said.

I had a feeling she was about to scold me, in her old familiar way. Sure enough, she waved at me imperiously.

"Attention, Emma, must you be so dramatic? A woman your age should show some maturity. It is undignified the way you carry on."

"If you're riding for your babby, Emmy, so be we," Robert said. He strode over to me and looked me full in the eyes for a long minute, then hugged me.

As we cried on each other, I didn't tell him he was hurting my dislocated shoulder, because it just felt so good.

WE RODE TWO more hours by the light of moon and stars and made it to an expanse of hilly plains in the crook of a river. The land felt fertile, seeming to exhale good, rich loam even through the snow. I assumed it must once have been farmland. The mists had been through and no buildings stood. There were no living beings to greet or accost us.

Suddenly the horses stopped and gathered themselves into a tight herd. Arthur, Theo and Nwokocha got out flashlights and shone them around. The beams of light finally settled on a herd of skinny cattle. We rode around them, and Donny and Theo each roped a cow to bring along with us.

We came upon a grove of trees and made camp for the night. Kangee and Nwokocha took first watch.

"Is this Battle Creek?" I asked Arthur.

He shrugged. He and Robert and Donny were stamping down a big patch of snow. Marco and Gaff gathered branches and sticks for a fire, while Jeannie oversaw their efforts.

Laurette tended to Brendan. "Don't go far," she called to me. "I'll look at your shoulder when I finish with the little man."

It was official: I was back in the family, and Laurette wanted to put her talons on me. It made me want to hug her, but it also made me want to avoid her.

We slept mashed together on a lining of blankets laid over plastic garbage bags, both taken from the cabin, along with all the other items we had ransacked. I slept more soundly than I had in months. Something about having my old mates near me. Or maybe it was Arthur clasping my hand in the dark.

BREAKFAST CONSISTED OF fresh milk and another quarter of elk. Marco trooped around in circles, looking uncharacteristically troubled.

"What's his story?" I asked Laurette, as Robert and Theo cooked the elk.

"We are near the settlement where his girlfriend lives,"

Laurette said. She rolled her eyes and made one of her expressive moues. "Silly little girl. I do not understand his taste. She cannot even finish a sentence. *Mon dieu*, the thing does not have a brain in her head. If it was not attached to her body by her neck, it would float into the air."

"I'm not sure he's looking for brains in a woman," I said, amused.

"I'm not," Arthur called, then ducked as I threw a snowball at him. He threw one back, with greater accuracy.

I wiped off my chest as Laurette lifted her eyebrow at us.

"I suppose it is only a matter of time before we are all forced to listen to you scream in a tent," she said.

"Gets you off, does it?" I asked.

She sniffed and flounced off.

Arthur came over and put his arms around me.

"How about it? Want to scream in a tent?" he asked. He held my chin and looked into my eyes. "The other half of your soul, huh?"

I made a face. "Please. That was just for dramatic effect. Don't let it go to your head—to either of them."

"Anything you say, Emma." Then he kissed me. It wasn't brief.

I wanted to think of a clever retort, but my legs felt spongy and my brain reeled in a way that defied even Kangee's magic muck. I mustered a husky, "You betcha!"

Whistling, Arthur went over to join Jeannie, who was calling something about wild turkeys and deer.

THE SETTLEMENT WAS gone, though it wasn't mists that had destroyed it; the damage had been wrought by humans. A cluster of ten homes, barns, and a granary lay in blackened, snow-covered ruins. Fallen timbers made pyramid shapes under glassy ice.

Marco dismounted and walked from building to building, his hands in fists.

Gingerly, I slid off my horse and went to him, put my good arm around his shoulders.

"They survive the mists, only for this *tragedia*," Marco said. He stepped through a vanished doorway into a roofless interior. He looked around at the crumbled, burnt wood and dashed tears away from his face. "She lived here. Lynsey."

"I'm sorry," said Arthur, who had followed us in. He stood next to Marco and gripped the boy's shoulder.

Theo came in, too. "This bad," he said.

"Brutal," Robert said gloomily, as he stepped inside. He looked around the bleak shell of a home. "My lady wants us to get going. Na farting around with trouble, she says." But he seemed frozen in place.

"*Il mio cuore duole*," murmured Marco. He backed out of the door, his usually merry eyes still and angry, with Theo and Robert in tow.

I took Arthur's arm. "When do you think this was done?"

He squinted and eyed the doorframe, then ran his palm along it. "Hard to say because of the snow and the storm."

"If the raiders came through here after Edmonton, they could have done this," I said in a sotto voce.

Arthur's eyes gleamed. "They might have Marco's girl and some of the others from here."

I nodded.

He touched my cheek with his gloved hand. "Another reason to track those bastards."

14

WE SAT AROUND ANOTHER CAMPFIRE beside a lake that, after some consultation with a map, Donny pronounced to be Creedman Coulee Reservoir. We'd left Canada and made it into Hill County, Montana—if the old divisions even mattered in The After. It was all one huge sky, one unfettered horizon, in these Northern prairies.

Robert, Theo, and Kangee plucked wild turkeys to roast on a spit; Jeannie and Arthur had shot them with their crossbows. Donny boiled snow for drinking water. Gaff and Marco stamped down a space for sleeping and laid out the plastic garbage bags. Most importantly, everyone was finally updating me about the new camp in the south of France.

I was astonished at the intensity of my feelings: I was starved for the information.

"After you rode off in a fine snit, we made it to Toulon," Robert said as he threw feathers off to the side.

"Hell of a straightener with a band of scallies by the port," Jeannie said. She looked crosswise at me. "You're a cool hand with a piece, Emmy. Woulda liked yer to be wi' us."

"Everyone pissed," Theo said. "Chop chop, kill most roguers right away." He drew a line across his throat.

"We were all tired and cranky, and everyone was upset about losing you. We ambushed the rogue band and killed most of them immediately," Arthur translated for me. "A dozen soldiers put up a nasty fight after that, but we put them down and suffered no casualties."

"We rescued thirty-two women from the roguers," Laurette said proudly. She reached across Brendan to pinch Theo's cheek. "Theo found a *petit chou*."

"Theo, you have a lady friend?" I cried.

By the golden, morphing light of the flames, his cheeks reddened. "No worry, Emmy. I love you still."

"Is she nice? What's she like? Where was she from, in The Before?" I asked. "What does she look like? What did she do?"

"Opera singer," Jeannie told me. "Berlin. Pretty bird, short-arsed, nice Mae Wests."

"I have heard better," Laurette said, tossing her head. "An alto with too much wobble."

"Anna's lovely," Arthur said. "She's been a fine addition to the camp. She's teaching our little ones how to sing."

"She speaks eight languages fluently," Nwokocha told me. He pushed his glasses up his nose and smiled. "The Romances, and not just the primary ones. Also Catalan and Romanian. I was glad to have her help with translating. We got 350 people back to shore safely off the cruise ship. A dozen different languages, with a few variants, were represented."

"Weren't there more than 400 onboard?" I wondered, casting my mind back to my final days with Arthur's camp.

"By the time we arrived, they were down to 350," Arthur said. "Starvation."

Everyone fell quiet.

"So you built the new camp?" I prompted. "Vasily complain much?"

"He was ill set," Robert said. "Couldna stop saying your name, Emma. His aching arms this, his aching back that. Told everybody that Emma could solve all his troubles."

"He did his share of work," Arthur said defensively.

"He was a creepin' Jesus with a long string o' misery," Jeannie said. "He found hisself a friend, Borys."

"Borys?" I repeated.

"Cute chap," Robert said. "My age."

"Also multilingual," Nwokocha said. "Though his languages are mostly Classicals: ancient Greek, Latin, and Aramaic. His primary tongue is "Polish."

"I guess the ancient languages aren't useful now," I said.

"Perhaps, but when we return to camp, I'll catalogue them for preservation," Nwokocha told me. "Also, we need a lingua franca. I will devise one, structured around English, probably, due to its flexibility. But Post-Achaemenid Aramaic has some fine features as well."

"That's my primary goal in The After, learning Aramaic," I said, mirthfully.

Robert, Theo, and Jeannie laughed, and even Arthur and Laurette smiled. Nwokocha gave me a dry, wounded-professor look. Brendan was watching us all, especially me, from beneath a somberly lowered head. I gave him a rueful half-smile, but I couldn't pretend I didn't care about the camp, my old friends who were my intimates, and what they were all up to. It was of the utmost importance to me.

"We built the camp—" Arthur started.

"We built a giant camp! You cannot believe," Laurette interrupted.

Arthur gave her a wry look which she pretended not to notice.

She ignored him and continued, "The walls defy imagination. We used every salvaged piece of metal, wood, or concrete we could find."

"Ay, it's big," Robert said. "The walls are miracles of nature."

"It's big but organized," Arthur interjected, as if that were in question.

"Same as the old camp, patterned after the Roman legionary camps?" I asked.

Everyone nodded.

"Caris came to help build it?"

"Tara sent a contingent of women to help," Laurette said. "I think she is considering moving the women's camp in with us. It would be safer. Arthur has cleared the mists from the area and we have excellent resources for food and water."

"We're also well defended, which must be her foremost consideration," Arthur said, "though she's certainly running low on supplies."

"The mists are gone from France entirely, now," Nwo-kocha announced. He nodded deferentially at Arthur, who looked away.

"Fifty more sane refugees moved in with us," Robert said.

"Tara, maybe, too, huh?" I looked at Arthur, who did not look at me. He had slept with Tara, and it gave me a pang to think of her close to him, within arm's reach. I realized I had to relieve myself, and I excused myself from the group, walked out a good distance in the quiet, snowy night to find privacy behind some trees. The wholesome sounds of my friends' laughter and conversation dwindled behind me.

When I emerged, Arthur was waiting for me. "Give me a minute," he said. He went behind the same tree.

I looked up at the white orb of the moon, which seemed to hover like a giant iridescent pearl just at the top of the treeline. *Is Kangee's potion entirely out of my system?*

Arthur came out scratching his chin. "I need to trim this, it's becoming a real beard," he said.

"I'll start calling you 'Fidel' again," I teased. When I had first met him in France, Arthur had worn a bushy black beard; it was that wildness that had given me the courage to approach him. If he hadn't looked so shaggy and untamed, I wouldn't have had the guts to make the fateful offer: my companionship for our safety, mine and the children's.

What the hell was I thinking that day? That survival vindicated anything?

Arthur grabbed me and backed me up to press me against

a tree trunk. "Emma, come with me."

"We're all going to Bismarck together," I said blithely.

"No, I mean come back with me."

My eyebrows knit themselves into a single skein, I looked at him so carefully. His gray eyes were huge, and he seemed to be holding his breath. It wasn't often that anyone saw Arthur uncertain; he was talking about more than Bismarck. I said, confused, "Come back here with you, after Bismarck?"

"Back to Europe, after Bismarck. After we rescue Beth. Come back with me."

"Back to Europe," I repeated slowly. I sagged.

He boosted me up to stand my full height. "Stand and listen," he said firmly.

"Do I have a choice?"

He shook his head and smiled. "Do you want me to get down on one knee? I will if you want. I'll do whatever it takes to get you to come back with me to Europe. As my wife. To the new camp. Someday it will be a new town—a real town. Our children can live and grow there."

"A town."

"Yes, a town—a new town in the new age of humanity. Come and rebuild with me, by my side. It will be hard. There will be many deprivations, little ease, and no luxuries. We'll face hardship, enemies, uncertainty. Every day will be precarious. I have to send the mists away. I'm the only one who can. It's my responsibility, so I'll be working to that end. I'll be working to rebuild civilization from the ground up, a better civilization than we've ever had before—one that's truly just, that's built on and for peace and personal human dignity. But I want to do that with you working alongside me, Emma." He was solemn now, poignantly so. His pupils were dilated and his cheeks were flushed.

I couldn't speak, so he continued. "That's what I can offer you—hard work and me. You'll never lack for anything I can give you or share with you. All that I have, all that I am will belong to you. You'll be my first thought in the morning and my last one at night. I expect to be yours too. I want to make love with you as many times a day as we can manage it. I also expect we'll argue a lot. You've always been stubborn and independent, and I think you're getting more so. But let you walk out alone into subzero weather with a gun and no horse? No way! Not if you're my wife. Then again, I'm a little bull-headed myself. I take risks, too, so I will always respect your determination, your will. I'll always seek out your opinion. I may not always follow it, but I'll consider it.

"While you're considering my offer, Emma, you have to know that I want as many children as we can make together. If Mandy and Beth come with us, I will love them as if they were my own blood. I'll protect and support them with my own life, and I intend to give them sisters and brothers."

He was quiet for a moment, perusing my shell-shocked expression. Then he said, "One last thing. I want sixty years with you, but I'll settle for fifty. I want to be clear about that up front." He kissed my lips gently, quickly. Then he stepped back and cocked his head.

I couldn't answer because of the tears running down my face. He clasped my hand in his and we walked slowly back to the campfire. I cried the whole way.

Such was the loving kindness of my friends that they pretended not to notice.

MEDICINE LAKE, MONTANA was a revelation. It was both civilized and completely unscathed by the mists, though the good folks there had managed to fend off several raids. We were seen by a sentry posted atop a thirty meter observation tower; the sun glinted sharply off the glass lens of a pair of binoculars. We rode alongside railroad tracks on the outskirts of town, and a couple of men on horseback rode toward us.

"That you, Arthur?" hollered one of the men, from a great

distance. He was a rangy cowboy type, leggy and long-haired. He sported a giant handlebar mustache and Texan hat and was dressed in a shearling greatcoat over jeans and distressed boots.

"Who else, Bill?" Arthur called. He cantered out fast to meet the men, whom he greeted with hearty handshakes.

I rode the chestnut gelding, a fine match for me, except that he was lazy and refused to go faster than a lollygagging half-trot, and even that only when I kicked him like crazy and called him unkind names.

The others raced out ahead of me, even Brendan, who rode a tallish tobiano quarterhorse with a very precise gait.

Bill and his friend seemed happy to see everyone, particularly Jeannie, whom they both hugged repeatedly.

I was the last to join them, and Bill and his friend, another long-haired cowboy, scrutinized me carefully.

"That's the gal you came all the way from France for?" Bill asked doubtfully.

"Indian togs but she's not Indian, with that yella hair," said the other fellow. "Maybe there's something worth seeing under all the Eskimo clothes. Not much to look at with all that gear on though."

"I'm Emma, screw you and the horses you rode in on," I said in a pleasant voice.

Arthur shook his head in mock-disgust but Jeannie and Theo chortled, and everyone else grinned.

"I might get the appeal," Bill said, with no small amount of irony.

"I'm really good with my gun," I told him. "Sit still and I'll show you. You fond of that hat?" I took my new gun out my pocket and aimed it squarely at Bill's forehead.

"Sure, I'm getting it now," he said, laughing. "Why don't y'all come into town? Arthur, most of the rooms are empty at the Club Bar and Hotel."

"Yes, but has Irna forgiven me yet?" Arthur asked. "If she

hasn't, we'll just ride all the way around Medicine Lake and not bother you at all."

"Well, about that Irna, you know women," Bill shrugged.

"Who's Irna?" I inquired in a suitably frosty tone. I returned my gun to its place in the caribou pants pocket.

"Mayor of Medicine Lake," Bill said. He winked at me. "Come on in, we'll give you guys a hot meal."

"Sounds aright to me," Jeannie said.

That settled it, and we all set out with Bill and Arthur in the lead.

I guided my horse over toward Robert. "Robert, who's Irna?" I asked.

"Irna?" Robert sighed.

"Yes," I snapped. "Who is she?"

"It goes back to a bottle of gin and me and Theo jamming with a couple of birds here. Don't fret. Arthur wasn't the bold one."

"Irna was the bold one?"

Robert cocked his head and looked off into the horizon. "Better ask Arthur."

We rode into a town that was still a town, past a stark gray building emblazoned with the words "Feed" and "Seed." Brick storefronts, shingled wooden buildings, and ice-sheathed trees lined the streets. All the houses looked lived in, and people walked, rode, or led horses down the streets. A number of dwellings that looked newer and hastily assembled stood between more established-looking buildings; some could only be called shanties. The town clearly took in refugees. Down the street, the lodging house flaunted a dilapidated, vaguely art deco-looking sign that proclaimed "Hotel and Club Bar." Artificial light shone out through some of the windows.

"There's power here," I commented when my recalcitrant steed ambled up to join the others.

Bill turned around in his saddle. "Solar panels provided

power for a high tensile, electrified fence in the refuge. We recycled those for the town."

"You've still got a fence," Donny murmured. His eyes were sweeping the snow-covered prairie, seeing something I couldn't.

"We were spared the mists, thank the good Lord, but the crazies come regularly," Bill said. "We do what we can to keep 'em out."

"You let us in," I said.

"You're with Jeannie," Bill said, with a jovial air and a wink at Jeannie. He dismounted in front of the Club bar, and so did everyone else. Boots and hooves stamped, and horses neighed while conversation broke out among our group. Bill stood near me, and his eyes flicked to my arm. "We got a doc in town who can examine that for you."

"That would be great," I said gratefully. My shoulder ached intermittently, and occasional bursts of pain reminded me of the original injury. Riding with one good arm for the past several days had caused me tremendous exertion, in terms of holding my balance from my seat and my core. Luckily for me, the lazy gelding was congenial to reins.

Arthur walked over to stand beside me and touched my arm gently. "I'll be glad to have your shoulder looked at." He grinned with half his mouth and leaned down close to me. "You know what this means, don't you? We'll be alone tonight, finally—indoors, in a room." His eyes glimmered at me.

"Hold your horses, cowboy. I'm bunking in with the girls," I teased.

"Try it, and I'll hoist you over my shoulder and carry you to my room," he threatened. "I've done it before and I'm not afraid to do it again. Besides, Jeannie will be with Robert and Laurette with Nwokocha."

"But Gaff and Marco need adult supervision."

Arthur grabbed my good arm playfully and dragged me

close to his chest. "I will make you pay for even pretending to deny me. All I can think about is that one night we spent together. I'm dying to repeat it."

I snuggled closer and giggled. "Dying? Such hyperbole."

"Our other guest," Bill said.

The Club Bar door opened. For a split second, the door trembled and hung open, and then the world split apart. A tall, lean man with graying auburn hair leapt toward me and pulled me out of Arthur's arms and into his own. "Emma!" said Haywood. "I knew I'd meet you here."

15

ARTHUR PALED TO HIS LIPS. I KNOW, because I craned my neck to see his face, instead of looking at my husband, as I should have done. I recovered myself and turned to Haywood, who kissed me gently on the mouth.

A shocked silence fell down over the group like stones falling down as a city wall crumbles.

It was Arthur who recovered first. "You're Haywood? I'm Arthur." He thrust out his hand. His face now bore bright slashes of red skin at his cheekbones.

Haywood maneuvered me around, close to his left side, keeping his left arm wrapped around me. He shook Arthur's hand with his right hand. Haywood's face wore a rare hostile expression. He was often quietly courageous, but Haywood was seldom confrontational. He said tightly, "Arthur, huh?"

I couldn't speak and didn't have to. My old friends once again came to my rescue. This time they didn't shoot me down from an executioner's noose, except metaphorically. Instead, they crowded around Haywood and Arthur, all of them babbling at once, separating the two men with their bodies and introducing themselves to my husband excitedly. Laurette even tried to wriggle between me and Haywood, but he wouldn't relinquish his grip on me.

Brendan remained apart, impassive. Finally it was his voice heard above the hubbub, silencing it. "Haywood, did you fly here?"

"Brendan!" Haywood's face brightened. Still gripping me, and thus dragging me behind him, he strode over to greet Brendan, and the two of them embraced. Brendan's tiny stature allowed Haywood to keep hold of me with one arm while leaning down to clasp him with the other. "Yes. I knew the time was right."

So he'd had a vision and he'd followed it. I swallowed and asked breathlessly, "How's Mandy?"

"Good," he said, nodding vigorously. "Safe with my mum. She was glad to know I was coming to look for you, and she sent a drawing she made for you." He squeezed me gently. "What happened to your arm, sweetie?"

Everyone started speaking again—except me.

It was Bill who broke up the faux boisterousness this time. "Irna here will see you to your rooms at the inn. Meantime, I'll take the filly to the vet." He reached through the crowd and plucked me from Haywood's grip as naturally and easily as snow falling.

More babble erupted.

A tall, raven-haired, high-cheekboned woman, luscious looking even in a drab parka, put her thumb and index finger in her mouth, shrilling a loud whistle that silenced everyone immediately.

Bill was practically galloping me down Main Street. "Didn't see that coming," he muttered. "Haywood's your husband? Nope. Sure didn't see it coming at all."

"That's Irna? Wow. What's with her and Arthur?" I asked.

"You're asking about those two when your husband is waiting here for you?" He shook his head. "Didn't see that coming," he repeated.

"You've said that, and I didn't know he'd be waiting here for me," I said. "I didn't know I was going to run into Arthur, for that matter. Last time I saw Arthur—"

"Yeah, yeah. He was in France, with some crazy dude holding a gun on him," Bill finished for me. He tossed a jaundiced look at me over his shoulder, then turned a corner and came to a stop. "Doc Kendrick is a family practitioner. Grew up here and happened to be home for the holidays on The Day. Good thing, 'cause he used to practice out of Williston, which got torn up bad by the mists. He'll take good care of ya." He pushed me to the door of a well-insulated house. "You know, we all like Arthur here in Medicine Lake."

"Do you think I don't?" I asked, plaintively. "I wish I didn't. It'd make things easier."

"Well, your Haywood's a good guy, too. I guess you'll just have to make a decision, missy." He stepped through the door. "Hey, Doc! We got an injured woman here."

HAYWOOD LET HIMSELF into Dr. Kendrick's makeshift exam room. "Dislocated shoulder?" he asked, but it was more of a statement. His lean face was taut with feeling. His eyes swept over me, and I knew he was upset. I'd known Haywood since I was a child, and even before we dated I could read him.

Doc Kendrick was in his early forties, a big, sturdily built man with a red complexion and white-blond hair. "It's healing. No fractures, I don't think. I've showed her some exercises she can do in another month to help her rehabilitate."

"How long until I'm completely recovered?" I asked.

"Eight to twelve weeks."

Haywood hovered near me, folding his arms across his chest. He peered at me intently. "They were going to hang you?"

"I was rescued," I said defensively. "I'm still here."

"Just a little worse for the wear," Kendrick said. He rose up from his stool and leaned against a cabinet. "You'll be more prone to future dislocations, so be careful."

"When can I take off the sling?"

"I'm going to give you a new one. Keep it on for another week. The thinking used to be to wear the sling for six weeks, but there wasn't good evidence that such a length of time helped the joint heal faster, and you want to avoid a frozen shoulder. It's important that you do the exercises. I'll write a list for you. Give me a moment, and I'll find a sling." With that, he disappeared, leaving husband and wife alone.

"So Arthur came by boat?" Haywood said, his mouth tightening into a thin line.

"Didn't you see him?" I responded quietly.

Haywood shook his head. "No. None of the paths showed him—not one. How's that possible? How would he be hidden from my vision?"

"Arthur's . . . got his own path," I murmured. I closed my eyes. I'd told Haywood that I'd given myself to Arthur, but the one thing I couldn't reveal was that Arthur had created the mists, that he could control them. Since the mists affected the human brain and imparted psychic gifts, perhaps Arthur, as their creator, was somehow obscured from their activity. Perhaps that was why he could dissolve the mists. I could only surmise though. I had never before heard that Arthur could not be seen by mist-given prescience.

"Of course he's got his own path. The question is, Emma, does he also have you to travel it with him?" Haywood asked. His face seamed in upon itself, and I was looking at naked loss.

What is it about human suffering that changes everything? It was a question I asked myself a few hours later. At dinner, we sat at a long table in the Club Bar. I sat on one end, with Haywood and Brendan. Arthur sat on the other end with Irna and Bill. We had roast duck and pheasant and sautéed fish, warm bread with honey and chokecherry jelly, and barley beef soup.

Irna, in a low cut shirt that exposed impressive décolleté, kept leaning over to drape her arm around Arthur. He seemed impassive to her shameless advances. When the meal ended, everyone rose and bid each other good-night. We all flowed toward the stairs.

On the second and third floors there were seven rooms. Brendan was bunking with Theo; Gaff and Marco had a room; Jeannie and Robert took one; Kangee and Donny another; and Laurette and Nwokocha had one. Arthur looked across the room at me. I dropped my eyes. Haywood took my hand firmly in his.

Half-way up to the landing, I cast a quick look back at Arthur. His handsome face was ashen with sorrow. I must have jerked my hand from Haywood's when I turned toward Arthur.

"No, Emma," my husband said in a voice of soft determination. He took my hand again. "You're with me." Upstairs in our room, Haywood wrapped himself around me and drifted off immediately.

But I could barely sleep, wondering if Arthur had availed himself of Irna's too-obvious charms. I wished I was lying beside Arthur, but I simultaneously felt guilty for not wanting my husband more. I still had no idea how painful it would get before clarity insisted upon itself and all other paths but one fell away.

WE RODE THROUGH oil rig country, though most of the rigs were long gone. Food was not a problem; there was an abundance of deer, antelope, elk, cattle, and even sheep, both bighorn and domestic. The people at Medicine Lake kindly replenished our supply of canned goods and gave us loaves of bread and bags of grain for our horses. They'd even made a gift of a few jars of vitamins, which we all prized for the Vitamin C.

Williston had been devastated by the mists. It was just gone, scoured from the Earth. There weren't even scavengers in the area, because there were no remains left from which to scavenge. We made camp near or on what once been the Bakken Oil Field, according to Donny, the site of an oil industry boom that had promised to yield over four billion barrels of oil for the United States. Like all promises in The Before, even the ones made before God, that one had been broken by the mists.

"I'M WALKING," KANGEE said, after dinner.

We were all seated around a fire. Robert had been singing to us. Haywood sat on one side of me, Brendan on the other. Arthur sat across from me. His gray eyes were quiet, but I was sure they were hiding storms.

"I'll go with," I said, rising and sighing. Conversation had been stilted. No one quite knew what to make of Haywood, and he was shuttered, laconic. Everyone, even Laurette, kept looking at me to provide small talk, to ease the impasse, but I didn't know what to say. Haywood shuffled his feet as if to join me but I gestured at him to stay. Arthur watched our interaction from a narrowed gaze.

"Not that kind of walking," Kangee said. She laughed and walked out away from the group.

I followed her.

She kept walking, faster and faster, though her legs didn't appear to be moving more rapidly.

I trotted to keep up, but then she was gone. I cried out. "Kangee? Where are you?" There was no place for her to hide, nothing to relieve the severity of snow-covered land and over-arching indigo sky. I turned around in a complete circle. No Kangee. I called her name again, and there was no response. I waited for a long while, my breath making white plumes in the night air. My gaze swept over ground that had once been studded with oil rigs, crawling with people and trucks; it was now barren with snow. Finally, frustrated and anxious, I retraced my steps to the camp fire. "She's gone," I said, tensely. I didn't sit but stayed on my feet.

"She'll be back," Donny said. "She goes. She comes back."

"You sure?" I asked, troubled.

He nodded. "Does it all the time. Started in The After. I don't know how she does it. Don't think she does either."

"Where does she go?" Arthur asked.

"She doesn't always tell me," Donny said.

"Do you ever ask?" wondered Laurette.

Donny shrugged and looked at Arthur. "Women. Sometimes they do what you want, but mostly they don't."

That made Arthur smile and look sidelong at me. Haywood bristled. Robert and Theo erupted into boisterous conversation at the same time. Nwokocha won: He challenged Brendan to a duel of Shakespeare quotes. Brendan accepted, and the tension was diverted.

I felt like vanishing, myself.

KANGEE WAS NOT present the next morning either.

Donny told us to ride on. "She'll find us," he promised.

"I don't like it," Arthur said, grimly. "We never leave someone behind—not ever."

"It's not what we do," Robert said. He looked at me and winked, reached across and tugged my hair. "We cross a bloody ocean if we have to, but we don't leave a man or a woman lagging."

"My wife does things her own way," Donny said. "It's pointless to wait for her. I wouldn't. Even if it was just the two of us out here. I'd keep going. She'll find us in her own time. Could be ten minutes from now, could be two days from now."

"Where she go?" Theo wondered.

Donny zipped his parka all the way to his chin and pulled his hood tight around his face. It was colder today, and we all felt it. "Sometimes she tells me, sometimes she doesn't." He swiveled to look at me. "She used to go watch Emma sometimes."

That made goose flesh on my arms. "I only saw her a few times."

"She thinks you're the key to something," Donny said. His voice was somber, and his eyes swung between Arthur and Haywood.

"That's not a responsibility I want," I said.

"Who would?" Arthur asked.

"How does she do it, disappear that way?" Laurette wondered.

Donny shrugged. "How do we do anything in The After? How does Arthur use his powers? Kangee says he has mighty ones."

Arthur walked away to saddle his horse.

Haywood took my elbow. "What powers?" my husband asked, scowling.

I shook my head. I'd never told Haywood about Arthur's control of the mists. Haywood would witness it for himself.

WE RODE ALONG the curve of Lake Sakakawea and slept on a cliff overlooking the glassy frozen lip of the lake, which had been created by the Army Corps of Engineers when they'd completed the Garrison Dam on the Missouri River. Arthur sat beside me over dinner, telling me the history of the dam and the Army Corps' work.

"Were you part of them, the Army Corps of Engineers?" I asked.

"No, though I based my command on their model, 'a great engineering force of highly disciplined people working with partners through disciplined thought and action to deliver innovative and sustainable solutions to the Nation's engineering challenges.'" He lifted one corner of his mouth in his old, ironic smile.

"A noble ideal," Haywood said, from my other side. "But sometimes ideals aren't enough." He glared at Arthur.

Arthur looked at me, as if to ask if I'd told Haywood his secret.

I shook my head slightly.

Arthur's eyes gleamed.

I knew what he was thinking: It was a small victory for him that I had kept his secrets from my husband.

Haywood sensed something and stiffened, and testosterone fumes growled at each other in the air around me.

I wanted to ask Arthur a million questions about his military work that had created the apocalyptic mists. There had been no opportunity for me to do so at his camp in Europe. I had learned of Arthur's involvement in the mists when I'd watched my sweet Newt die. I'd immediately confronted Arthur, and he confirmed my worst fears. Then, shattered, I rode north with Alexei and Mandy.

Newt, the little English girl with prescience but no memory, had become a daughter to me. My heart trembled, remembering her. It was so small a slip into a palpable feeling sense of her: the skinny girl with stringy hair, the big eyes that softened with prophecy, the bony shoulders. I'd held her hand and hugged her a thousand times.

How could she be gone when I can feel her standing close to me, her head resting against my chest? Of course, as special as she was to me, Newt was only one of billions.

My appetite fled, as did my taste for this rivalry between the husband I was bound to and the man I loved, but wished I didn't. I rose and went to join Jeannie and Laurette, who'd walked down over the cliff to take in the frozen lake.

Jeannie's back hurt her today and I thought to offer her some of the healing energy from my hands.

"WAKE UP! WAKE up!" Kangee was shaking me.

It was the next night, and I was curled up under one of the blankets we'd taken from the cabin, situated apart from everyone because the emotional undercurrents roiling through the group gave me a bellyache. I sat up and blinked at Kangee. "I don't want any of your sorcerer's potion," I said. "The pain is mild, bearable."

"Get Arthur," she said, in a low voice. She walked away.

I contemplated lying back down and returning to sleep.

Kangee cast a warning glance back over her shoulder.

I groaned and clambered to my hands and knees, then made it unsteadily to my feet. It was the middle of a moonless night, but a diffuse milky shimmer glossed over everything. As I came to complete wakefulness, I wondered where the light was coming from. It was too profligate to be starlight.

I walked quietly to where Arthur lay sleeping. For a moment, I just stared at him. He slept peacefully, relaxed and at ease, his handsome face much younger and softer than it usually appeared. Even the crow's feet by his eyes had smoothed over. I seldom saw him in such a state—not once since Haywood's arrival. I watched him, enjoying with yearning and wonderment the strong beauty of his repose.

I could never feel this way about Haywood.

I wondered if it was fair to stay with Haywood when I longed for another man. Even if it hurt Haywood for me to leave him, I wondered how I could possibly stay. *What about Mandy and Beth? How will it affect them if—when—I leave their father? How might it affect them if I stay with Haywood, always yearning for another man?*

I leaned close and whispered, "Arthur."

His arms encircled me, and he drew me down into his chest, an embrace I didn't resist. His lips brushed my forehead, and for a moment I let him hold me against him.

Finally, I pushed up. "Kangee asked me to get you."

He rose like a big cat, soundless and dangerous, and I pointed toward Kangee's retreating back. He took my hand, and we followed, picking our way through sleeping forms and standing horses. "Something's wrong," he said in a low voice. His long stride picked up, and I hurried to keep pace. We trotted out more than two hundred meters to where Kangee stood.

She pointed out over the prairie.

It took a moment for our eyes to adjust to the pale light. Then we saw it, far in the distance: All along the horizon, white tongues of fog licked slowly along the ground. Tiny, dark throngs scurried ahead of the white tendrils, which emerged randomly from a glowing wall of white. Small, dark swirls rose up ahead of the white fog. It took me another few beats to understand what my eyes perceived.

The diffuse white luminosity was cast by a vast bank of mists rolling toward us, driving people and animals ahead, marking them for destruction.

16

"ARTHUR," I SAID.

He seemed stunned, frozen.

I yelled, "Arthur!"

"Yes!" he said. "Emma . . ."

"Are the mists——"

"They're herding people," he interrupted. He stared and blinked.

"How is that possible? I've never heard of them doing that before!" I said.

He didn't respond.

I grabbed his arm. "Arthur! Do something!"

"I've never felt them like this. They're . . . different now," he murmured. He stroked his face. "How could this happen? They were programmed to evolve, but this? This is . . . they're just different—stronger."

I shook him. "So are you! Come on, or we all die here, tonight, and so do they!"

He glanced at me, then visibly steeled himself. He nodded and held out both his hands at shoulder level. His eyelids drooped. He was doing what I did when I set about healing with my hands. He was sinking into himself, cohering into a peaceful state. I felt him shift. It was as if his hard edges melted. He soon radiated peace. Feathery light surrounded his hands, and just standing next to him calmed me.

But it wasn't enough. The mists went undeterred. They

continued to approach us. The dark upward swirls around the mists resolved into birds—prairie chickens, falcons, ducks— that flew up to escape.

Theo and Robert came to stand beside us. They didn't speak; they just gazed out over the prairie at the mists, which grew larger, a white wall moving inexorably toward us, bleaching out everything. Ahead of the white wall was a shifting mosaic of animals and people. The ground rumbled, as if there was an earthquake.

"Mary, mother of Jesus," Robert whispered. "That's terrifying."

"Get women on horses, get out!" Theo commanded, smacking Robert's arm.

Robert dashed away, pausing to call over his shoulder, "Em, you coming?"

"I'm staying with Arthur!" I called. "But get Jeannie the hell out of here!"

Robert nodded and raced toward the basin in the snow where everyone else still lay sleeping.

The air brightened with white light. Then it hit us: a sickly smell of sweet lilacs and sulphur.

Theo gagged and I drew back. Even Arthur recoiled. The ground rumble grew like surf swelling, and the Earth shook with the pounding of many hooves and feet.

"Arthur, now's a good time to dismiss the mists," I said, softly but tensely.

"I'm trying," he grunted.

Cries went up from the campfire.

I turned and spied our friends mounting horses. "Theo, go with the others."

"I not like you. I not leave. I stay," he said, in a crisp voice that brooked no argument.

I argued anyway. "Theo, get on a horse so you can rescue us at the last minute, if necessary!"

He glared at me. Another gust of the mists' cloying odor hit us. The wall of mists was coming closer. It was still distant but now ominously loomed into the air, rising several stories above ground. It curved for many kilometers around the south and east, blotting out the land and sky, erasing the horizon.

We could make out animals racing in groups: elk, deer, horses, wolves, lynx, rabbits, foxes, coyotes, and moose, along with domesticated animals like dogs, horses, cattle, and sheep. Behind them came human runners, men and women running alone, in groups, sometimes carrying children or adults. They trotted ahead of the huge embankment of thick, writhing, pearlescent white fog. The mists were moving fast enough that they sometimes rolled over a lagging runner or an exhausted animal.

Bird crap and feathers rained down on us. I hadn't realized there would be so many birds still lingering around in February. *Or is it March already?*

Then screams shrilled through the air. The first runners sprinted past us. They were a pair of men, one black and one white, their heavy winter clothes soaked with sweat and their eyes huge. A few seconds later, a group of six or seven people came. Minutes later, a big, silent throng of people ran by. This peloton included women and children, most above the age of twelve or so. They stormed past us, as if they didn't even see us. They did not waste energy speaking.

"Arthur," I warned.

"Emmy, help Arthur!" Theo commanded. Then he raced back toward our horses.

Of course I could help Arthur somehow. The healing energy that poured through me for sick people would surely bolster him. I tore off my sling and put both hands on his shoulders. It was difficult to focus with terrified people streaming past us, sometimes brushing alongside, but I'd done it in the past. I'd managed to achieve focus while under extreme pressure. When Alexei had kidnapped me, he'd held a gun to my head until I healed his son Mikhail. I knew what I had to do now.

I forced my breath to slow, coaxed my pulse to relax, and concentrated on Arthur. I merged myself into his strength, his need. The scent of the mists became a roar like an ocean thundering over us. The white luminescence shone like a moon planted within fingertip reach of the Earth.

Haywood rode up on a horse and screamed for me to come with him. He leaned down over his horse and tried to grab me, but I shifted out of his reach.

Women carrying children struggled past. The mists were only twenty meters away. Screaming rose up as stragglers fell, unable to rise, and were subsumed.

All at once, everything inside me opened. I dissolved. I became the river, and the river ran into Arthur. Arthur exclaimed. An inner vision irradiated everything. In it, Arthur grew to stand as tall as the mists. The waves pouring out of me into him flowed through his heart and out his hands.

The wall of mists stopped, just five meters from us.

I let myself flow along the river, the interminable river. The tide moved through Arthur. His thoughts were clear to me, intricately patterned like snowflakes and cochlea: He was determined to stop the mists permanently, to rebuild civilization better than it had been before, to be with me.

There was a well of suffering in him: his pain over the creation of the mists that had destroyed the world. I knew he carried pain, but the intensity of his remorse and sorrow shocked me. It would have killed a weaker man.

Then the inner vision took over everything, highlighting empty space and turning objects into voids, like a photonegative. In the center of it all stood Arthur, facing white mists that wore billions of faces. *The faces of the dead,* I thought.

And then he roared—not audibly, but a silent thrum, vast and unforgiving. It was like a cyclone rushing against the mists, and they retreated. First one centimeter, then another. Arthur's roar was visible to the inner sight as concentric circles, spreading and widening, a colossal round wave of percussion that forced the mists to submit. The mists retreated several meters, followed by several more.

Arthur lifted his face to the sky and howled physically. It came from his gut and the mists obeyed it. They lifted; they hovered. Once more, Arthur howled, and the audible and inaudible sounds merged. Pure force exploded, shoving me to my knees. Blood trickled out of my nose and ears.

I fought to keep my hands on Arthur, to keep channeling the healing energy into him. I gripped his calves to stay connected. Next to me, Haywood's horse stumbled to its knees, then flopped over on its side, pinning Haywood. Everywhere on the snow-covered plains, people and animals collapsed.

The world writhed with light. It reminded me of what I'd seen after tasting Kangee's potion, except this writhing light didn't alleviate suffering. It intensified it. It filled me with sorrow, ache, and guilt. I've cheated on poor Haywood! I've made him suffer! *Why haven't I already found Beth? Is she enduring torture and horror? I'm a worthless mother, so incompetent in my attempts to rescue my child . . . If I leave my family to be with Arthur, as I long to do, what will they do without me? How will Mandy cope? But, oh, how I want to be with Arthur.* It was awful. Every scenario was torturous, with no possibility for joy or redemption. It was like thick gray paint spilled out everywhere, coating everything. I had never felt such a suffocating agony of despair.

Poignant images from my life wracked my being. I saw myself as a young bride. I had married Haywood one month after I'd graduated art school, while he was in law school at

Penn. We'd known each since I was seven; he was fourteen then and mowed our lawn. He was already interested in being a pilot and used to show me pictures of airplanes in flying magazines. I'd loved him with a child's intensity, and I'd pursued him while I was in high school and he was in college. Always the gentleman, he refused to take me out until I was eighteen and in art school in Philly. *How could I love another man? Yet how could I live without Arthur?* It was an impossible dilemma. My face grew wet with tears.

Then it wasn't just about Arthur and Haywood and the girls. Every regret, every misdeed, every nastiness—small or large—that I'd ever perpetrated flooded my memory. I suppose my sins were no worse than most people's, but I hadn't been Mother Theresa, and I felt intense shame. I was awash in knowledge of my own ugliness, stained at the core with no possibility of salvation. *What is the point of it all, anyway, in the face of the destruction of everything?*

Then, the mists vanished.

I would not have noticed, so riveted was I with my personal hell, but Arthur grabbed me up off the ground. He kissed me hard, wiping my nose with his hand. "Are you okay?" he asked. It sounded as if he was calling to me from a far distance.

What's going on? I struggled to return to the present.

Arthur's hands steadied me.

I looked around, trying to get my bearings.

Haywood still thrashed about under the horse. Arthur and I went to help him. Arthur pulled the horse's reins. As the horse rolled and twisted to its feet, I dragged Haywood out of the way. His nose and ears were bloody.

"Arthur can control the mists," Haywood said. His face was twisted with despair, his eyes dull and veiled. I could see from the working of his throat and Adam's apple that he was screaming, but his words were faint; something about losing me, about everything being lost.

Arthur grabbed my shoulder and pointed.

Hundreds of people lay on the snow, under the tangerine sky of dawn. Slowly they stood and looked around at one another. Nearby, a man in a thick Icelandic sweater took out a gun and shot himself in the head. The woman standing next to him, her chest still heaving with exertion, pried the gun from his hand and swallowed the muzzle. After a muffled *pop*, she fell to the ground. Behind them, two white-haired women with a group of teens stabbed the youngsters, who stood with their necks obediently bared for the knife blade. One woman then slit her wrists, and the other stuck the knife into her own throat. All over the mist-less plains, people were committing suicide.

Arthur ran out, shrieking. He grabbed a mother who was trying to strangle a baby in a front-carrier. His shriek pierced the murk in my brain.

I ran out and laid my hands on a man who had pointed a gun at a woman. I managed to intercede with him, but a few yards away, a panting man set his wool jacket on fire. He stood and screamed while burning, but he did not drop and roll, which would have extinguished the flames. I pleaded with him to no avail. I moved on to others, hoping to wake them and stay their undoing.

Haywood saw what we were attempting. He blinked and his face registered cognizance. He joined our efforts, but the snow was turning crimson, steaming with bright, warm blood from the people we could not reach in time.

IT WAS MIDDAY before we quieted the swell of self-destruction. We organized the survivors, treated the wounded, stacked bodies, and teased out the story. For a long time, we tended the injured. I fell in beside Laurette and Jeannie, just as I had done before, in France. The three of us moved through the masses of people, triaging.

The living were exhausted and demoralized. A dozen people had fallen and then lost part or all of a limb during the last few seconds, before Arthur had sent the mists away. Amidst much cursing, Jeannie got sick, so Laurette and I cauterized and then bound four arms, six wrists, two knees, and two ankles.

It went slowly at first, but all the injured seemed happy to be alive.

Dozens more had survived their suicide attempts. There were stab wounds, bullet wounds, and bruised necks to contend with. Some had tried to smother themselves in the snow. They were numerous head injuries; people had tried to bash in their own skulls.

After a while, I became light-headed and thirsty, and I made my way back to the campfire. Arthur stood with Nwokocha, Theo, Robert, and Brendan. Donny, Haywood, Marco, and Gaff worked the people, moving through groups and asking questions. Kangee stood apart, watching. Arthur saw me coming and tossed a canteen to me; I drank gratefully. Conversation lulled as I joined the group.

"What?" I asked. "Why did you stop talking?"

"Emma, we've gathered some intel. The mists originated in Bismarck," Arthur said. He gripped my arm to steady me when my knees went weak. "Don't panic. There are hundreds of people here. We haven't talked to them all."

"The mists started slowly in Bismarck," Nwokocha said. He pushed his glasses up his nose. "There was time for most people there to scatter. The mists kicked up outside the city, in what was left of the city."

"It had become a fort for raiders," Brendan said.

"The raiders who have Beth," I said tremulously.

Brendan nodded. "It's very poetic, really—the way these

survivors are speaking of the mists' first appearance—'fluffy cotton balls' or 'white cotton candy floating through the air' and 'pearl fibers bouncing through the atmosphere.' Then the small mists found each other. They combined into larger mists, and large mists merged to become huge, all soft and powdery looking. 'It is amazing how complete is the delusion that beauty is goodness.'"

"Ay! They're a bucket of snots," Robert muttered. "The question is, what caused them to behave in such a way?"

"The mists are evolving," Arthur said, his voice bitter and angry.

"They took shape and herded like sheep those poor sods who didn't leave immediately. They cast an enchantment on our minds to madden us," Robert said. "Arthur, if I didn't have you at my shoulder, these mists'd sicken my pish."

"Don't put the wagon in front of the horse. They'll be harder for me to fight." Arthur gave me a level look. "Emma, I couldn't have dismissed them without your help."

"For now, we're in the clear," Nwokocha said. He turned to me. "A large contingent of raiders, with accessory personnel—"

"Snappers and birds to serve them!" Robert interjected, scowling.

". . . left as soon as the mists were first seen," Nwokocha continued. "The group with an entourage was led out of Bismarck by the man they call The One. He has some sort of prescience. His visions told him to leave."

"Do we know where they went?" I cried.

Everyone shook their heads.

"Scotts Bluff, Nebraska," Haywood called. He walked up to join our circle. He gave Arthur a sour look, then looped his arm around my waist. "They're headed to Scotts Bluff, and they have Beth with them. I spoke to a woman who had met Beth in their camp. She saw them take her."

"The mists didn't get her!" I cried. I grabbed Haywood's arm. "Which woman?"

"There's something else," Haywood said slowly. "I think this fellow they call The One is someone you know."

Arthur's eyes narrowed to thin gray lines. "What do you mean?"

"The woman, Linda, was confused, no question. The mists squeezed her mind like a rag. She slit one of her wrists from the mount of her thumb almost to the crease on the inside of her elbow. Lucky I got to her before she cut the other one. I was just in time to bind her and stop the bleeding," Haywood said quietly. He glared at Arthur. "Do you know why the mists affect people's minds?"

I didn't want that confrontation to occur right now. Haywood had a right to know about Arthur, but we had more pressing matters at hand. I asked, "Is Linda okay?"

"The mists operate on the human biomind," Arthur said, crisply but evenly. "The biomind is our faculty for extrasensory perception—clairvoyance, telepathy, telekinesis."

"Precognition," Haywood said. "You know a lot about this."

Arthur nodded. He opened his mouth to say more but I cut him off.

"Haywood, what about Linda and The One?"

"Linda's very pretty. She was kept by one of The One's generals, someone who's been with The One from early on. The One knows Beth is our daughter, Em," Haywood said. He turned his eyes to me, and his face softened. "He knows you."

"Me? How could he know me?" I cried.

Haywood said, "Linda said he calls Beth 'daughter of my friend' and that he's singled her out specially. She doesn't stay with the other women and children."

"That could be good news. Perhaps she's not being

abused," Arthur said, giving voice to my urgent, unspoken plea. Arthur exchanged a look with me, as if we were still linked by the healing current, and he shared my thoughts. Then he asked, "Does this woman know anything else about The One and how he might know Emma?"

"He's called The One because he only has one arm," Haywood answered.

Arthur's face pinched in on itself as if he'd been sucker-punched. "My God! He survived," Arthur murmured.

I didn't understand and looked back and forth between Arthur and Haywood, confused.

"He's Russian. His given name is Alexei," Haywood said. "Wasn't that the name of the Russian sociopath who held you hostage?"

17 FOOD WAS THE NEXT ORDER OF BUSI-
ness. These desperate but fortunate people
hadn't had time to pack. The mists had
started slowly in Bismarck and then gath-
ered speed. They'd also spread out in space as they moved
across the land, destroying what buildings remained and
obliterating people who didn't move away fast enough.

The last hour, before Arthur dissipated the mists, had
been the worst. The mists pressed forward at a rapid, relentless clip. Half those caught in the glowing white net had been
killed.

Theo, Jeannie, and Donny went hunting with the
crossbows.

I questioned Arthur about Alexei, but all he had to say was,
"I left him for dead." Arthur rubbed his shoulder where he'd
been shot, and then stomped off in one direction to question
people, while Haywood stomped off in another direction.

Unsettled by Alexei's reappearance and seething with
unanswered questions, I went back out into the groups. I
walked far out into the plains, to the periphery of where people were resting. That was when I came on three men sitting
in a tight circle around a sixteen-year-old girl. A body lay near
them, another girl, fourteen or fifteen years old, her head
bashed in by a stone. "Hi folks," I said, approaching the group.

The living girl's angry dark eyes peered up at me from

under a hood that was closed tight around a grim, blanched face. She was in trouble and afraid to say so.

I stiffened but I tried to disguise my reaction. I made my voice friendly as I said, "I've got some questions."

"We don't need to answer no questions," said one of the men. He was small and blade thin, with a handsome, angular face, but there was an unmistakable errant spark in his eye. His parka was spattered with blood and bone. He sat closest to the girl, and her lips paled when he spoke. "It was a mistake that our girl was killed. The mists put everyone out of their minds. Nothing more to say. No need for questions."

"Everyone answers questions," I said, pleasantly but firmly. My hand went to my pocket. "We saved you, and now we're gathering intel."

"We don't have intel," the man said.

"You want food, don't you?" I asked tartly.

The man's eyes locked onto mine.

I smiled, as if to calm him. "We've got a hunting party out shooting game."

"You guys have bullets?" he demanded. His eyes swept out to where our horses stood in a tight group, guarded by Nwo-kocha and Marco.

I nodded but didn't bother to explain that we were saving our ammo. "We've got a fire started, and we're gonna have a big ol' barbecue. Delish, you betcha."

"We'll be on our way. There're animals everywhere. We'll feed ourselves," the man said. He rose suddenly. His hand snaked out as if to grab the girl, but when my gun appeared in my hands, aimed at his forehead, he only laughed. "Look again, lady." His hand hadn't grabbed the girl, but a gun. He grinned wider, showing me all his stained and yellowed teeth. "Looks like we got ourselves a standoff, missy."

His two men rose from their seated positions into crouches, one on either side of me, preparing for battle.

I was about to get jumped.

But the mists had grabbed my mind, too, and left a residue of knowing. I knew something about this man, something true. I smiled. "You asked about bullets. That means you don't have any."

His smile broadened. "All I need is one."

"Maybe, but you don't even have that," I said.

His other hand made a motion, but I was waiting for it. The two crouching men sprang at me, but I got a shot off and hit the leader in his throat. Scarlet spattered everywhere. The two men froze, then howled as they turned toward their fallen mate.

But the girl was quicker. As the leader lay there gasping and spewing blood, she grabbed a knife from his belt. In one smooth motion she pivoted and thrust the knife into the chest of the guy closest to her. I took that as an opportunity to hit the other guy hard in the head with my gun.

"Nice," the girl drawled, praising me. She stamped heavily on the bloody throat of the leader, causing his body to jerk and flop. Then she kicked the stabbed man in his gut, so he rolled over onto his face, moaning.

"Back at you," I said, amused and horrified, all at once.

She straightened and let down her hood. Her face was heart-shaped and lightly freckled, her eyelashes long and minky. She was tall and very slim and had a spill of blond hair, a deep honeyed color, darker than mine. "I'm Susie."

"Emma," I said.

"Mind if I kill him, too?" She pointed at the man I'd knocked out.

"Better for us to question him," I said.

"Can I kill him after?" she persisted.

"Maybe."

"He deserves it!" she shouted.

I put my hand on her shoulder. "I'm sure, Susie, but let's give him to my folks and see what they get out of him."

The girl cursed, but she acquiesced. She flung the dead

leader onto his back, unzipped his coat, and ripped a leather belt off his waist. Then she jerked the unconscious man's arms behind his back and tied his wrists together with the belt. She lifted the man's arms away from his body by the belt ends and dragged him along the snow, face down. "Let's take him to your people then." She set off toward the campfire.

I took the guns off the two dead guys and raced to keep pace with her. "Were you with the raiders a long time?"

"Uh-huh, since before they were organized." She looked over her shoulder to eye the man she was dragging face down behind her. "These guys took me out of Minneapolis right after The Day, when the city was mostly destroyed."

"I'm sorry."

"I'm alive, aren't I?" she responded acerbically. "You think your guys will torture him? Hot knives, make him eat shit, cut his hamstrings, remove his thumbs, something?"

"I don't know," I mumbled. I felt awkward in the face of her cool vengefulness, which I was sure was warranted.

"I saw them do stuff like that to people. He ought to know what it feels like."

Maybe I could distract her. "My daughter was kidnapped out of Edmonton by raiders who rode on to Bismarck—a blonde girl named Beth."

Susie pursed her lips and shook her head. "I didn't know her. Sorry she was kidnapped, but I'm not surprised. The One trained raiders and then sent them out on missions in all directions from Bismarck, the old headquarters for his army."

"Did you see him? The leader?"

"The One? Sure. He likes to give speeches and hold big, drunken dinners. He walks around talking to the men about how he's going to rule Europe and the Americas. He promises them the spoils."

"Ambitious."

"Impossible!" Susie laughed. "He flew here from Europe, I heard, but that won't happen again. The mists tore up his airfield in Bismarck, ate the planes he was collecting and scattered his men."

"But if he found a plane . . ."

"There's fewer of them around and no fuel," Susie said. "Air travel is dead, like all the old good things and all the good people. It was a freak miracle that he got over from Europe that way. It'll never happen again."

"Did he ever mention his name?" I asked, thinking maybe it wasn't Alexei after all.

"Nope. Everyone just calls him The One, because of his one arm, and because he was the one man who can unite the raiders. You know," Susie said, looking pointedly at my head, "The One is always looking at blonde women. He once came and touched my hair. He pulled it over my shoulder and rubbed it between his fingers, all intense and silent for a long time. Finally he said, in his thick accent, 'Girl, you remind me of woman. Woman with magic hands. One day I find and take her.' Then he smiled at me, all cold and creepy, and walked away."

So it was Alexei, and he was looking for me. I felt nauseated. *Is that why he's here? To find me? What does he want with me? Is it the same as before, to keep Arthur from having me? Is this still about his hatred of Arthur, or does he have some new, cruel agenda? Is he serious about controlling two continents? What is he doing to Beth? Will he release her peacefully or hold her for spite? Is this going to turn into a full scale war that won't end until either he or Arthur is dead?*

BETWEEN THE ANIMALS that were shot and the ones that were killed during the last few seconds before Arthur dissolved the mists, we had a lot of food—enough, in fact, to amply feed ourselves and the 582 survivors. People lined up by the two fires and waited patiently for chunks of meat. We also gave them water boiled down from snow; children and the seven pregnant women got fresh milk from the cows.

Arthur stood by the main campfire, speaking with people, organizing them into groups of fifty or sixty. Nwokocha assisted him, while Robert, Donny, Laurette, Susie, Haywood, and I served food. Marco and Gaff continued to work the crowds and gather information. Kangee did whatever she did.

Theo went around gathering domesticated animals: eighty odd horses and a few dozen cattle, dogs, mules, sheep and goats, which Arthur planned to distribute as equally as possible to the various groups he'd organized. Jeannie and Brendan each held a cocked gun and protected our horses and the cows we'd picked up earlier. We didn't want the survivors acting on a notion to add our livestock to their own.

Arthur directed people north and west, toward Medicine Lake. "Ask for Irna or Bill, tell them Arthur sent you. They'll take you in. You'll find a home."

During a lull in the conversation, as one group set off together clutching scraps of food, I approached Arthur. "Are these people going to make it to Medicine Lake in the snow, most of them on foot, many of them injured? What about raiders, mists, and the cold—not to mention starvation?"

"Should we take them with us to Scotts Bluff?"

I shook my head. "It'll be too dangerous. Plus, they'd be a hindrance. We have our work cut out for us getting Beth back from Alexei."

"You betcha," Arthur said in his old sardonic tone.

"When are we going to talk about what went down between you two?"

"When we're alone, after these good people have gone on their way toward the little civilization that's been spared by the mists. I think they'll be happy in Medicine Lake, and I'm sure the town will be glad to take them in, despite the trouble."

"I hope they make it," I muttered. At least a third of the survivors were under the age of twenty.

"So do I. It's not a perfect world, Emma," he said somberly, "but many of them are smart, competent people. They have a strong will to live, stronger now that so many have died. In each group, there are a few who seem to have solid sense and strong grounding. I've appointed leaders from those individuals. They'll make the right decisions. They have as good a chance as any of us."

I eyed him, hoping he was right. Something about the way he spoke made me believe him and bolstered my faith. Arthur was like that: He always saw the best outcome in a given situation. Knowing now, after my time merged with him, of his constant internal agony about the mists, I marveled at his optimism. I asked, "Shouldn't we warn Medicine Lake that we're sending them some five hundred people?"

He grinned, his eyes lighting with merriment. "Irna likes surprises."

I made a face and turned to walk away.

Arthur grabbed my arm. "When are you going to tell him?"

"Tell who what?"

"You know what. You were inside my being. I felt you." Arthur drew me closer, so I could feel the fire emanating from his chest. He searched my face. His own relaxed into a frank, unguarded expression. "Tell Haywood that you're coming with me."

I shook my head. "First things first, and my daughter is first."

"I need you, Emma," he said. He took a breath. "I need you to help me with the mists. I won't be able to send them away for good without you by my side."

"You're powerful," I demurred. "Sure, the mists are evolving, but so are you. You're getting stronger, more articulate with your ability to control the mists, more sure of yourself, and—"

"I'm sure of one thing. We wouldn't be standing here

now if you hadn't put your hands on me and reinforced my control. I couldn't have done it alone. That energy or force that runs through your hands gives me a whole new range of possibilities."

"You'd have managed. You're underselling yourself."

"I never undersell myself. That wall of mists would have killed us and all these people on these plains. I don't know what would have stopped the mists. Maybe they would have kept going until they swept through the Safe Zone. I don't know, because they were different from how they've been. They've changed, evolved in a way I couldn't have foreseen."

"When you were developing them, back in your lab in England?" I said softly. "As the ultimate weapon to end all need for weapons?"

"It seems bitterly stupid now, but that was the intent." He nodded. He took a breath and tugged on my sleeve. "I know that *you* are essential—to me, and to what we have to do. Emma, our mission is to send the mists away so the world can rebuild."

"I don't want that mission," I said softly. "I want to raise my children in peace and safety. That's all I've ever wanted."

"Sometimes you don't get to choose," he said. "There's a higher calling, something greater at stake."

IT WAS TWENTY-FOUR hours before we got the last of the survivors on their way. When Arthur objected to killing her remaining captor after questioning him, Susie refused to leave me. She couldn't believe Arthur was just going to send the man with one of the groups; binding his hands and warning the others wouldn't be enough, she claimed. She cussed Arthur out in a way I'd never heard anyone dare. He smiled and told her she was welcome to ride with us. We were now fourteen.

Brendan proposed that we chop up the last of the cooked meat, mount the horses, and eat as we rode.

"I agree," Nwokocha announced. "It's about eight hundred kilometers to Scotts Bluff, nearly due south. Let's get on with it."

"We want to avoid Black Hills Forest," Donny said as he hacked up well-cooked elk ribs and packed them with snow inside a deerskin.

"Why is that?" Arthur asked, packing his saddle bag, checking his gun, and counting his remaining bullets.

"Special women's camp," Kangee said and laughed raucously. "Susie will like them." She climbed up on her horse.

"I don't like that woman," Susie said in a sotto voce. For someone as fierce as she was, she had glued herself to my elbow like a child half her age.

"She grows on you," I said.

"Liar," Arthur said and chortled. He swung himself up on his horse.

"Emma's full o' fibs," Robert called. He was kicking snow on the campfire closest to us, and Gaff and Marco were doing the same at the next campfire, some twenty meters away.

"Fibs and no small amount of acting ability," Arthur added.

"I find Emma full of truth-telling," Haywood said. He stood next to his horse, waiting for me to mount mine and ride over to join him.

"That shows how well you know her," Arthur said coolly.

"I've known her since she was a child," Haywood said. He stood with a stiff back and bristled with anger.

"You know the events of her life, but do you really know her?" Arthur asked. His horse danced and Arthur wheeled him around and rode to the front of the group.

Haywood's eyes, glowing with hate in a shuttered face, followed him.

I touched Haywood's arm. "Let's go rescue our daughter," I said, a little wearily; the men with their competing prerogatives exhausted me. It often felt as if I stood in the middle of a shadowed path that was blocked both forward and backward.

There was nowhere for me to proceed, nowhere to retreat to. I measured off the stirrups against my arm.

"How are we going to do that?" Haywood demanded. "Have you planned that far ahead, Emma? How are we going to retrieve her without dying ourselves? Especially since that Russian has separated Beth out from the others."

"I figure we'll come up with a plan after we get there and survey the raider camp."

"Oh. So you think we'll just ride up and ask nicely for Alexei to release our daughter?" Haywood asked. "If we say 'pretty please,' maybe the one-armed monster will release her to us? That's how you think it's going to work?"

"I don't think so," I said quietly.

"Me neither," Haywood said. "In fact, for whatever reason, if Alexei really knows she's your daughter, I think he'll fight like hell to keep her."

"Probably."

"And it probably has a lot more to do with Arthur than with you, though you and I will pay the price, since she's *our* daughter and *we* love her. Of course, she's just a pawn between those two," Haywood said.

My throat clutched and I couldn't speak. It hurt to hear Haywood speak aloud my private fears.

He continued, "It's probably best if he doesn't know you and Arthur are the ones trying to rescue Beth."

"He might be holding her because he knew that would draw us," I said softly, miserably. "If he knows Arthur's crossed the ocean..."

Haywood nodded slowly, and his gaze on me was piercing. "I'm sure you haven't told me everything about Alexei and your experiences with him. I'm not stupid. I know there are big gaps in what you've said about your time in France. But I don't take you for a liar, Emma." He mounted his horse and rode toward Arthur.

Kangee rode up beside me. "We can all have tea and cookies," she said and laughed hard.

Laurette overheard and guffawed. "You are in a fine pickle now, Emma," she said. "What did you think you were going to do with two men? Do you not have any sense?"

"I wasn't thinking," I said wearily. "When I met Arthur, I was desperate to keep seven kids and my daughter safe. I didn't think I'd ever see Haywood again."

"You should be more like me. I always think," she told me. She made her dismissive moue but then patted my arm. "Well, we are a family, so we will see this through—for you and your daughter. Then you will have to make the balance right."

18

THE ROAD TO SCOTTS BLUFF WAS cold and windy, more of what we'd experienced on the aborted journey from Outpost City toward Bismarck. The sky above the plains was unabashedly, overbearingly, inescapably huge. After my years in Manhattan, with its lush skyline, and my time in rolling, forested France, followed by the year and a half in Edmonton, I was unused to the unmitigated expanse of elements that formed the prairie. We were all glad when Arthur detoured us into the Little Missouri State Park, with its Martian-like topography of jagged outcrops, primeval ridges, rugged mesas, and peaks.

The park offered running water and, on north-facing slopes, trees. The trees were our objective: We needed arrows and spears. Our bullets were running low and had to be conserved. We took a day for Theo to carve two bows out of ponderosa pine logs that someone had cut and left stacked near the park ranger's office, which was uninhabited. Jeannie made arrows.

Arthur called the rest of us over and told us we had to know how to draw a bow and shoot an arrow.

"I am quite excellent at archery already," Laurette said gaily. She held a bow and came to stand next to me. She spread her feet and pointed the bow toward the ground, then placed the arrow, nocking it into the bow string. She raised and drew in one fluid motion, then aimed at the green door of the park ranger's office. She let go, and the arrow flew straight, hitting the center of the door. "Nice, yah?" she crowed, giving me a triumphant glance.

"I want to learn how to do that," Susie said. "I'll be able to kill a man from far away. I won't have to risk letting him get close to me."

"That's why it was invented in the late Paleolithic era," Arthur said.

"It must be hard to do on horseback, but it seems really useful," Susie said. "Teach me how!"

"That's the plan, since we're running out of bullets and not making new ones," Arthur said. He then lectured us on the history and development of archery, before describing the basics of shooting an arrow. I had to smile, remembering that he was once a military professor of sorts.

Haywood had been a competitive archer in college. He quietly observed as Arthur talked. When Arthur finally put the bow in my hands to demonstrate how it should be held, Haywood cleared his throat. "Emma's right-handed, but she's left eye dominant," he said.

Arthur swiveled around to give Haywood a stony look.

Haywood walked over to me. "Here." He shifted the bow so I was holding it with my right hand and would pull the bowstring with my left.

"How does it feel, Emma?" Arthur asked.

"A bit off," I muttered.

"You're left eye dominant?" he asked.

I nodded.

"You have to try it this way first then," Arthur said, but his voice had dropped in pitch.

"Maybe I'll help everyone figure out which eye is dominant, since it's the starting point," Haywood said, as if correcting a recalcitrant teenager. He grinned a little and strolled over to stand next to Susie. "Hold your hands out at arms length," he told her.

Arthur continued to glare at Haywood.

I said, sharply, "Are you going to teach me how to do this, or not?"

He turned back to me and his mien softened. "Show me your stance."

IN THE RANGER'S office, we found a cache of canned goods, including several cases of liquid nutritional supplements. Someone had clearly used the ranger's quarters after The Day, but she or he was long absent. Dust sueded every surface, and a family of mice had taken up residence under a desk. We felt no guilt when Arthur and Theo removed an entire pane of glass from one of the windows.

"Good tips for arrows," Theo sang, with a grin.

Donny used a knife and carefully etched lines into the pane, painstakingly breaking the glass into large triangles, which Theo told us would be shaped into proper arrowheads.

Beside a giant bonfire, over which we roasted wild turkeys and a deer, we chowed down on the carrots and peas as if they were the finest delicacy in the world. To us, after days in the cold, eating only roasted meats, they were. We toasted our absent benefactor with cans of strawberry-flavored supplements which were only a few months past their expiration date.

That night we covered the window with a blanket and slept indoors, all except for Marco, who claimed he liked to sleep outdoors, and Arthur, who took first watch.

In the morning we packed the liquid supplements up and scoured the park ranger's office for useful objects.

ONE MORNING I awoke with a start, feeling a thousand eyes watching me. I looked up into cushiony grayness. I couldn't see them, but I still felt the staring eyes. I wriggled free of the blanket that was my bedroll, and then the puppy huddle in which we all slept, and walked out a distance to relieve myself.

Brendan was on watch. He pressed his index finger to his forehead, saluting me. His lips were moving, and I knew he was reciting poetry to himself.

On the way back to the bedroll, the feeling of being watched sharpened. I stopped and turned around in a complete circle. Nothing on the horizon. I looked up. This time, I saw the eyes. Where the clouds were parted, white mists lowered through. Like soft wax embossed with seals, the mists were impressed with thousands of faces, their eyes gleaming. Noses and mouths were vestigial, but the eyes were large, staring, and intelligent. I exclaimed and went to wake Arthur, who was asleep between Laurette and Donny.

Arthur struggled to a sitting position. As he rubbed his eyes and looked up, the mists sucked themselves back behind the clouds. "Hmm," Arthur rumbled.

"What was that?" Laurette asked. She pushed herself up on her forearms. "What have you discovered now, Emma?"

"Nothing I went looking for."

"The mists are changing," Donny said.

"They're growing," Kangee said, popping up beside him. "I wonder what's next."

OVER THE EVENING fire, Haywood forced the issue of Arthur and Alexei. We ate roasted grouse and pheasant with canned asparagus tips, and we drank fresh, warm milk and old, cold strawberry supplements. Haywood finished his can of supplements and put it in the pile with the other empty cans, which we were saving for reuse. He walked back to the fire and sat beside me, then took my hand in his.

"Arthur, we appreciate you coming along with us to rescue our daughter. Beth means the world to Emma and me. Now it's time for you to be straight with us. We're riding into

a situation with this Russian, and we need to know what it is."
Haywood paused and fixed Arthur with a gimlet stare. "We
all need to know."

Arthur looked away, but he nodded. He wiped the poultry
grease off his mouth with the sleeve of his coat. "A few days
after she left, I rode after Emma. I arrived in Le Havre just as
the plane doors closed. Alexei was waiting for me there. He
held a gun to my head to keep me from stopping the plane."

My throat and stomach clenched up as I remembered looking out the window of the small plane Haywood had flown, at
such great risk to himself, to get me and Mandy.

As if reading my thoughts, Haywood squeezed my hand.
"What happened then?" he asked in a dispassionate tone.

"When the plane disappeared into the blue sky, I didn't
care anymore. I attacked Alexei with my knife. We scuffled.
I lodged the knife in his firing arm, but he grabbed another
gun with his left hand. He got a shot off into my shoulder. I
pounded the blade deeper into his forearm, felt the humerus
shatter. I got back on my horse and rode off. I left him bleeding out on the ground." Arthur absently rubbed his shoulder.
"Someone saved him."

"His whole camp was in Le Havre," I murmured. I thought
of the beautiful Thai girl, Kulap, and Dmitri, the doctor with
the scar that drew up one side of his mouth. I hoped they were
still alive and that they were well and whole and happy.

"So what happened before that moment that led up to
it?" Haywood asked. His voice was soft but commanded an
answer.

The group fell into a hushed silence.

Arthur rose and paced. He kicked a clot of snow and
watched it arc up and vanish into the dark. "I told you I was
in charge of the special projects army group that invented the
mists." He paused as if waiting for Haywood to answer, but
Haywood didn't. Arthur didn't look at him. He walked back
and forth, rubbing his eyes. "I had this dream when I was in

college—a dream to start a new era in human history, an era of peace. I had an idea for ending war as we know it, this controlled force that would dissolve munitions so they couldn't be used to kill." He came back to the fire and seated himself again.

"It became an obsession. I thought I could help humanity by ending war forever. By the time I reached grad school, I knew I had to go further. The force had to affect more than matter. It had to affect the mind, or else people would find other ways to destroy each other. It's in our nature, the worst part of our human nature. We have better selves but don't always choose to be them.

"So I studied biology, physics, chemistry, and materials engineering. I was interested in nanoparticle liquid suspension and colloidal suspension. I brought my idea to the army, and they were interested. In fact, they gave me carte blanche. I had the finest minds and best laboratories in the world at my disposal, along with unlimited funds." He rubbed his fist over his scarred shoulder as he stared into the fire. He lapsed into quiet but none of us spoke, so he continued.

"My work was comprised of two parts: One, I had to engineer something light, something vaporous so it could move without being stopped, something that would dissolve the metals commonly used to make munitions, such as steel, polymers. Two, I had to find a way to impregnate the dissolving force with the ability to influence the human mind. So that people would *want* to disarm." He looked up into the sky. "My team studied everything—every crazy theory about human psychic abilities, every far-out, super-specialized scientific paper. We started experimenting. It was an exciting time, every day brought a new discovery, a new idea.

"My childhood friend and colleague Will brought me the latest work on AI, artificial intelligence, and bio-nanotechnology. We invented a way to make chips just two nanometers wide. Then we invented a way to suspend them in gas in an organized fashion, to control them, so they were like a fog under our direction. It was all very technical. Then it all went wrong," Arthur said. He rose again, still staring out into space. He wrapped his arms around his chest and rocked back and forth on his feet.

I had never seen him look so bereft, so vulnerable.

"How did it all go wrong?" Haywood said.

"There's already programming out there, on ambient molecules," Arthur said. "That was what we discovered. There's already programming, in a language we can't understand, but that interfaced with our 1's and 0's. That made our fog particulates unstable, unpredictable. I tried to halt the experiments but by then they'd gone too far. The mists had developed crude AI of their own, and they were . . . well, extrapolating. They were defending themselves."

"They were thinking for themselves?" Haywood asked, incredulous.

"Sort of. Not exactly." Arthur shivered. "I bolstered the containment structures and told command it was time to shut down the project and destroy the prototypes until we understood the existing ambient programming. I spoke directly to the President and the Prime Ministers of Britain and Germany. They all disagreed emphatically."

"What do you mean by 'existing ambient programming'? What does that mean?" Nwokocha asked. The pitch of his voice was raised far above usual. For a reserved man, he was suddenly aquiver with curiosity, practically wriggling with the desire to know.

Arthur didn't acknowledge him. Instead, he walked out from the campfire a few strides. "We started losing control of our mist specimens in the lab. Accidents happened. People died. The mists slipped back inside their containment structure so we never saw it happen. They dissolved the cameras we installed. It was clear they were leaving containment at will, and I knew I had to shut down the project, with or without authorization and by any means possible."

"That was when you met Alexei," I said. I remembered what Alexei had told me: that Arthur had gone to him, asking Alexei to find him a nuclear bomb. Alexei had imparted this information after I watched little Newt die. But even my voice didn't distract Arthur from his introspection, his confession.

"I asked around and heard about a Russian arms dealer with a special reputation. They said he could get anything, as long as the price was right—anything. I knew there was a serious problem building. I didn't know how serious, but I suspected. How could I not? So I set up a meeting with the Russian, Alexei. I met with him and his wife, an Estonian woman named Helina. She was so beautiful, brilliant, and special. Alexei was obviously off, but that beautiful, intelligent woman loved him. He adored her. It was Helina who told Alexei that he had to help me, that he had to get me a bomb so I could destroy the lab and the mists. It had to be a nuclear bomb, so no trace of the mists would be left, not a single molecule."

"Where's Helina now?" Haywood asked.

"The mists got her," I said. "Alexei put a bullet into her brain so she wouldn't suffer."

Jeannie made a mournful noise. "He must be devastated."

"I always wonder, what if Alexei had come through one day earlier? What if I hadn't delayed after the President and Prime Ministers refused to stop the project, but had immediately taken action anyway? What if I'd stopped the project as soon as Xavier told me there was ambient programming? All those billions of people might still be alive."

"So you went to Alexei to get a nuclear bomb, and he delivered, but it was too late?" Haywood queried.

Arthur nodded. "The mists broke the containment structures and vanished. There was no sign of them. For a while I thought it might be okay. Six weeks later, it was The Day. The mists attacked in full force, and they'd proliferated.

They consumed anything comprised of the metals we'd programmed them to dissolve—iron, zinc, cobalt, nickel, and
copper. Human bodies contain those elements too."

"You'd have bombed England," Robert said bitterly. "I
wish you had."

"Then the mists killed Alexei's wife, and he blames you,
because he knows the truth about their origins," Haywood
said.

Arthur nodded again.

Haywood said, "I take it he hasn't forgiven you. Alexei
wants you to suffer."

"Yes. When he held the gun to my head as your plane took
off, he told me that leaving me alive would be a crueler fate
than killing me, that I would suffer more this way," Arthur
admitted in a distant voice.

"So he looks for ways to hurt you, and he knows how you
feel about Emma. This isn't about her at all! She's just a pawn
in his vendetta against you, an innocent bystander, and so is
Beth. In fact, the probability is, if Emma goes to get Beth,
he won't release her. He'll just hold both of them until he's
got you. Then maybe he'll kill them in front of you so you'll
grieve as he does."

Arthur cleared his throat. "That sums it up."

"For what it's worth, your dream wasn't stupid," Haywood said. His eyes filmed over with mist-imposed prophecy.

I was desperate to ask him what he saw, but I didn't dare
do so in front of the others. It wasn't my place to reveal Haywood's gifts to them; I had to honor that.

He dropped my hand, which he'd been kneading, and
went over to the sleeping area we'd tamped down earlier and
spread over with animal skins: deer, elk, and cattle hides.
Then he lay down.

"I still want to know," Nwokocha said, "what the hell is the
existing ambient programming?"

But Arthur was walking out alone into the darkness. He made soft sounds, as if he were moaning.

The rest of us were too disturbed to talk, and we followed Haywood to the sleeping area. Gaff and Marco had first watch, and even they were uncharacteristically quiet.

Susie, sleeping on my other side, grabbed my arm. "That was some story he told. Is it true?"

I nodded.

Susie grimaced. "The world would thank us if we put a bullet between his eyes. He probably would too."

"Probably, but he may be the only one who can save the world," I said.

"Will there be anything left to save?" she asked scornfully.

I shrugged.

IN THE MORNING, Haywood was gone. He'd ridden off on his horse sometime in the night. The boys had fallen asleep on their watch and didn't notice his absence when they awoke and roused Robert for the second watch.

Horse hoof prints led due south, toward Scott's Bluff, but I didn't need to track them to know where Haywood was headed: My husband had gone to save our daughter. He didn't trust that Arthur and I could do that.

Haywood was probably right, and I hoped he survived. I was tempted to pray, except I still couldn't believe that God cared one whit if people lived or died.

19

RAIDERS ATTACKED A HUNDRED kilometers north of Scott's Bluff. Even at a distance, we knew they were Alexei's men; they all wore an outer garment without a right sleeve. In place of the missing right sleeve, they wore a black leather gauntlet.

Robert and Theo had been patrolling ahead, but they galloped back. "Men!" Theo called. "Bad men!"

Arthur's eyes swept over our group. We were thirteen plus extra horses, a few cattle, a mule and some sheep. "Can't hide," he said.

We'd reached the southernmost tip of a woodland area that Donny said used to be the Nebraska National Forest, the largest hand-planted forest in the United States. We'd taken a day in the forest to carve more bows and arrows and to practice with them. Many whole trees were dead, felled by the ravenous bark beetle, so Theo found a plethora of excellent wood. He'd presented me with my own bow, a rough-hewn thing he'd insisted that I finish, rub, and polish myself, with a small knife, a stone, and a knot of coarse horsehair cut from the tail of my horse.

"We fight!" Brendan said. He still wore a bandage over his eye, though he said the daily healings helped. I was doing my best with the healing current, but I doubted he'd ever see out of that eye again. It made his archery awkward, but he could hit a big target. He'd made some javelins for himself, and since he had excellent upper body strength, he was good with the weapon. He pulled one from where he'd slung them on his back. "Time to pierce some gonads. 'I throw a spear into the darkness. That is intuition. Then I must send an army into the darkness to find the spear. That is intellect.'"

"We get to kill them, don't we?" Susie asked sharply, jerking her horse so it danced nervously. In just a few days, practicing at night and during every meal break, she'd become adept with her bow and arrow. She practiced as if possessed, with utter absorption. I pitied her targets.

Arthur's mouth lifted in his old ironic grin. I was glad to see it; he'd been unnaturally dour since the night of his revelations. "Yes, but if we can question one of them before he dies, that would serve us well."

"I hope Haywood didn't encounter these guys," I murmured anxiously.

Jeannie and Laurette, riding nearby, exchanged glances, then drew their horses closer to mine, so they flanked me tightly.

"Maybe a few of us can ride out, circle around, and get them from behind while you're engaging them," Jeannie suggested.

"I don't want you engaging anyone," Robert said in a crisp, authoritative voice. "You're fighting for two, and that means you don't fight at all!"

Arthur pulled his hat further down on his ears. It was bright but bitingly cold, our breath making plumes of frost in the clear air. "Let's modify Jeannie's good plan. Jeannie, you, Brendan, Susie, and Nwokocha fall back into the treeline. The rest of us will engage. Then you come out, two to the right, two to the left, like scissors closing."

"I want to stay where the action's good," Susie objected. "I'm better with the bow and arrow than anyone besides you and Laurette. Send Emma into the woods."

Arthur looked amused but he nodded and gestured at me.

Susie brightened. "After you question these bastards, then I kill them?"

"You're a bloodthirsty bird," Robert commented. "Don't you think there's been enough killing, between the mists and the roguers?"

"Nope, and I can't wait to make these bastards pay for what their friends did to me," Susie growled. She was restless on her horse, which reared a little.

Arthur leaned over and grabbed her horse's reins. "You'll get your opportunity," he said sternly. "For now, this horse is mannerly, but he's picking up your cues, and you're not properly contained. Settle down."

Susie scowled at him but quieted herself. "I'm just saying that they deserve it," she sulked.

Arthur ignored her. "Places," he said. "Arrows, people, unless they start shooting. We want to conserve our bullets for the real fight." He nodded at Jeannie, who clicked her tongue at her horse for a fast trot and then led me, Brendan, and Nwokocha back to the woods.

"I want to know if they've met Haywood," I called back.

Theo waved.

Around the boles of pine trees planted in snow-covered prairie grasslands, we watched a dozen raiders approach our group. A tense conversation took place, and then one of the raiders drew his weapon. Susie was even faster with her bow and arrow, and he slumped on his horse, gushing blood from his throat. Laurette was drawing and letting fly, as was Arthur.

"That's our cue," Jeannie yelled. "Emmy, you're with Brendan. Nwokocha, follow me. Ya!" She steered her horse out of the pine trees to the left, so Brendan and I raced around right. I watched in amazement as Jeannie stood up in her stirrups, nocked her arrow into her bow, and shot one of the raiders in the heart at a trot. Laurette was still shooting fluidly.

I was going to have to practice diligently with my bow.

If I couldn't kill at least one of the raiders with an arrow, Laurette would lord it over me for weeks.

Brendan hoisted his javelin, which, when we were mounted, had to be called a lance, according to Arthur. Brendan flung the thing; it flew with grace and accuracy toward a raider, who didn't see it coming from the side.

Before I could draw an arrow, shots rang out. The remaining raiders were firing. I drew my gun and got the one with a shotgun before he squeezed off a round. The next few seconds were noisy with gunfire, and then everything was shockingly silent.

"How we doing?" Arthur called.

"Good!" Robert called.

"Good!" Jeannie called.

"Good!" Nwokocha said.

"Good!" Kangee said.

"Good!" Donny said.

"Hit, upper arm!" Laurette said.

"Good!" Marco and Gaff chorused.

"Good!" I called, and trotted toward Laurette.

"Good!" Susie yelled.

"Good!" Theo said.

"Good!" Brendan said.

"Grazed, rib cage!" Arthur said.

We all stopped in our tracks and looked at him.

He shook his head. "It hurts like hell, and Laurette and I need any remaining antibiotic cream, but I've had worse."

"I killed two of them and took a bullet. I am a hero," Laurette said and then slumped in her saddle.

Arthur, as always, was the one to grab the reins of her horse, and Theo and Nwokocha took her down off her saddle.

I TENDED LAURETTE immediately. Kangee and I peeled off her coat and layers of sweater, shirt, and long underwear. A deep red line creased across her upper right arm, but there was no penetration. We managed to stop the bleeding, and I smeared the wound thickly with the antibiotic ointment from my backpack.

"Can you get the bullet out?" Laurette asked as her lids fluttered open. "If you have to dig for it, I will need some of Kangee's magic potion. I will take it right now. Kangee, fetch it for me."

"There's no bullet," I said. "You were only grazed."

"*Merde*, it burns like hell. There must be a bullet in there." Laurette struggled to see, flailing her arms and making things difficult for me.

"I can give you some of my stuff. If you take too much, it will be poisonous," Kangee said. "I'll get my jar." She scooted off, and Laurette redoubled her flailing.

"Lie still," I commanded sternly. "Laurette, there's no bullet! It's just a terrible scratch."

"Just a scratch? I am in severe pain! I am going into shock! What if I die from infection?" Laurette scrabbled around harder.

I waved to Theo to come hold her down. "I put enough antibiotic ointment on there to kill germs for the next ten years," I said. "Hold still. I'm going to wrap it lightly."

"Do you know what you're doing? Oh, maybe it should be cauterized!" Laurette's eyes rolled up in the back of her head, and she fainted.

"Should I put some on her lips?" Kangee asked, from behind my shoulder.

"Hell, no! She's hard enough to deal with when she's sober," Arthur grumbled.

"No. Come on. Be nice," Nwokocha said in a tone of mild reproof.

"The big mister has a point, but she might be more fun if she's not the full shilling," Robert said.

"Robert and Arthur, I will ask you to refrain from insulting my significant other, who was wounded on the field of battle," Nwokocha started, pushing his glasses up his nose. His mouth tightened.

"You're poking her. That don't mean we have to love her," Robert said. "Don't mistake me, for she's a fine thing, but she can be a real puss face."

"That's me friend. Purra zipper on it," Jeannie announced, which quieted the men.

BEFORE HE LET me tend him, Arthur questioned the two raiders who remained alive. Robert and the others stripped the fallen raiders of their weapons, clothes, and other belongings, while Laurette lay resting on a pile of deer skins. With a gun in one hand and knife in the other, Susie stood with us, guarding the raiders.

"How long have you been looking for us?" Arthur asked the two men.

One scowled at him, and the other looked away. Both had the gleam of madness in their eyes, and both were wounded. One guy, tall and lean with a long brown braid, had caught Brendan's javelin in the thigh, close enough to the femoral artery that we'd scrambled to stop the bleeding. The other, a gray-haired Asian in his fifties, had an arrow sticking out of the right side of his chest, just below his collarbone. I couldn't imagine how he was still alive. He appeared unfazed, though, and didn't seem to register any pain.

"If I have to repeat myself, there will be consequences," Arthur said.

Neither man spoke.

Arthur raised his eyebrows at Susie.

She leaned down and twisted the arrow in the gray-haired man's chest.

He screamed, pain registry. "Stop! Stop! Please! Are you Arthur? How did you know we've been looking for you?" he asked.

"I didn't. You just told me," Arthur said.

"Han, shut your mouth!" the man with the leg wound yelled.

Susie kicked him in the thigh.

He screamed and clutched the binding on his thigh. "You made me bleed again, you stupid bitch!"

"What'd you call me?" Susie said. She kicked him again, harder.

"Did you encounter a man riding by himself before us?" I asked anxiously, when the screams died down.

"You must be the healer woman, like The One said," Han muttered. His crazed eyes went to my hair, and he giggled. "He likes your little girl. We all do."

Panicked, I opened my mouth to ask him what he meant, but Arthur preempted me. "Did you encounter a man riding alone?" Arthur asked quietly.

Susie reached for the arrow in Han's chest.

"Wait! No, we didn't see anyone. You're the first people we've seen in a week. A big group came by after we did, saying the wall of mists that started in Bismarck was chasing them. No one since, but we're not the only watchers. There are other groups out here." Han panted and licked his lips. His eyes flicked to the arrow tail. "Could you help me with this? I'll answer all your questions."

"Hey, you bogtrotters, we've got a big cat on our tail!" Robert called to us from where he knelt, stripping a dead raider. He stood, holding a holster with two guns in one hand—a big prize—and pointing with the other hand. "Incoming!"

"More raiders?" Arthur called back. "Weapons, people!"

"No, a cat," Robert said.

We all squinted into the sun. Twenty meters away slinked a familiar muscular, tawny form.

"I close, I take care," Theo called. He raised his bow to his shoulder.

"No!" I shouted. "Leave it be!"

"Hold your fire," Arthur yelled.

Theo paused.

Arthur lifted an eyebrow at me.

"Friend of mine," I said. I owed the cougar my life.

Arthur studied my face, then shrugged. "Watch but don't shoot unless necessary," Arthur yelled.

"So are we all set here?" Susie asked. "Han is gonna talk?"

"I'm talking," Han assured her, sweating despite the cold.

"Shut up, dickhead!" screamed the second captive.

"We don't need this one then," Susie said. She jammed her knife into the raider's throat, spraying blood on Arthur and me.

"Jesus priest, Susie!" Arthur snapped. "Get hold of yourself. It's time for more humane behavior."

"Humane? I'll tell you what humane is. Humane is when you've been starved for a week and these assholes let you eat a meal before they gang-rape you," Susie hissed. "You like that definition?" She stalked off, her knife dripping scarlet tears.

"I hope Alexei doesn't let them hurt Beth," I whispered. My heart jigged inside my chest like teeth chattering.

"Beth is kept apart, remember? Emma, go help Susie. I'll question Han." It was a command, and one glance at Arthur's face told me he meant it. I wanted to argue, but I didn't. Arthur knew that if I stayed for the questioning, I might fall apart.

ARTHUR'S WOUND WAS more serious than Laurette's. I gestured for him to take off his shirt and he smiled while wincing. "Last time I took off my shirt for you—"

"I was dolled up to be a tarty brunette." I cleaned his cut with hot water boiled out of snow and a rag torn off one of the dead raiders.

"I like brunettes," he said in a suggestive tone, "especially tarty ones." He put his hands on my hips. Despite his pain, his gray eyes cleared.

"Irna?" I couldn't resist teasing him.

"You!"

"It was a mistake," I said softly.

"Best mistake you ever made though, right? Best night of your life and mine too. It wasn't a mistake at all, Emma. Nothing between you and me could be a mistake." Arthur's breath drew in with a rasp.

I pulled the rag back. "Does that hurt?"

He nodded. "Bullet probably cracked a rib when it passed."

I laid my hand gently on the swollen red mound. The healing current gushed immediately, and an image like a photograph posted itself on the screen of my mind: two cracked ribs. "Two cracked ribs. How did one bullet do that?"

"Just the way my body was positioned, I guess," Arthur said, shrugging with the opposite shoulder. "Truth is, bullets aren't friendly creatures. They leave pain and suffering in their wake. I've never liked them."

"Hence your dream to end war," I murmured.

"Exactly." He sighed and pulled my hand away from his wound and laid it on his chest, which was warm despite the frigid air. "I miss you, Emma."

"Let me work on you," I admonished. I placed my hand back over the deep red scoring on the side of his ribcage. "What else did Han tell you, after I left?"

"They didn't see Haywood, and Alexei has kept Beth with a group of women and children that no one touches. He confirmed what the woman told Haywood."

"Thank God," I cried, "if there is such a thing."

Arthur smiled, a solemn, reflexive act. "God helps those who help themselves, and Alexei is trying to help himself to North America. He's organizing the crazies here, promising them spoils and women. He left his son back in France, in charge."

"That will be good for France. Mikhail is cut from different cloth than Alexei," I said. "He's kind, gifted. He must be more like his mother. So Alexei knows who Beth is for sure?"

"He knows she's your daughter, and he knows I'm coming," Arthur said. "He's using her to draw us out, as we expected."

"Maybe she'll be okay when we get her. It's almost more than I've let myself hope for." I imagined holding Beth again, feeling her blonde head against my chest, wrapping my arms around her so tightly that every angstrom of my being could squeeze her into me. *I am coming for you, Beth. I will keep my promise. Hold on.*

"She'll be okay," Arthur said. "Does she look like you? Mandy resembles Haywood so much that I imagine Beth takes after you." His eyes were soft and warm on my face.

I nodded.

He murmured, "Haywood's a good guy."

"I know that."

"Brave thing to ride out alone like that. He wants to reason directly with Alexei. He hopes Alexei will be open to him because there's no history between them."

I nodded. The healing tingles swept out my hand into Arthur's torso, which looked more dinged up with red and white scars and bruises than it had in France; Arthur never complained. I couldn't help but feel profoundly connected to the man even as I thought of my affection for my husband. Arthur and I had begun as a business transaction, but it had become so much more—everything my soul knew. But still I loved my husband. I sighed. "Haywood's brave and good. I love him."

"We'll get Beth," Arthur said with confidence. "Alexei is using her to get us, but we know that, so we have the advantage."

We both fell silent, and finally the healing current slowed and ended. I smeared the wound with ointment, then stepped back and handed him his shirt and coat.

He took them from me with a smile, though I knew his ribs ached. Something about the healing current seemed to make the pain a little more intense initially, even as it sped up the healing process in the tissues. "You love me more," Arthur said in a low voice. He took my hand in his big one and kissed the center of my palm.

Everything in me melted and opened. Then it ached. The truth hurt as much as any bullet.

20

WE MADE CAMP IN THE RUINS of the town of Scottsbluff, across the North Platte River from the rugged beauty of Scotts Bluff, where Alexei had built a camp with his raiders. Han, terrified that we'd turn him over to Susie, informed us of the location of every patrol as we rode into town, so we came in unhindered. We rode through a desolate town inhabited by snow and ice, scattered detritus, and the shells of buildings, imploded automobiles and the dusty yellow grit excreted by the mists.

Ashley Furniture Homestore on West 27th Street was mostly intact, so we set up camp in and around it. As soon as we had the animals tied up and watered, Arthur set Han to drawing a detailed map of Alexei's camp. Theo, Robert, and I set out cold meat and strawberry supplements inside the store on a plastic-wrapped Sealy Posturepedic.

"I never thought I'd say this, but the pink stuff is getting old," I said.

"It's shite," Robert said blithely. "We're lucky to have it."

"Shit with vitamin C," Theo said, with a droll expression.

I laughed.

Theo grinned at me. "Too bad no fire."

"Another reason to hate those buggery raiders. They're keeping us from a hot meal. My beauteous wife needs one, you know. She's got my babby bakin' in her oven," Robert said. He turned to face Jeannie, who sat with Laurette on a loveseat they'd dragged close to the mattress. He touched the back of his hand to Jeannie's cheek and the two of them shared a smile.

"I'll forgive them the meal. I just want my daughter back," I said. I popped open a can of supplement and drank it. It only made me shudder a little.

"The question is, what now?" Robert asked.

"I've been wondering that myself," Brendan said. He dragged up a rocking chair and perched himself in it, balancing a can of supplement on the arm as he rocked. "You know that cougar is still following us. I saw it when I went outside to relieve myself."

"I'm going to walk in, reintroduce myself to Alexei, and demand that he give me my daughter, if he hasn't already given her to Haywood," I said fiercely. "He's going to give her to me. He has to. I saved his son! Mikhail is alive today because of me."

"No way. You're not going to do something so obvious and doomed for failure," Arthur said. He strode up behind me and kissed the back of my head, then stood behind me, holding me gently by my upper arms. "Haywood has probably already tried that tactic, and we haven't seen him riding back north, so either they're holding him or something's happened to him. We have to find another strategy. I've been thinking about it. We need to apply force. I can send in the mists, the way I did in France to get Alexei to release you. We'll have an armed party waiting outside, behind the mists."

"You can't send the mists in. There's too big a risk that Beth and other innocent people could be killed. The mists are evolving. You said yourself that they're unpredictable," I objected.

Robert nodded. "Neither can we send in an armed party.

There are a lot more of them than there are of us. If we go in brutal, they'll just kill us all."

"It has to be a small party, unthreatening, a woman alone. It has to be me and me only," I said loudly, pointing to my chest for emphasis.

"Not you. It's too dangerous," Arthur said.

"Arthur is correct, as Haywood pointed out before he departed," Nwokocha said. He stood beside the loveseat with his arms crossed and his expression somber. "Your appearance is exactly what he wants, because it signals that Arthur is close behind, and Arthur is the true prize. It would in no way induce Alexei to release your daughter. We will need to apply force somehow, not tempt him to retain the girl or worse, as a way to thwart Arthur."

"We will go," Marco offered. "Me and Gaff can go as emissaries of the family, friends of you and Haywood from Edmonton. *Magari*, that Russian will not remember me, a boy from our camp in France. That was a long time ago now." He stood very tall, his chest lifted. "I am looking for a girl too. I must find Lynsey."

"No! No way. You're too young. I won't be a party to putting you in danger," I exclaimed. "Tell me what your girlfriend looks like, and I'll try to find her!"

"Wait a minute. Marco's idea has some merit," Arthur said. "Let's think about it."

"Beth is my daughter. I'm going!" I snapped.

"The One knows Emma. He's looking for her," Susie said. She smiled, a timid expression that none of us expected, one that surprised and quieted us all. As usual, she stood close to me. She touched the hair on my shoulder. "Orders are to check every blonde woman who comes into camp for any reason, whether they're brought in as captives or refugees who come looking for food and shelter."

"I like your pretty cat, Emma," Kangee said, towing

another rocker toward the mattress. "He wants to be close to you."

"Yeah, what is it with you and that big cat? He looks so fierce," Robert said.

I shrugged.

Robert shook his head, then returned to the topic at hand: rescuing Beth. "Maybe you shouldn't go into Alexei's camp if he's scouting for you. That would be giving him what he wants. Can't be a good move strategically."

"I will make the sacrifice, I will go," Laurette announced. "I am wounded, but I can enter a camp."

"My daughter, and I'm going," I insisted.

"Emma can't be Emma. If she wants to go in, she has to be someone else," Kangee noted.

Arthur's eyes lit up. "A disguise! Emma, a real one this time."

"What do you mean, this time?" Laurette asked.

"*Si, certo*, when was Emma in disguise?" Marco wondered.

Arthur and I grinned but looked in opposite corners of the big furniture floor room, with its aisles of sofas, sectionals, chaises, dinette sets, and media storage towers.

"I smell a secret," Laurette said.

"Yeah, it stinks in 'ere. You can smell the pile," Jeannie said.

"I could cut my hair, but it's still blonde," I noted. "How do I disguise myself?"

"I knew my herbs would save the occasion! They are so often the solution to a crisis," Laurette said, preening. "You are lucky to have a trained herbalist such as me with you. Emma, I can make you a dye. Chestnut brown! With the herbs in my possession." She straightened. "Even with my injury."

"Emma will make a wonderful brunette," Arthur said. He stroked my hair.

"You go in under cover, and then what?" Donny asked, frowning. "Say you get in. How do you spring your little girl?"

"A distraction?" I mused.

Arthur shook his head. "Can't be an obvious distraction. Alexei is no fool."

Susie raised her hand, as if she were in school, and then cleared her throat. "They'll take any weapons she has. Then they'll rape her, if they don't recognize her as who she is, the woman The One is looking for, because they'll think she's just another refugee woman, a slave."

Everyone stopped breathing.

"I'll survive," I said softly.

Arthur's strong arms encircled me, but before he could argue, I pushed him away.

"I'm strong. I'm prepared to go through a lot more than that to get my daughter back."

"I bet they don't rape the crazy ones," Kangee said, shifting in the rocking chair.

Susie shook her head. "No, not usually. They're afraid the madness is contagious. I mean, they're half-mad anyway— mostly mad, some of them. But they fear crazy women. They think the women will put a spell on them."

"Okay, good. Then I'll go in as a crazy brunette," I said with a shaky laugh. "I can play that. It's just acting."

"You won't be able to fake it. They'll be able to tell," Susie said. "If you act too crazy, they may kill you immediately."

"A little bit of my medicine," Kangee said. "That will help you."

"No way," Arthur exclaimed. "She wasn't crazy on that stuff. She was out of her mind and totally vulnerable."

"I can dilute it," Kangee said. "Besides, Emma knows about being crazy." She gave me a clear-eyed, knowing look, as if she'd been present when I was mad in France on that long ride north to Le Havre.

"Yes, I know about it," I said softly. "I can be crazy for real."

"No. I forbid this. You can't endanger yourself. This plan

has more holes than a sieve! I'll go alone and trade myself for Beth," Arthur said, scowling.

"It's not your kind of plan, mister, but it's the best we've got," Robert said.

"I'm what he wants. He can have me," Arthur said. He straightened. "I can't bear to think of Alexei hurting Emma or of Emma being hurt because he doesn't know who she is. I cannot stand by and let those monsters have her."

We all looked at him.

I said, "He wants you, but he may not release Beth. As Haywood said, Alexei could kill her and make you watch, just to hurt you, because of his wife. Besides, Arthur——"

"You're too important to trade for one child," Nwokocha finished for me. "If this world has a chance to be rid of the mists, *you* are that chance. You're the only one who can control them. Your purpose is bigger than one girl, even Emma's daughter."

"You cannot make that sacrifice," Laurette agreed.

Arthur opened his mouth to argue, but Robert clapped his hand on Arthur's shoulder. Robert said, "You're the big mister and a grand leader. I'd follow you to the burnin' gates of bloody hell, but sometimes you have to listen to us."

"True word," Theo said earnestly. "Emma go in with pretty brown hair. Marco and Gaff go next day, day before. Emma have back up."

"Me too! I'll go," Kangee said. She gave me her strange placid smile. "After you're settled."

"You'll walk in!" I said. "The way you do . . . but why?"

"So I can bring you my stuff and you can poison the raiders. There's enough in my jar to kill a hundred men." Kangee gestured with her hands. "Who says the distraction has to be outside the camp?"

"I love it," Jeannie said. "Emma will give those scallies a bellyache!"

"More than a bellyache," Laurette said, narrowing her eyes at Kangee. "Death."

"A plan, weak, yes, but almost feasible," Arthur said reluctantly. "I can't believe I'm going to agree to this." He nudged his way in to stand next to me. "Emma will disguise herself and then drug herself. Great! Gaff and Marco will join the camp separately, so they can support Emma. At some point, Kangee does her thing—"

"I'm good at it. I can carry a few things in," Kangee said. She folded her hands in her lap. "Not too much, nothing too large, but I can bring Emma her gun and my jar."

"Nighttime," Arthur said.

"Dinnertime," Theo said. "Everyone eat. Put stuff in scallies' food."

"But I don't want Kangee to come too soon," I said. "I have to locate Beth."

"Will you be able to get back out again, Kangee?" Arthur asked.

Kangee nodded.

"Can you bring anything back out, or better yet, can you carry a child out?"

"I never tried," Kangee said, looking startled.

I'd never seen her look that way, and it made me wary. "If it's dangerous to Beth—" I started.

Arthur waved me to silence. "Can you try, Kangee? We're just brainstorming here. If you can bi-locate in the way you've been doing, deliver the jar and a gun, a knife too, and then carry Beth out, we'll have solved the biggest problem of getting her out safely. If a number of men die inexplicably, attention will be focused on that, not on one little girl. Emma can meet the boys and sneak out, shoot any patrol who tries to stop them. Susie, how well guarded are the women at night? Do many try to escape?"

"Not many," Susie said. She wore a chagrinned expression.

"No matter how bad it is, it's better than the mists, the winter, the starvation, and the other raiders. Course, that was back in the old camp in Bismarck. I don't know what the new camp in Scotts Bluff will be like."

"It'll be the same." Arthur nodded and stroked his face. "This could be a bloodless op. Get in, spirit Beth out, and Emma and the boys sneak away. Maybe we won't even have to alert Alexei that Emma and I are here. Maybe we can avoid a battle."

"Those are a lot of maybes," Kangee said uneasily, her round moon face puckering. "I don't know if I can carry Beth."

"Will something happen to her if you fail?" I asked.

Kangee shook her head. "I may have to put her down and walk out myself. I'm not entirely solid when I do it."

"Still, that's a neat gift," Robert said. "All the mists gave me was dead kin."

"Kangee, you have to be like lightning, quick in and quick out," Arthur said. "Whether or not you can get Beth out, you're our communications."

"But if she can't carry Beth out?" I asked. "Then what?"

"Plan B," Theo said. He smiled his old grim smile, the one he always wore when we were about to face a battle.

"Poison as many men as you can. Then, during the uproar, we attack," Arthur said. "Kangee will tell us where to find you. We'll fight in and get you. Otherwise, intel from Kangee gives us Plan C. We can pass information back and forth through her."

"I don't know which is worse, Plan A, B, or C, but at least there's a plan," I muttered.

"Not so much a plan as a train wreck we're hoping to surf for a few kilometers," Arthur said. He rubbed his beard. His gray eyes pierced me as they swept over me.

"Train wreck, plan . . . same difference," I said. "Let's do it. Right now. I'm not waiting one more minute to find my daughter. Besides, it'll be dark in a few hours, and I can go in then, when there's less light to see my face. Just in case Alexei looks at it despite the dark hair. Laurette, what do you need to mix your herbal dye?"

ARTHUR STOOD WATCHING as Laurette took a switchblade to my hair. She slashed close to my head and carved a chin-length bob out of the yellow thicket. The long blonde locks of my girlhood fell away. I closed my eyes and surrendered; hair was nothing in the face of my beloved daughter's need. Even though the wild mane had characterized me all my life, it was only an extraneous part, whittled away by necessity.

A small thing, and I would have given so much more for the people I loved.

When I opened my eyes, Arthur was stooping to retrieve a handful of my hair. He stood and combed it with his fingers into a long strand, then carefully coiled it and placed it in the pocket of his coat.

"Arthur, are you really that sentimental?" I teased.

"Only about you, Emma." He smiled. "Remember when I combed the lice out of your hair? I still remember that soft sensation, like yellow silk on my hands."

I smiled at him, but I couldn't answer because of the lump in my throat.

Laurette made a harsh raspberry sound. "Bah, silly people, it is hair. It grows back. Emma, you are long overdue for a cut. This mop is too unruly. You carry chaos around on your head. It is no wonder that your life is in chaos."

"My life isn't, isn't in chaos!" I sputtered.

"*Oui,* chaos. Two men and a missing daughter and a hand-ful of shitty plans to save her," Laurette said. "If that is not chaos, what is? Now, let us make you truly beautiful, *vraiment,* with hair like mine."

AT NIGHTFALL, SPORTING a short mop of muddy-brown hair, and having exchanged my Inuit gear for a dead raider's parka and snow pants, I mounted my horse. It was chilly through the parka, and I missed the caribou fur, which had kept me comfortably warm for so long, since I first set out from Edmonton to steal a horse.

Arthur and Theo rode with me, accompanying me to the border of Alexei's camp. Arthur carried Han's map of the usual patrol spots. He steered his horse close to mine and teased, "It's a cold and lonely night. Should I call you Angie?"

"Only if the fun's about to start," I teased back.

"Good fun," Theo called.

The smiles vanished from our faces and Arthur and I both grimaced.

"Laurette is right, it's a shitty plan," Arthur said. His strong, symmetrical face wore a pained expression. "I hate to admit it."

"We've done the best we could in the time we had, with limited resources," I said. "I'm more grateful than I can say for what you've done. I wouldn't have made it this far without you—all of you." I peered through the dark at the forms of my friends who stood around us, seeing me off and wishing me well: Jeannie, Laurette, Robert, Nwokocha, Brendan, Kangee, Donny, Marco, and Gaff. The latter two planned to approach camp the next afternoon and ask to be taken in as fighters. Kangee was scheduled to make her appearance the following evening, giving me twenty-four hours to find Beth. I hoped that was enough time. "Guys, thank you . . . and I love you," I said. I didn't think there was more to be said than that. They knew it came from the heart.

A chorus of well wishes answered me.

"It is just another impossible mission," Laurette said lightly. "We do this all the time. *À bientôt.* See you soon. Try not to brag too much when you return. It is so hard for the rest of us."

"Knock down some scallies for me," Jeannie said. She punched my thigh lightly. "Yer a git, but we're maybe naming our boy Emmet."

"Good luck," Donny called.

"If anything happens to you, I'll be really angry," Susie said.

"May fortune smile upon you," Nwokocha said.

But it was Robert whose words touched me the most deeply. "Bring Beth back to us," he said. "I can't wait to meet your little bird. I already love her."

21

ARTHUR AND THEO MADE QUICK work of a two-man patrol on the Old Oregon Trail along the river, slitting their throats and dumping their bodies into a ravine. They were the only raiders we encountered on our jaunt into the bluff site. There were over three thousand acres of unusual land formations in the area, but Han had drawn us a map showing Alexei's camp and the most and least traversed paths to it.

Alexei had centered his new camp at the northern base of the eponymous bluff by the north overlook. Tunnels in the area provided shelter, and the jagged sandstone and limestone rock formations served as fortress walls, controlling the influx of other raiders, bandits, and refugees. The Old Oregon Trail was watched but sparsely used. Alexei preferred the south and north trails; that pavement had survived the mists' incursions.

When we could see the patch of parking lot that remained from the days when the area was a national monument, I dismounted. "This is my cue. Wish me luck."

Arthur got off his horse. He stood in front of me, a tall, pulsing form, the sclera of his eyes very white in the moonlight. He grabbed me roughly and kissed my lips. "Stay alive, no matter what."

"That's the intention," I said wryly. I yearned to press myself against him and rest my head on his warm shoulder, to melt into him. I couldn't let myself. It was all still too unresolved.

Haywood stayed stubbornly on the periphery of my mind. He'd left the relative safety of our group and set out alone to find our daughter. I loved him for that, but I loved Arthur, too; he'd crossed an ocean to find me.

It was an impossible choice.

"I mean it," Arthur said hoarsely. "Stay alive. I'll get you out. Know that. I am here for you. I won't abandon you. I'll fight Alexei and the raider army if necessary."

"I know," I said softly. I went to my tiptoes and kissed him gently on his cheek.

His arms tightened around me as if he could keep me next to him. He released me suddenly and stepped back. He passed me a small folded envelope of animal hide.

I unrolled it and found a tiny dab of paste: Kangee's potion. I scooped it off with my index finger, steeled myself, then sucked it off my fingertip.

"Emmy, good luck," Theo called.

Arthur remounted his horse. They waited for a moment, and I could feel them staring at me, willing me to succeed. Then I heard the rollick of their horses cantering away.

I couldn't see the horses anymore because the bluffs had burst into flame. Around the flames flew giant blue butterflies wearing red cowboy boots. An hour later, when the patrol found me, I was singing Christmas carols.

I CAME TO in a pen. The sun was warm on my face. I sat up groggily, staring around a pit of slushy mud at two dozen ragged, dirty people. Some sat and babbled, and others crawled on hands and knees. Two women peed in the corner. An elderly man beside me cackled. He had a black eye and a bloody mouth, vacant of teeth that had been knocked out.

My face hurt. A little exploration with my fingertips found a swollen eye on one side, a split bottom lip, and a jagged cut on the other cheekbone. My shoulder that was still healing also felt tender. I had no idea how I'd come by these injuries.

"Oh, no," I said and moaned. I was wracked with heaves. Only a little pink bile came up, a remnant of the strawberry supplement last night. Wincing, I sat up and blinked in the bright sunlight, taking in the gorgeous towering rock faces that reared up out of the snow. It was a geological Shangri La, with the ridges' weathered layers of pale brown and light gray, dark gray and gray black.

"You're a pretty thing," the old man said. "Such ugly hair." He touched my head with a quavering finger.

"Back," I muttered, pushing his hand away. I wiped my mouth, and felt the shudders quiet. "Is there any water?"

"The guards will bring you some," the old man said. He giggled. "But you have to pay for it. That's how I lost my teeth. I accidentally bit—"

"How many guards? Will they let me out?" I interrupted him. "How do we get out of here?"

The old man shrugged. "We don't. But sometimes some of the women bring us food and drink, and we don't have to give the guards blowjobs for that."

I spoke to the other prisoners, but the old man was the only other person in the pen who was lucid. He leaned against a post and dozed off.

Two guards circumnavigated the pen, which was roughly ten meters square. They saw me eying them and clutched at their crotches and yelled foul suggestions at me.

They'd be the first two raiders I poisoned.

The pen was positioned near the northern edge of camp, offering a good view of the camp and the northern plains. I passed the time by observing the frenetic activity around me. Wagons from which people took various items were parked in a haphazard border along the camp. Raiders, horses, cattle, goats, women, and children swarmed everywhere, and a great cacophony seethed through the air: shouts and rattles

and bangs and clanks and thuds and the cries of animals. The
women hurried to and fro, lugging items that ranged from
water jugs to suitcases to wooden planks to tools. A group of
about a dozen women were engaged in digging something not
far from the pen: latrines, I guessed.

The men constructed shanties out of materials they must
have brought with them: tents, wood, sheetrock, plastic sid-
ing, and cinderblocks. I recalled that Alexei had had time to
pack, back when the wall of mists first appeared in Bismarck.
It looked as if he'd planned ahead and was now settling in for
the long haul. I wondered if he expected the mists to avoid
the area, and then I noted the giant barrel-drums positioned
between the wagons along the periphery of camp. Rhythmic
percussion was the only defense against the mists, besides
Arthur's power over them.

I counted but lost track around three hundred sixty men. I
was sure there were at least double, if not triple, that amount.
They all appeared armed, and they all wore a black gauntlet
on their right arm.

Alexei was assembling a formidable army. I wondered
which of his old mates had come with him to North America,
but I saw no one whom I recognized.

I kept searching the children for Beth, but I saw no sign
of her among them. Haywood was not in sight either. I eaves-
dropped on conversations as people passed the pen, but not a
word was spoken about my daughter or my husband.

A few hours later, some women carrying buckets
approached the pen. With downcast eyes, they exchanged
a few words with the guards. The guards seemed reluctant,
but they swung open the gate and let the women in. They
passed out food: chunks of roasted meat and cold boiled potatoes, only a handful for each of us. It didn't look too rancid,
though, and I was starving.

"I'm not crazy," I said softly when one of the women
offered me a potato.

She gave me a sharp glance. She was young and petite, slender even in a heavy wool coat, and very pretty with curly red hair. I felt like I knew her even though I'd never seen her before. "Maybe you want to be crazy," she said. "Women who aren't get used."

"Do I know you?" I asked softly.

She pursed her lips and shook her head once, then moved on to the old man, who sat with his hands piteously outstretched. "Here you go, Jeffer," she said, giving him a potato.

"Jeffer likes yummies," the old man sang, mashing the potato with his blood-crusted gums.

"I need help please," I said quietly. "I'm not crazy. I'm looking for someone."

"Give up on that," she said without looking back at me. In a few moments, the women had emptied the buckets, and they left the pen almost at a trot.

For the next few hours, we prisoners were ignored. The red-haired woman's face nagged me. *Where have I seen her before?* I finally let it drop into my unconscious, and I went back to observing the camp.

The time that Gaff and Marco were supposed to join the camp came and went, and I neither saw nor heard any sign of them. Day was wearing into late afternoon, and I had no idea about Beth or Haywood or how to free myself from the pen. Then I remembered where I had seen the young redhead's face.

THE WOMEN CAME back with their buckets in the evening, as the sky glossed over with lavender and orange. The red-haired woman was with them. She gave me two boiled carrots.

"Thank you, Amy," I said, smiling.

She stiffened. "How do you know me?" she hissed.

"I sketched your portrait for Norman, for the sign he made

offering a reward for you," I replied. "I'm Emma."

Her large eyes filled with tears. "Norman? He must be worried sick."

"He is," I said. "He keeps offering more and more credits to anyone who knows your whereabouts."

"My poor Norman." Her head drooped with her low, mournful voice.

"How'd you get here?" I asked.

"Kidnapped when I came home from the market. There are spies in Outpost City," she said. She shrugged, as if answering the question she knew I was thinking about how she'd been treated. "At least I'm alive."

"Norman would be thrilled to know that," I said.

She fixed me with an intense, compelling gaze. I had to admit that Norman's rhapsodic description of her was justified; Amy had mesmerizing eyes. She asked, "What's your story? When did you leave Outpost City?"

"A few weeks ago now," I said. "I'm looking for my daughter. She was kidnapped from Edmonton."

Amy asked, "Is she blonde?"

I nodded.

"She must be one of the special ones, kept apart. They're on the south side of camp, backed up close to the bluff. That's where the special ones are."

Of course. Alexei had stratified his camp in France, and he would do the same everywhere. It was the way he saw the world: as divided between those who were important and privileged and those who were expendable and miserable.

"I'm here to rescue her. You can come with me if you want."

Amy gave me a sardonic smile. "You're in a fine position to rescue anyone, and why would I come with you? So I can die in the frozen wilderness?"

"There's a group waiting for me in Scottsbluff town, and

we have horses and food," I whispered. "If we can escape here, we can take you back to Outpost City. Please? You have to help me."

Amy narrowed her eyes and stepped past me to hand out food to the rest of the prisoners. She passed by the other women who had walked in with her. After fifteen minutes, she returned. "Here's what you're going to do. You're going to stand up casually and take one of the buckets. Then you're going to walk out with us. Just act as if you belong and don't look at the guards."

"I can do that," I said, rising.

"You'd better, because if you don't pull this off, they'll kill you, after raping you," she said. She put her bucket in my hand, and we walked over to join the three other women. They didn't look at me; they'd been briefed.

Jeffer was watching us. "Pretty girls, wait! I can help."

The guards saw us women huddled together with the pails, and one of them opened the gate.

Jeffer smirked. "Hey guard boys! You with the small dicks!" He trotted to the opposite side of the pen and leaned against the railing. "Hey, crazy guys with the teeny tiny Johnsons!" The guards ran around the pen to smack him with the butts of their guns, but Jeffer kept calling insults.

I walked out with Amy and the others. My heart stammered out a staccato rhythm in my chest, but I kept my eyes down and my face neutral, just like the other women. I didn't look back but I heard a *crack* and then silence; Jeffer had been knocked out.

We walked south, a circuitous route through throngs of people. Camp conditions improved the closer we got to the bluff. Nice wooden shanties were built, and the raiders were more orderly. I smelled something delicious cooking and inhaled deeply, savoring the scent and salivating. Then my eyes fell on a man and a little girl walking together ahead of us, and I froze.

I only spied them from the back, but they were unmistakable. It was the empty sleeve that told the story. With his remaining hand, the tall blond man clasped the little girl's hand.

The little girl wore a blue ski hat. Her long blonde braid snaked down her back. I recognized the form instantly and would have cried out, but Amy clapped her hand over my mouth. For a young woman, the redhead was immensely strong.

"Holy shit, are you *her* mother? Are you the woman he's looking for, the healer he knew in Europe?" she whispered furiously.

I nodded.

"Damn it," she swore. "Don't say a word. I'm going to take my hand away." She released me.

My eyes filled with tears. "What's he doing with her? I've got to get her away from him," I said desperately.

"Not right this moment," Amy hissed. She grabbed my wrist in a vise grip, squeezing so hard that I could feel her fingers through my coat. "You're coming back to the cooking area with me, then we'll figure things out. Don't tell anyone who you are, do you hear me?"

"But Alexei has my daughter!"

"The One'll have you, too, and it'll go badly if he recognizes you," Amy said. "Keep your head down."

Walking past Beth without greeting her was the hardest thing I'd ever done. I had to keep my head down, as Amy commanded, to hide my tears.

A LARGE CANOPY tent, probably fifteen by twenty meters, overhung the food staging area. Its side panels were tied back around the poles, exposing the interior, which was lit with candles and the flames from the central fire pit. Big cast-iron cauldrons hung over a series of smaller cooking fires, and tables were set up for food preparation. Some raiders strolled around the tent, but only women worked inside it.

I sagged against one of the tables as soon as I was under the tent.

"Who's she?" asked one of the women.

"Don't ask," Amy said flatly.

"Sheesh. You're touchy." The woman sniffed and squinted at me.

"Here. Look busy," Amy said. She thrust a knife and some potatoes in my hand.

I stared at them without comprehension. I kept seeing Alexei holding Beth's hand.

Amy was talking, but I only caught one word: ". . . husband . . ."

"Huh?" I asked.

She leaned her head next to mine. "I suppose that's your husband The One's put in the cage?"

"Haywood?" I squeaked. I closed my eyes. I had to pull myself together. I had to be strong for my husband and daughter. Haywood was being held there in a cage, and Alexei kept Beth with him. I took a deep breath. "Where?"

"By The One's tent," Amy said.

I was going to question her, but someone approached and stuck a fur bundle in my face. I took it. "Kangee!"

"How's it going?" she asked. "Where's Beth?"

"Alexei has her. I have to get her away from him," I answered in a low voice.

Amy and the other women looked shocked speechless at Kangee's sudden appearance; all motion in the tent had ceased.

"What about Marco and Gaff?" she asked.

"Who are you?" demanded Amy.

"How did you get here?" asked someone else.

"I'll check on the boys," Kangee said and vanished.

The women in the tent gasped. They all stared at me.

I shrugged. "She does that, ever since the mists."

"What's that she brought?" asked Amy.

Several women gathered around me.

Hands shaking, I unwrapped the fur. Inside was my gun and Kangee's jar of thick, dark paste. I smiled. "Is the men's food separate from the women's?"

"Partly," Amy said. "Why?"

"Spread the word that the women shouldn't eat tonight, and think about which hundred men you want to kill." I handed the jar to Amy, whose eyes gleamed.

She held the jar up, and the women cheered.

22

I WAS BRINGING A TRAY OF food to a group of raiders when my name was called, and a cry went up. It was an hour later, and my senses were on high alert. I didn't need the heightened perception to know who had identified me.

"That's her! That's Emma!" Gaff called.

I turned around slowly.

Gaff raced toward me, a dozen raiders at his back. He was pointing at me. "Get her!"

Gaff betrayed me, even after we saved him? And where is Marco? I wondered. *Is he alive?* I caught a glimpse of Gaff's face, bruised and bloodied. Then raiders swarmed me, grabbing and prodding me. Someone bashed me on the head.

I CAME TO because I was being pulled upright by the roots of my hair. "Ow!" I yelped.

A man laughed.

I opened my lids, with great effort, because my head rang with pain. The craggy features and implacable eyes gleaming with madness: I recognized him at once.

Alexei stood in front of me, laughing, with his one remaining hand practically woven into my scalp, hurting me terribly. "Emma, you sneak into my camp like thief?" he boomed. His blue eyes filled with recrimination. "Is that proper way to greet old friend?" With a shake he pulled his hand away, taking chunks of my cropped dark hair with it.

I fell to my knees, crying out and rubbing my head.

"Mommy!" Beth cried.

I struggled to my feet and looked for her.

She strained against two men, who pinned her arms and kept her from running to me.

I nodded at her.

Beth stopped struggling and gave me a fierce and trusting look. She was alive and she was well and now it was up to me.

"I want my daughter and my husband, Alexei," I demanded, loudly. I looked around. We stood in a clearing near the food staging area, in a kind of square lit by torches.

"We all want. I want my wife," he said. "I miss her every day. Mikhail mother." His accent was as turgid as ever, his face as shuttered over with the same old, unrelenting anger.

Would he never learn? "I saved your son for you," I said. "You owe me!"

"I not kill Arthur and friends for you. Debt is paid," he said, shrugging. "How is Arthur? He come, yes? When does he come?"

"Alexei, Beth is my daughter. A mother's bond with her child is sacred. Release her to me!"

"Beth make good wife for Mikhail," he said. "I send pretty girl back to France."

"No!" I yelled.

"You be happy." He thrust his index finger into my chest. "Beth be queen of world. I think when I send men to Edmonton, they bring your little daughter. 'Bring back healer woman and daughter,' I tell men. They come back with older daughter, better for Mikhail."

"You cannot do that to Mikhail," I said wildly. "You can't choose his wife for him. Mikhail has to find his own wife, someone he loves as much as you loved Helina."

Alexei recoiled. "Do not speak her name to me!" He struck me on my mouth, sending me to the ground, bleeding.

From the ground, I said, "If you try to choose Mikhail's wife, you will take away his manhood. How can he rule then?"

"Manhood? What you know of that?" Alexei walked in a circle around me. He cocked his blond head, thinking. His empty coat sleeve swung as walked. "Ah, manhood. You have husband who is man. You want daughter and husband, so we have contest of manhood." He stopped pacing and raised his voice. "Bring Haywood Anderson!"

"No, Alexei! Please don't hurt my daddy," Beth called, her voice shrill with terror.

I scrambled to my feet and put my hands on Alexei's remaining arm. "Alexei, what are you going to do to my husband? Please stop this. You don't have to do this. Release me and my family—"

"What are you doing with your hands on me?" Alexei roared. "Where your healing hands when arm bleed out? You were on plane, go home. I send you home with husband and child. I give you gift—your home, family. Then I pay price. Arthur your lover stab my arm off!" Clearly he blamed me, in part, for the loss of his arm.

I took a deep breath and dropped my hands. "I'm sorry that happened to you, Alexei. I wish I could have healed you."

"I was good to you, and you were not there to heal me," he said. "You selfish woman. Selfish woman with lover whose mists kill my wife." Alexei leaned down and grabbed my hair again, dragging my face close to his. "I should have make you my woman when I bring you to my camp. Mikhail love you—"

"Yes, Mikhail loves me, and he wouldn't want you to hurt me and my family," I cried. "Mikhail would choose kindness. He will be that kind of leader."

With his mouth narrowing, Alexei seemed to consider my words. He glanced at Beth.

"Alexei, please," Beth said softly.

Alexei looked back at me.

Are his eyes . . . softening? I felt myself hope.

Then a tall, lean form was thrown down in front of us: Haywood. I knelt and touched him. He was conscious, though very weak. He smiled at me. "Sorry, Em," he croaked, in a voice so low that only I could hear it. "Don't be sad. I always saw this. I knew it was coming. But I think you'll get her out."

I was about to answer, but Alexei laid his hand on my shoulder and hurled me away. "Haywood Anderson, you are man. You have manhood. With manhood, good husband and father fight for wife and child. I would fight for my wife, but no one can fight the mists. Only Arthur, because he create them. I cannot fight to save her. But you, you are willing to fight for your wife and child?"

"No!" I cried out. I lunged toward Alexei, but two of his guards caught me and restrained me the same way Beth was being held.

"Yes. I'll fight for my wife and daughter," Haywood said. He struggled to his feet. He moved awkwardly, as if he'd been injured. Broken ribs, probably. Nevertheless, he stood straight and looked Alexei in the eye. I'd never been so proud of my husband, or so terrified for him.

"A contest," Alexei said. "I like contest. I make it easy for Haywood Anderson. He fight one-arm man. Me. If he win, he take woman and girl away. If he lose, I kill him and Emma. Beth marry Mikhail." He slipped his coat off, then his sweater and shirt. He stood bare-chested and pointed his jagged stump. It ended in a purplish twist close to where his elbow once was. "Is no contest, I have one arm." Then he laughed. Even with one arm, Alexei was terrifying. His tall, broad frame rolled with lethal, bulging muscles over which thick blue veins coursed. His skin was mottled, as Arthur's was, with scars, both old and fresh. He emanated fire and anger. Alexei looked like a damaged but deadly bear, full of sharp claws and toxic teeth.

Haywood didn't have his coat off the first time Alexei

punched him, low in the gut. Haywood doubled over, and Alexei swung his fist upward in an arcing hook, slamming Haywood's cheek. Haywood sprawled over backwards, but he pulled himself back to his feet, amidst the cheers and boos of gathering onlookers.

"I like your gallant husband," Alexei called. "Your lover Arthur not gallant. I hurt him when he come for you. But this husband? I like him."

HAYWOOD SWAYED BACK and forth on his feet. He was bleeding from a dozen cuts and bruises. His eyes were swollen, his lips and nose broken, his knuckles thickened. Alexei kept hitting him, pummeling him with his single fist, which moved so fast it was almost a blur at times. Haywood kept his hands up defensively as best he could, but it was clear he was outmatched. Haywood was weak; he'd probably been starved. He was painfully thin, thinner than I'd ever seen him, his ribs bulging out through wasted skin.

"Ugh," he said, as Alexei got him with a jab to his chin. Haywood took a deep breath and then roared and rammed forward, thrusting his head deep into Alexei's gut.

Alexei went down onto his back, laughing.

"Everything's on fire!" screamed the guard holding my left arm. Then he fell over, dead. The other guard jumped back. He vomited black blood and then fell, and several other raiders in the crowd keeled over as well. Chaos erupted around us.

I ran to help Haywood, who finally had the advantage. Weak and battered, he sat on Alexei's chest with total determination and slugged Alexei in the face repeatedly.

Alexei heard the uproar and struggled ferociously to sit up. He howled and swept out his thick, blood-spattered arm and knocked Haywood off. Alexei jumped to his feet and looked around. Ten or eleven of his men lay dead around us, and screaming sounded all over the camp. Raiders and women shrieked and rushed everywhere. It was bedlam.

"Emma, what have you done?" Alexei shouted. He grabbed my throat and squeezed.

But he only throttled me for a few seconds, because a muscular golden form leapt, snarling, out of the darkness, and the cougar took him down.

"Let's go!" I said to Haywood, urgently.

In the panic, the guards had released Beth, and we pushed through the shrieking throngs toward her. He grabbed one hand, and I grabbed the other, and we raced away from the clearing. Beth's face was as set as ours.

Total pandemonium reigned over the camp. People ran around in all directions, screaming and ululating with fear and panic. We ran past dead bodies and through crazed crowds. I glimpsed a group of women killing a raider, tearing him limb from limb, seizing the opportunity to rid themselves of captors they truly hated.

Someone caught my hand. It was Amy, running with us. "You promised," she yelled, to be heard over the hubbub.

"This way," Haywood yelled, pointing. He was panting and drooling blood, but he set a fast pace and kept us to it. We ran north toward the pen where I'd been held. "There are horses near the wagons."

The four of us made good progress and were soon at the horses. Three guards lay dead near them. A fourth guard sat on the ground with his head in his hands, weeping; we ignored him. Haywood took a coat off one of the dead guards.

Without bothering with saddle or reins, I grabbed Beth and, with more strength than had ever coursed through my being, I tossed her up on a horse. She cried out, but I didn't heed her. If she was in pain, she'd heal. I scrambled up behind her. Amy and Haywood mounted bareback too. I reached around Beth, circling her with my arms, and grabbed the horse's mane. I kicked his sides. He neighed and reared. We gripped him even tighter, and he set off at a gallop.

"Hang on tight!" I yelled to Beth. She leaned forward and clung to the horse's neck, and we flew away from the camp.

We rode north, hard. It seemed to be forever before the sounds of the melee at Alexei's camp diminished behind us. When there was finally some quiet, we slowed the horses to a walk.

Beth was shaking and breathing hard. "That was scary, Mommy, but I'm so glad you came for me. I knew you would!"

Amy said, "I thought we were going to Scottsbluff town. That's east of here."

"North and east," I answered.

"Emma," Haywood groaned. He slumped over his horse, draining dark blood onto its withers. As I steered our horse over to him, he turned his battered face toward me. "Just as I always saw. I'm not going to make it. Take Beth home. Be safe." Then he tumbled to the ground.

Beth and I, as one person, screamed and dived for him.

SOME LITTLE WHILE later, as night deepened into indigo lit by the silver radiance of moon and stars on white snow and the healing current through my hands finally slowed, Kangee arrived. "Found you," she said. "What happened to Haywood?"

"You again!" Amy yelled, jumping back.

"I have another gun for you, and a knife," Kangee said. "Arthur thought you might need them."

I sat on the snowy ground beside my unconscious husband. "Kangee, Where's Arthur? Has he attacked?"

"Not yet. He's waiting on the top of the bluff, hiding with the others. I'm supposed to tell him where you are and give the go-ahead if everything's in place," she said. "Hi, Beth."

"Hi," Beth said, waving. She sat on the other side of Haywood and smiled tremulously. Her beautiful oval face was tense but open, her attitude scared but accepting.

I let myself take in for the first time that my daughter was fine. She was healthy, both in spirit and in body. She was alive, and she was with her father and mother.

As if reading my thoughts, Beth laid her hands on her father, mimicking me. She wanted to help heal her father. I'd poured into him all the healing current at my disposal, and Haywood was just barely alive. I hadn't mentioned that, but somehow she knew. My daughter didn't want to lose half of her foundation, especially after how close she'd come to losing me. She gave me her sweet, serious smile.

It crystallized something in me—like opening a cage full of winged creatures to set them free. Doves or butterflies, which were never meant to be domesticated.

Beth and Mandy were everything to me—to me and Haywood. I had been willing to sacrifice my life for either of them, and so had Haywood. I knew he still might pay that ultimate price for his daughter's freedom. I looked at my husband, the man I'd known since I was a little girl, and I admired his courage.

Cool, clear understanding broke over me: Who we were as a married couple was more important than who either of us was as individuals. I'd made that vow, and I would keep it. Beth and Mandy deserved that of me. So did Haywood.

I took a deep breath, taking Beth's hand and pressing it to my chest. "Tell Arthur we've escaped. Gaff identified me to the raiders, but I think he'd been hurt, possibly tortured. I don't know where Marco is. You need to find him. Alexei was attacked by the cougar who's been following me."

"Good cat," Kangee said. "Hope he's okay."

"Me too." I rose and stared up into the sky, at the white cold flow of Milky Way and the myriad icy stars that glittered like shards of my heart. "Tell him to expect Amy. She'll ride into town, to the furniture store. She has to be taken back to Outpost City."

"I like Outpost City," Kangee commented. She eyed Amy closely. "Aren't you Norman's friend?"

Amy nodded, then turned to me. "What about you, Emma?"

"I'm taking my husband and daughter back to Edmonton."

"Are you sure?" Kangee asked doubtfully. "You don't have any supplies or anything."

"I'm sure," I said. "Give Amy the extra gun you brought. I'll take the knife."

"If you say so. See you," she said, handing us the weapons, then vanishing.

"How does she do that?" Amy exclaimed.

"Hell if I know," I said, laughing shortly.

"She's magical, like a dragon or an elf," Beth pronounced.

Amy and I smiled at each other in the dark.

I touched Amy's arm. "Amy, continue north, then take the old highway east. My people have made camp at a furniture store on West 27th Street. You can't miss it, it's just about the only intact building in town. They might not be there at the moment, because they were preparing to attack Alexei's camp, but they'll be back shortly."

"There'll be patrols on the highway," Amy said uneasily.

"You'll be able to avoid them," I said. "If you can't, use the gun. You know how?"

"Yes," she grunted, and examined it with quick, practiced motions. She smiled. "This is The After. Doesn't everybody know how to use a gun?"

"We had a map of Alexei's camp, drawn by a raider we captured," I told her. "There are two small groups of patrols along the highway, two-man patrols, but only one rides at night. Stay alert and you'll hear them."

"Come with me to Outpost City," Amy said quietly. "We've got a doctor for your husband. Norman will be so glad to get me back that he'll make you rich."

"I can't go near Outpost City." I grinned. "They tried to hang me. There's a noose waiting for me there, along with some pretty pissed-off folks."

"Ouch," Amy said. "I've had enough Outpost ale to last me a lifetime, but I can't help you get to Edmonton. I'm sorry. I have to go back to Norman. He loves me. I mean everything to him. He takes care of me."

"Of course. You need to go where you're loved," I said quietly. "Where you love. That's Norman, in Outpost City."

Amy hugged me, briefly but fiercely. "Norman had you draw a picture of me? That was really how you recognized me?"

"Two sketches. He paid me three credits each," I said.

"He must really want me back," she said wistfully. She mounted her horse. "Sure you'll be okay? With a child and an injured man?"

"Hey, I'm a big girl now," Beth said. "Alexei said I was brave and strong and special. I can help my mom!"

"I'll be okay. We will," I said firmly. "We're together, and I have a gun."

Amy walked her horse over to stand beside me. "Is this what you're doing, going where you're loved, where you love?"

"What else is there?" I asked. I didn't tell her that another love awaited me, that part of me hurt with a fierceness I didn't expect to ever go away, a hurt that came from not being with Arthur. I couldn't tell her, because if I gave voice to my feelings, I feared they might consume me. I feared I might yield to the deep impulse like a craving that led me back to Arthur. I couldn't do that to Haywood, to Beth, to Mandy, or to the vow I'd made.

Amy wished us well and set off. I watched her go, then Beth helped me settle Haywood on the horse. He was awkwardly situated, but at least the horse was carrying him, and we didn't have to. With Beth walking beside me, I led the horse into the night.

Love would not be denied, but it could be sacrificed.

ACKNOWLEDGEMENTS

MANY THANKS TO the brilliant Lori Handelman, for her wonderful editing skills and kind support.

Thanks to Autumn Conley for the copyediting.

Many thanks to Gerda Swearengen, Mark Swearengen, Chris Gartner, Stuart Gartner, Rachel Leheny, Mary T. Browne, Komilla Sutton, Don Steelman, Sarah Novotny, and Michelle Czernin von Chudenitz for the warm support. I love you all.

Thank you also to Carole and Stefano Acunto, for good wine, great opera, and fantastic company.

Thank you to Dr. William Chambers.

Thank you to Joe and Maria Mills, Lisa Brewster, and everyone else at Black Sheep Design for the brilliant covers.

Thank you to Drew Stevens for the beautiful work.

Thank you to Sarah Miniaci.

Thank you to Adrienne Rosado.

Many thanks to the readers and bloggers who read and loved FALLEN and asked for more.

Thank you always to my daughters Jessica Hendel, Naomi Hendel, Julia Howard, and Madeleine Howard. Thank you to Sabin Howard.

TRACI L. SLATTON is a graduate of Yale and Columbia. She lives in Manhattan, and her love for Renaissance Italy inspired her historical novel *Immortal* (Bantam Dell). Also the author of novels *The Botticelli Affair*, *Fallen*, *Cold Light*, *Far Shore*, and *The Love of My (Other) Life*, Slatton has published *The Art of Life*, a photo essay about figurative sculpture; *Dancing in the Tabernacle*, a book of poetry; and *Piercing Time & Space*, a non-fiction title on science and spirituality.

www.ingramcontent.com/pod-product-compliance
Lightning Source LLC
Chambersburg PA
CBHW071235250626

47163CB00001B/183